Mark
Of The
Jaguar

Mark Of The Jaguar

A Book of Mormon Adventure in the Land of the Maya

Mark F. Cheney

authorHOUSE®

AuthorHouse™
1663 Liberty Drive
Bloomington, IN 47403
www.authorhouse.com
Phone: 1-800-839-8640

Published by AuthorHouse 04/29/2014

ISBN: 978-1-4969-0808-7 (sc)
ISBN: 978-1-4969-0806-3 (hc)
ISBN: 978-1-4969-0807-0 (e)

Library of Congress Control Number: 2014907424

This book is printed on acid-free paper.

CONTENTS

About the Book. ix

Acknowledgment. xi

Introduction xv

List of Illustrations xvii

List of Characters xix

Yax Kan And The Mark Of The Jaguar

Chapter 1   The Mark of the Jaguar 3

Chapter 2   Zapotecs!. 15

Chapter 3   Education 19

Chapter 4   Tonala 28

Chapter 5   A Farewell. 37

Chapter 6   Adventure 43

Chapter 7   Discovery 48

Chapter 8   Escape! 64

Chapter 9   Teotihuacan, City of the Ancients 71

Chapter 10 The Potter's Daughter 75

Chapter 11 Avenue of the Dead 84

Chapter 12 Beneath the Pyramid of the Sun 93

Chapter 13 Opposition 100

Chapter 14 Captured! 103

Chapter 15 The Assignment 112

Chapter 16 Liberation 126

Chapter 17 The Ritual 134

Chapter 18 Temple of the Descending God 139

Chapter 19 The Prayer and the Blessing 150

Chapter 20 Yax Kan's Legacy 160

Chapter 21 Reunion in Lamanai 162

Yax Kan And The Skull Of Doom

Chapter 22 The Wedding 169

Chapter 23 Stranger in Need 175

Chapter 24 The Cave 183

Chapter 25 Lubaantun 189

Chapter 26 The Skull of Doom 195

Chapter 27 The Plan 205

Chapter 28 Justice and Emancipation 224

Chapter 29 Salt Marsh 235

Chapter 30 Departure to Comalcalco 244

Historical & Explanatory Notes 249

Glossary of Terms 261

About the Author 265

ABOUT THE BOOK

MARK OF THE JAGUAR is a landmark novel in that it is the first work of LDS fiction that connects Pre-Columbian people with the stories and archaeological remains of the Book of Mormon people and times (2200 BC to 421 AD).

Yax Kan's story takes him from being orphaned in his childhood, through his training as a shaman, healer, scribe and stonecutter, and on the quest set out by his mentor to find the lost truths of the ancient religion of the people of Mesoamerica.

This is a story of adventure, danger, beauty, romance, and spiritual growth which attempts to shed light on what it may have been like for some of the people living between the time of Moroni and Columbus.

Follow Yax Kan's quest from near Comalcalco on the Gulf of Mexico to Izapa, then to the ancient city of Teotihuacan, and onward to Xbalanque (now Palenque) and then through Chichen and Tulum, down to Lamanai and Lubaantun in what is now Belize. See how jaguars go from foe to friend!

ACKNOWLEDGMENT

I wish to express my sincere gratitude to my friends and family, but especially to my eternal companion, Sally, for support and love during the writing of this, my first novel. I give special thanks to my daughter, Anika and her husband, Paul, for their review and suggestions in helping me improve each draft; Anika also did the cover painting and other artwork. The technical assistance of my good friend, Morris Grover with the cover and illustrations was invaluable. Also, I express appreciation to those select friends who read and made suggestions to help me along the way. The encouragement given by fellow writer Kerry Blair was a tremendous boost to morale, as well. However, in the end I am solely responsible for the contents, and I hope the errors are few.

"For none of these iniquities come of the Lord; for he doeth that which is good among the children of men; and he doeth nothing save it be plain unto the children of men; and he inviteth them all to come unto him and partake of his goodness; and he denieth none that come unto him, black and white, bond and free, male and female; and he remembereth the heathen; and all are alike unto God, both Jew and Gentile."

2 Nephi 26:33

INTRODUCTION

The story of Yax Kan (pronounced Yawsh-Kawn) could be similar to the account of other individuals throughout various 'dark ages' of time. This particular adventure is set at the latter end of the seventh century in part of the land of the Maya, known as the *Mayab*, in Southern Mexico, the Yucatan Peninsula and Belize. The writing of this story was inspired by a study of archeological evidence which seems to support the claims of the Book of Mormon, a number of trips by the author to Mexico and Central America over the years, and reading about the historical setting of the time. This book is not an attempt to prove the Book of Mormon true, but only to show possible connections to ancient finds.

After beginning the book, I was encouraged to continue by a statement I found while preparing a Sunday School lesson from an Institute of Religion manual, **The Book of Mormon for Religion 121 and 122**, referring to Mormon 1:14-15: "…No environment can become so corrupt that a private individual cannot have the sweet influence of the Holy Ghost." This struck me as an irrefutable statement indicating that man may forget God, but God will never forget man. At any time, in any place, if a person has righteous desires and sincerely prays for truth and guidance, that child of God will have his prayers answered in God's own way and time. This is the basic premise of the story of Yax Kan's quest and his ultimate discovery.

I would ask scholars and scriptorians to forgive me if I have made anachronistic, linguistic, or factual errors in presenting this story in a historical context. It has been my great pleasure to attempt to get it as close to the true geographic, historic and cultural setting as I possibly could. Many modern Mayan terms were not used by the Maya, circa A.D. 700, and the ancient words and names are no longer known as certainties. Also, the author has taken some liberties in using ancient locations which may not yet have been developed during this time period (ca 665-685 AD), since it is only important to the story that they occurred after the close of the Book of Mormon record.

To any who may read this book I would suggest that it is best understood after reading the Book of Mormon. The Book of Mormon is a volume of scripture which supplements the Bible with an account of God's dealings with ancient inhabitants of the Americas through prophets and rulers between approximately 2200 B.C. and 421 A.D., including wars and times of prosperity, but particularly including an account of a visitation to the Western world by Jesus Christ shortly after his resurrection in Jerusalem. It therefore probably includes much of what would be Yax Kan's spiritual and cultural heritage in Ancient America. Finally and foremost, it is my solemn testimony that although this book is a work of fiction, the Book of Mormon truly is not.

LIST OF ILLUSTRATIONS

Subject   **Page**

Map of the route of Yax Kan's journey xxiii

Yax Kan's worm-eaten leaves 8

Utchi "And it came to pass" Glyph and Glyph
    of the Sacrificial Rite 13

Tree of Life Stela (Izapa, Mexico) 33
    (With permission from V. Garth Norman)

Yax Kan meets the great Kan Balam 106
    (With permission from Anika Ferguson)

Pakal's tomb lid (Palenque, Mexico) 121

Pakal's tomb lid (Jaguar God overlay) 122

Pakal's tomb lid (Bat God overlay) 123

Descending God in Tulum 149

Tutoma sings under Crystal Skull Altar in Lubaantun . . 234
    (With permission from Anika Ferguson)

Note: Illustrations not attributed are by the Author.

LIST OF CHARACTERS

BELEB CHO, or Nine Rat—The evil High Priest of Huyub Caan in Lubaantun.

CHI KAL—a resident of Lubaantun who seeks Yax Kan's help.

CHUN CHUKUM—a resident of Lubaantun who goes with Yax Kan to the salt mines.

COROZCO—temple guard in Lubaantun

HUN'TUL—the chief shaman to Kan Balam in Palenque

IXKEEM—Guard at the salt mine of Lubaantun

KAN BALAM, or Snake Jaguar—the king, keeper of the mat or ahau of Palenque, and an actual historical figure, also known as Chan Balam.

KA'WUN, or Coyote—pot-bellied Zapotec guard from the mines.

KECHIKA COC—a scribe to the king of Lamanai

KWIUTUL (Quee-ootul)—a shaman in Lamanai.

LEMNOCH DOUBLE REED—the dwarf potter in Teotihuacan, and Tutoma's father.

MAKIN PAKAL, or Great Sun Shield—the deceased king of Palenque, father of Kan Balam, and an actual historical figure.

MALOCHI—a senior priest in Tulum.

MAZCO—Zapotec guard from the mines.

NAHOMI—Yax Kan's mother.

NATANA—Yax Kan's twin sister.

NAZ-HANI (Nas-hawnee)—Yax Kan's adoptive grandfather and teacher, an elderly shaman

PALAK—Yax Kan's pseudonym during his rescue of the people of Lubaantun.

PEPEM, or Butterfly—a woman in Lamanai with an interest in Lemnoch Double Reed.

PY'ISHKA—Priest and overseer at the salt mine of Lubaantun.

RAGNOTH—A priest in Tulum.

RAMARKIAH—Yax Kan's father, a hunter.

RIBNAKI—a boy in Chichen who acted as guide to Yax Kan.

SASAK KUKUM (nicknamed 'Sak'), or White Feather—A metalsmith working for the Zapotecs.

SEVEN FROG—Naz-Hani's friend in Tonala, the place of refuge.

SHEMITZAH—A shaman from Tonala, traveling companion who took Yax Kan to Izapa.

SMOKING SQUIRREL, or 'Pulque Breath'—A priest of the Temple of Kukulkan in Teotihuacan.

TUTOMA—The daughter of a potter in Teotihuacan and Yax Kan's love interest.

TWELVE TURTLE—a slave at the salt mine of Lubaantun, brother to Chun Chukum.

UXPEQ (pronounced 'Oosh-peck')—meaning "frog"- a merchant-priest in Lubaantun

WAN-ZAC—high priest in Teotihuacan

WI'TZIN, or Little Brother—Yax Kan's jaguar companion, a gift from the great Kan Balam.

YACH'KA—a servant woman to Belem Cho, High Priest of Lubaantun

YAXAM—Guard at the salt mine of Lubaantun

YAX KAN (Yawsh-Kawn)—Apprentice shaman and stone carver, and the main character. At one point he uses the fictitious name Palak in Lubaantun.

ZACONIUH, or Big Zero—man first met on the road to Teotihuacan.

ZAN LOC—a temple guard in the city of Lubaantun.

ZOMER—a helpful young man Yax Kan met on the road to Teotihuacan.

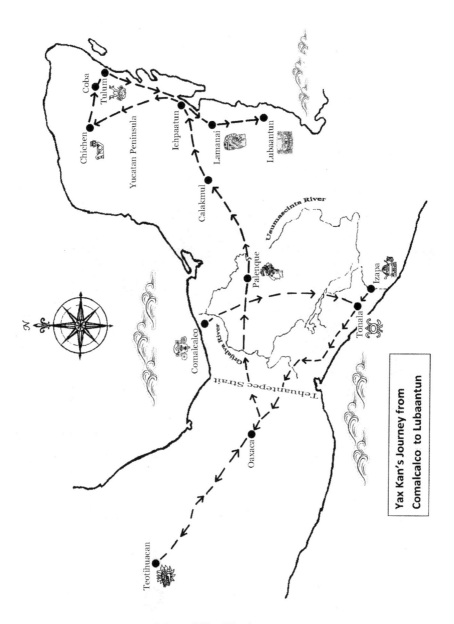

Map of Yax Kan's journey

Part 1

YAX KAN AND THE
MARK OF THE JAGUAR

1

The Mark of the Jaguar

In the lowland swamps near the sea to the north, the tropical jungle threatened to engulf the small human domain of a thatch-roofed village. A bronze-skinned toddler, playing in the warmth of the spring morning, wandered close to the jungle at the edge of the clearing, his playful activities within sight and sound of his family's thatch and pole home. He bent to examine a dung beetle struggling with an oversized load. Out of the dense foliage bright yellow eyes watched the child. Swiftly and silently, a sleek black jaguar lunged out of the broad leafed calathea, swatted the boy to the ground and seized him by his tiny shoulder, immediately leaping back toward the haven of jungle leaves. Before gaining another foothold in the dense stand, a poisoned dart pierced the cat's haunch, causing it to stumble and then lay nearly motionless, paralyzed by the deadly substance on the dart's sharpened bamboo tip. The powerful animal lay twitching, while still holding the child by his small shoulder.

The small boy, Yax Kan, too frightened to cry out in pain or fear, remained clamped in the immobilized jaws of the big cat. The boy's father dropped his blowgun, ran to his son's side, and desperately pried the animal's jaws open in order to rush Yax Kan's shivering, bloody body to his mother for her comfort and healing ministrations.

"Here, Nahomi, our son has been badly hurt, but with your care he will survive," Ramarkiah said. "Dress his wound and help him sleep to bring healing upon him."

Nahomi, suppressing her own panic and concern, tearfully sang a soothing song to little Yax while dressing his wounds with a healing yellow salve made of crushed red grubs and pungent herbal leaves. Then his father re-entered the forest to dispatch the luckless predator and claim his glossy fur. The smell of musk was strong on the great beast. It was an older male and Ramarkiah was astonished that the poison acted so quickly on the cat's system, even though it was a fresh mixture he had just smeared on the dart in the hut.

Ramarkiah marveled at the turn of events. If he had not picked up his blowgun in anticipation of a morning hunt and walked out of their hut just as the jaguar appeared, he could not have saved his only male child. He was certain the jaguar god had chosen his son, Yax Kan, for a special destiny by allowing them the privilege of taking the sacred beast's life to preserve the life of the child. The boy of two *tun*, or short years, would bear the marks of jaguar tooth and claw from that time forward to remind him of his destiny. It was highly unusual for a jaguar to attack a man, especially a child, and even more unusual in the daylight. Legends told of young jaguars emerging from the forest to play with children unaccompanied by adults, but Ramarkiah had never seen that happen, and the great cats seldom attacked when not threatened.

Yax Kan's father was typical of most Maya men in his belief in the gods of forest and field, especially as a hunter. He was a good father, husband and provider for his family. He decided to present the glossy black pelt to the village shaman, as an offering for the continued safekeeping of his cherished only son. He prepared the hide skillfully and carried it to the old shaman, Naz-Hani, and proudly related the curious story of the unlikely kill.

"Naz-Hani, I have a gift for you from the jaguar god for I know that the jaguar is the guiding spirit of a shaman. He has allowed me to preserve my son this morning, and to take the life of one of his children in so doing."

Visibly impressed, the shaman made a formal promise to the father. "Ramarkiah, I am honored by your gift, and I will gladly watch the boy's growth for any other tokens given by the gods portending to his future." From that moment old Naz-Hani doted on the boy and in the following years spent as much time with him as opportunities allowed.

Yax Kan's mother was not a demanding woman, and since she was kept busy teaching Yax Kan's twin sister, Natana, the arts of hearth and home, she welcomed the old man's help with her young son, especially when his father was off hunting. Natana was a quiet child, especially compared to her sibling, but her beauty was beginning to compare to that of her mother's, which was notable among her people. She often quietly listened to Yax Kan's adventures with admiration for his growing strength and skills. Even though they were twins, he was the first born and Natana looked up to him.

Naz-Hani also watched the boy grow and listened to his

parents' stories of his escapades as though he truly were the child's grandparent. Nahomi and Ramarkiah, surprised by the old man's interest, were also flattered. Yax, too, learned to trust and love the old man and asked him questions continuously.

"Why, Nazani, why?" was Yax Kan's most common pleading by the age of four, and unlike some children, Yax did not rest until given an answer he could comprehend. "Why does the night swallow the sun at the end of the day, Nazani?"

As they walked through the nearby forest, Naz-Hani patiently explained the ancient beliefs of their people, hoping his words were sufficient for this most unusual of small ones. "Yax Kan, the path of the sun, Yax-Balam, the younger of our ancestral hero twins, passes through Xibalba, the underworld. This allows all things on the land to rest, while Ixchel, the moon goddess, looks over the things of her responsibility. Ixchel, whom we also call Lady Rainbow, is the goddess of weaving, childbirth and medicine. She bestows the healing qualities on the plants at night, while the sun is in Xibalba. She watches over the women who labor to bring forth the young of the true people, the Maya, and checks on the correctness of the weaving being done every sun. Ixchel also watches over the mothers, teaching the young girls the arts of weaving and household healing with herbs."

"How do the plants know how to heal us, wise one?" Even at this early age Yax learned that respect helped keep the old shaman talking at times when he would rather be observing and ruminating on his own thoughts.

"Now you have asked a key question, Yax Kan and not one I can answer all at once. As the oldest child in your family, you are destined to become a shaman, with powers to heal, and the keys of written knowledge, because this makes us true people. Writing is more powerful than weapons. Knowledge is the key to our power, boy, and you seem an unfillable jug when it comes to learning."

Naz-Hani could not know at the time how much Yax would learn, how important it would be to his future, or how he would come to rely so heavily on the boy's thirst for knowledge, so like his own. Old Naz-Hani had been alone for many years and would normally not have taken another person into his meditative world. His hair was long and turning white, and his muscles, once firm, were becoming wiry and weak with age. His mind, however, was still strong and clear. He had a strong desire to learn more during his lifetime, especially about things of the next life and man's purpose upon the earth as taught by the great god, Kukulkan, who had visited his ancestors long ago.

Little Yax lifted the broad leaf of a large tree searching for the small insects that chewed many holes in the leaves. His mother, Nahomi, had shown him the holes and told him they were caused by small green creatures living under the leaves, but she said he would not be able to find them. Defiantly, he accepted her statement as a challenge. Yax Kan was now five years, and he was not only inquisitive, but also very determined.

Yax Kan found worm-eaten leaves

He learned numbers, and counted everything he encountered, lining up rocks and sticks in the way of Maya children, he kept track of the number of things. If he counted the fingers on one hand, he could represent the number five by using one stick; ten was shown by two sticks and so forth. Each stick served as a five, and any number less than five was symbolized by individual rocks. Thus the count of fourteen was kept by using two sticks and four rocks lined up in the dirt:

O O O O

———————

———————

Later he learned to merely scratch marks on a soft tree trunk or in the dirt to represent the sticks and stones in the abstract. The counting system of the Maya was based on the number twenty, the total number of fingers and toes on a person's body.

His parents were surprised by his abilities since they were simple folk without much education. The shaman had taught Yax Kan to count to satisfy his endless curiosity. Naz-Hani also taught him to date important events, and how to indicate the dates of those highly important events. Some of these events, which Naz-Hani told him were most sacred, were the Great Flood, eclipses of the sun and moon, and the feast times when Venus was aligned with the moon and the earth. Time was an integral part of the religion of the Maya and each *kin*, or time of sunlight, was taken seriously; each period considered a god in its own right. All important activities, especially attacks by their rulers on neighboring clans, were planned based on the position of the planets and the galaxies in the sky.

Yax Kan's own birthday was a propitious date on the *Tzolk'in*, the sacred Maya calendar—which further encouraged old Naz-Hani's attention. Yax was born on the 10th day of the sixteenth *uinal* (13-day period) which was 12 Manik' 10 Mol.

"You understand, small one, that 'Yax Kan' means 'green snake' because that is the name-sign of the day when you were born," explained Naz-Hani. "Every important person is born on an auspicious date, which proves that you are very important to the gods. You have been marked by the claw of the jaguar, young 'Yax Kan Balam', Yax Kan of the jaguar, and you must be constantly aware that you may someday be called upon to perform some special duty."

"What will it be?" young Yax inquired, "Will I become a

great hunter like my father, or a great warrior?" He looked at the old man wide-eyed in anticipation of the answer.

"I do not think so, but I am not yet sure. I only believe you are special, Yax Kan, and that we must keep this in mind and in our prayers." A frowning Naz-Hani turned away, his body language telling Yax the discussion was concluded. He would probably have preferred that Yax had asked if he would someday become a great shaman.

Although dissatisfied with the answer, Yax went back to his play. It was his and Natana's fifth name-day and special foods were being prepared for their family by his mother -- honeyed coconut milk and roasted wild turkey. Yax loved the taste of freshly roasted meats with skin that crunched in his teeth. His family had domesticated some of the large birds for their eggs and meat and kept them in a small enclosure behind their hut. There might even be gifts if they did nothing to displease the household gods, or their parents. He did not forget his teacher's words, but he put them into the recesses of his young mind to ponder later.

While walking near the lagoon the boy spied a tiny nest made by small leaves being folded and fastened together; he pulled open the sticky edges and finally discovered within this nest one of the small, elusive 'eaters of leaves.' His mother would be proud of him for taking the challenge. He counted its legs and the segments on its tiny body, smaller than the half moon in his smallest fingernail. He noted the feelers projecting from its head near its eyes. He also observed the minuscule mouth parts which were directly responsible for the holes in the leaves. Young as he was, Yax wondered about a god who was concerned enough to design each creature so carefully. He cupped the small creature in his hands and ran back to share his discovery with his mother and Naz-Hani.

Yax had been studying all living things since he could walk. He watched the trails of the parasol ants carrying their cargo of leaf segments in small parades through the forest, and studied both the green and the gold iguanas that hid under the mangrove roots on the edge of the nearby green lagoon.

When his father brought home fish, animals, or birds for their meat, skins or bright plumage, he would examine each part of the creatures with great interest. Further, he remembered everything he saw, heard or smelled. He saved so many things of interest he had to keep them outside their hut in a hollow stump with a rock capping the top to keep out curious mice and other prowlers.

Constant labor was necessary to survive in Yax Kan's world. Although he was still too young for most work, he was occasionally asked to carry a small load, or help to prepare a yam or plantain for his family's supper. Too, he was given a small blowgun to practice his skill as a hunter. He learned to roll the fluff from the kapok or 'ceiba' tree around the shaft of a long bamboo sliver and blow it through the long tube made from a 'Cho Otz' tree branch. Later he would be taught to hunt wild game with a throwing stick or spear-thrower, which was used to fling darts, arrows or longer arrow-like spears, accurately and swiftly.

His father was a practiced hunter and provided much of the game upon which his village depended for their communal meals. The villagers gathered wild edible plants and some food was cultivated in small patches after the heavy undergrowth had been burned away.

Theirs was a small community and the head man was only a minor *cahal*, and did not require much from the villagers. Mostly, he was an organizer of hunts and other expeditions, and a judge when others were unable to settle their minor disputes. Yax learned much as he grew and very little escaped his notice. Over the years he took advantage of his association with the shaman, Naz-Hani, to learn more than he could have from his family and villager friendships alone. In this Yax was very fortunate, for old Naz-Hani had traveled much and had a great store of knowledge of the history, religion, writing and healing skills of the Maya, and their Olmeca predecessors, as well. They grew close and the old priest purposefully directed much of Yax Kan's education by encouraging his inquisitive nature in a way that would one day lead him to levels beyond his teacher.

Yax was taught the beliefs and traditions of his people by Naz-Hani, and was trained in reading, writing, forming in stucco, and carving in stone the glyphs which made his people unique. For long hours he practiced etching them on large castor beans with a fire hardened wooden awl and black ink. The beans made an excellent, smooth cartouche for the glyphs.

Each character had a special meaning and they were often combined into one glyph. A common glyph, which told of time passing and was used throughout many of the stories written by the Maya, was the date indicator 'utchi', meaning 'And then it came to pass.' There were forms of the same glyph indicating past and future events passing, as well. Because time was a key to the Maya theology, this glyph was used often, as was 'uti,' meaning: 'It happened.'

Another common glyph, which was used in various ways to depict the sacred ritual of blood sacrifice, was depicted by a human hand with a circle in its center. Sometimes drops of blood were shown falling from the hand. Yax wondered about the origin of this glyph since he was unaware of bloodletting by the priests or kings from their hands. When he asked Naz-Hani about this, the old man scratched his belly a long time before answering him.

The Utchi 'And it came to pass' Glyph and the Glyph of the Sacrificial Rite

"Boy, you ask questions even another shaman would not dwell upon. I know of no other but myself who has pondered the origin of this glyph. There are legends older than this baktun, or sacred calendar round of 52 years, which speak of the great god Kukulkan coming with a wound in each palm, having allowed his blood to be shed to propitiate the wrongdoings of all men and to intercede with the father god for mercy. The *ahau,* or king, of each great city now pierces his own foreskin in the bloodletting rite because it is where new life comes forth, but as I have told you, even this could not be effective unless the king truly was a god."

Naz-Hani was beginning to be fearful for this young boy who thought so deeply. He must be taught to keep his thoughts to himself or he would be judged harshly for questioning the accepted ways of the priests and kings. Naz-Hani himself was always cautious of the ideas and beliefs he shared with other shaman. Yax must learn to keep his own counsel, as Naz-Hani had for many years, about anything differing from the orthodoxy of the polytheistic Maya religion. People had been chosen as sacrificial victims for asking questions of far less import.

2

Zapotecs!

It was the time of resting in the heat of midday and young Yax was dozing under a small lean-to he had created with some palm fronds left over from the thatching of huts. The boy liked to go there and pretend he was a great hunter preparing for the hunt. At eleven years he was still too young to have poison on his darts, or to accompany the men into the forests to hunt. At times he allowed his friends to join him in play, but they were often too noisy for Yax to fully enjoy his imagination, so he preferred to play alone. In his sleepy state he could hear the cacophony of the birds squawking and the monkeys jumping and chattering in the trees. An abrupt silence in the forest brought him fully awake, and Yax wondered what might have quieted the creatures of the forest.

A moment later Yax heard shrieks and frightening sounds coming from the farther huts. Quickly crawling out of his make-believe hunter's hut and peering out through the dust and smoke, he saw his neighbors running being chased by strange painted and feathered warriors and realized something was very wrong. A cold hand gripped his heart. The huts were aflame and villagers were screaming in panic! His eyes burned, and he choked on the smoke and ashes flying through the air. As he was about to run home to the safety of his parents, he saw them and his sister being led out of their hut bound by their wrists. His father, head bloodied by a war club, staggered as he was pushed along. Yax started to cry out, but a strong hand clamped over his mouth and he was lifted and dragged into the nearby forest.

As Yax struggled in panic, he looked over his shoulder. Recognizing old Naz-Hani, he trustingly relaxed in the old man's grip and watched from their hiding place in the trees. After sounds of the brutal raid coming from the village had died down, Naz-Hani gently released him. Yax Kan's heart ached within his chest and he fought back tears that a boy of eleven years among the Maya must not shed. The old man and the boy gazed into each other's eyes and a solemn understanding passed between them. There was nothing the two of them were strong enough to do that would help the others. Desperately they fled together, escaping their burning village south of the city of Comalcalco, with throats still dry and still stinging from the smoke.

In the following days they journeyed down toward the western sea on the south of the Isthmus of Tehuantepec, far from those who had destroyed their village. It was the start of a long and dangerous journey for a boy and an old man, but young Yax instinctively sensed that the shaman believed his life to be worth saving. This gave him added resolve to follow and not to add to the burden his mentor had accepted by useless complaining. Yax would grow stronger as he took more responsibility for their survival because although the old man had great knowledge, he did not have great physical strength. Yax often felt the terrible loss of his parents and sister throughout the journey, but he could not let this slow them down. He would miss them greatly in the coming years, however, as was the way of his people, he kept such sorrow within himself.

Their village had been located near a long swampy stretch of the Grijalva River running north to the sea. Over the next few days they followed the river southerly until it turned up into the Chol highlands toward the west, and then they continued southwesterly, detouring to miss the last of the swamp as they headed into the drier hills and valleys of Tehuantepec. The greens of the trees were lighter hues as they came out of the low, damp forest, as though the trees on the hillsides knew that being closer to the sun would always guarantee sufficient light.

Often the old man and the boy skirted villages where the inhabitants might be unfriendly to those of an unfamiliar clan. Warfare was a way of life in the *Mayab*, the country of the Maya, and the two travelers did not desire to confront any enemies. Naz-Hani knew that travel was relatively safe during the times of planting and harvest; at these times the life-giving crops were all important and warfare was mostly forgotten. However, they were now traveling during the dry season after harvest, so it paid to be cautious.

They foraged as they traveled, seeking the wild fruits, nuts, roots and fat grubs to be found in the forest. Having fled from the village so quickly, they had no weapon but an old obsidian knife. Naz-Hani was not the hunter Yax

Kan's father had been or they would have stopped to fashion weapons for hunting larger game. Naz-Hani had relied on the villagers to supply most of his physical needs, as he provided them with medical and spiritual guidance. As it was, they were forced to rely on the old shaman's knowledge, and the pack of ritualistic supplies which he always carried. Some of these items were not very practical for an exhausting journey of over two hundred miles, especially the black jaguar skin. It had been given to the shaman by Yax Kan's father, and the old man prized it dearly and would not consider leaving it behind.

3

Education

After five days the two fugitives had come down into the Southerly rain forest. The old shaman took this opportunity to share with Yax his knowledge of the varied plant life they encountered. He taught him which of them was useful for food, medicine and other practical tools.

"Yax, this is the 'give and take' plant, whose thorny trunk leaves a painful, stinging rash on any who accidentally brush against it," Naz-Hani explained. "The creator wisely supplied a means to take away their pain if they strip away the spiny bark and apply the inner sap to the painful rash." Not long into the trek, Yax had first-hand opportunity to use this wisdom. He also discovered that the same sap took away the sting and burn of insect bites and other scrapes and scratches as they bushwhacked their way along.

One morning they walked into a clearing next to a large leafy tree where two coati mundis were hissing over something edible on the ground. The two looked up, grabbed their prizes and ambled away as the humans approached. Naz-Hani said, "Here is the Chi Abel, or hog plum tree, which also provides fruit to the banded peccaries, tapirs and other wild animals." He picked one up and gave it to Yax. This one was just ripe, but the pungent, sweet smell of the rotting fruit on the ground came up to Yax Kan's nose as well. "As you can see, it is tasty for man to eat as well. You may remember your father using the bark and leaves of this tree to tan the hides of the animals he killed. When the time is right, I will show you how to use this stripped bark to make an astringent concoction to heal sore throats, mouth sores and other similar ailments." At the mention of his father, Yax felt a sadness tug at his heart, though he was too young to fully comprehend the possible fate of Ramarkiah, the great hunter, and his wife and daughter.

They soon came upon a tree that was as tall as the sacred *ceiba*, but which had a distinctive red bark that made it easy to remember. "Here is the Chacah, or naked man tree, Yax Kan," Naz-Hani said. "It is one of the most valuable trees in the forest. The creator plants it close to this Che Chen or Black Poison vine because the one will purge the pain from the rash caused by the other. It is used for healing both outside and inside the body. A tonic tea made from the bark purifies the blood and cures afflictions in that part of the body which distills our yellow water. This is one of the nine most important sacred healing plants I will show you. As I've told you before, nine is a sacred number. An extract from this plant, together with the others, concocts a powerful medicine for use in the direst emergencies."

They walked farther along the game trail they were following through the rain forest. "Here is another of the nine, the Pay Che or skunk root plant. Here, Yax, smell this root I have cut."

Yax wrinkled his small nose in disgust. "Ewww, Naz-Hani! It smells just like the striped bandit, himself! It must be a very strong medicine."

"It is, boy, and it may save your life someday, so remember its leaves and branches well. See how the branches cross the vine in the shape of the One Tree. Both the roots and bark are used to cure many ailments, especially sores growing inside the stomach."

Naz-Hani had long since ceased to be amazed at how he could show this young one something only once and have it remembered. He knew that teaching Yax these secrets was not done in vain. They walked a little farther to another tree, this one growing out of the mulch of many years.

"This Pa Sak tree has many uses. Its name means 'for the skin,' but that does not mean it is not useful inside the body as well. Boil this tree bark into a tea and it will cure loose bowels and give a healing sleep to the patient. This, too, is one of the sacred nine."

They collected bark, roots, leaves, blossoms, fruits and nuts as they went. Some were for consumption or use on their journey, and others were put into Naz-Hani's healing pouch for future use. Occasionally they came across a Chicle tree and ate its tasty fruit. If there was a gash in the tree, Yax would save some of the oozing sap for later chewing by wrapping it in a leaf. It helped keep his mouth moist while they hiked. They also found the fruit of the Mammee Sapote trees, and feasted upon their spicy, orange-fleshed fruit called sapotes.

The old man seemed to know every tree and plant in the rain forest, as one would know an old friend. He treated them as though they also knew him. He spoke to them and asked permission to partake of their useful parts, never destroying the whole plant unless absolutely necessary. He always thanked the plant for the portion taken.

"Here is the Pixoy tree, Yax," Naz-Hani again began his teaching.

"Oh, I know that one, grandfather," Yax cried as he recognized the tree. "We call it 'plug you up' tree because it stops you from going for a long time if you eat too many of the tasty nuts." Yax remembered greedy friends who had paid the price for their gluttony with their bellyaches.

He often called the old man 'grandfather' and it made Naz-Hani glad in his heart to have this young companion in his later life. All of his own children had long since left to start their own families, and his wife had died many years before. Now he was responsible for the total upbringing of this precocious boy and he took the obligation very seriously. He, too, sorrowed for the loss of Yax Kan's family, but he had done all within his power by saving the boy.

"One more lesson today, Yax, then we will find a place to rest for the night." Naz-Hani spied something further along the path and motioned for Yax to hurry along.

"This vine is Ha Ix Ak, the wild grape," he said. "It is not used for medicine or its sour fruit for food, but it may save your life just the same. Watch!" The old one slashed at the thick vine with his obsidian knife and it squirted Yax right in the face. "Aha! You see? It wants you to taste the sweet water it has stored for you!" He then showed Yax how to cut a piece of the vine to be carried with them, much like a skin water sack. It pleased the boy to learn so much in one day and he relished the lessons as some children relished sweets.

The next day, the forest thinned out and they moved faster, stopping less often. Naz-Hani continued pointing out various plants and their uses at their rest stops, and Yax practiced identifying the ones he had learned. Once they stopped under a large breadnut tree, called Cha Cox, to gather nuts Naz-Hani would later grind up to make into flattened bread-cakes for their dinner. It was one of Naz-Hani's favorite foods. He loved them toasted and hot for they reminded him of his childhood and meals that his mother had prepared for him.

Another time they stopped below an elder tree so Yax would learn to recognize the spiked white blossoms and to gather the root used for snake bites. "This will slow the heart down if someone is bitten by a snake, so the victim does not die before you have time to give him a purgative to remove the poison from his body. See how the root resembles a snake?" Naz-Hani asked Yax as he pulled one out of the shallow pit he had dug and quietly thanked the tree for its gift before cutting the root.

Naz-Hani often told Yax the parables of the Maya, and the snakeroot had reminded him of one. That evening, as they sat in the light smoke of their cooking fires which kept the swarms of mosquitoes away, he began his tale with a serious look, "I will tell you the story of the green iguana whose tail was always quarrelling with his head because it wanted to lead the way. 'You are always in the lead and I am unfairly left to drag behind in the dirt! You must let me lead some of the time!' the tail exclaimed.

"The head answered, 'It was ordained by the creator that I should be the head and lead. I cannot let you blindly lead or we would soon be lost!'" Naz-Hani looked very somber in his role as storyteller, and Yax frowned appropriately as he listened.

"The argument continued until one morning the tail wrapped itself around the base of a small tree and would not let the head of the iguana pull the body forward. When the head and body finally wearied from the struggle, the eyeless tail prevailed and began to lead the body. Almost immediately the iguana fell into a deep ravine and died from the fall. Yax Kan, that is why the creator made the iguana's tail so weak, to come off quickly if it ever tries to take the lead again!"

"The world is a place of order, Yax, and everything has its own role to play. If this order is upset it will disturb the way the plants, animals and men work together. Most people do not see beyond the plantain leaves they eat their meals upon, and so do not understand this principle." It pleased both the man and boy to end the day with a story, and they were content as they retired.

Most nights they slept up off the ground in the hollows of dead tree stumps on beds of soft fern fronds, or their bodies tied into the broad crooks of great trees. They drank from small springs gurgling beside the game paths. Yax found himself missing the common luxuries of shelter and well-prepared meals, taken for granted until now in his young life. The adventure of travel and new surroundings was such a challenge to his inquisitive mind that he often stopped worrying about his sister and parents. Although he never forgot them, his tender years and the distractions of the journey helped him to suppress the mourning he otherwise would have felt at their unexpected disappearance from his life.

One morning after they had awakened and eaten the remains of a scant meal from the night before, Naz-Hani made a hand sign for "Quiet!" and drew Yax Kan's attention to an ocelot, or striped and spotted wildcat, sitting up-wind and below them, bathing her alert young kittens. They watched as she taught them to catch mice and lizards in the grassy hillocks below their roost in a large fica tree. Yax was fascinated by these smaller cousins of the jaguar, and they watched until the cats left to find a place to sleep through the light and heat of the new day.

Naz-Hani spoke to Yax about the great jaguar often. He revered the animal and felt the boy should learn all he could about the beautiful cat. Yax learned that the jaguar is a solitary animal as an adult and seeks out another only during mating season with a compelling, coughing love call in the night.

Although the old shaman pushed on as fast as he could manage most of the time, it was not unusual for him to stop for some lesson about the natural world for Yax Kan's education. The drier country they were crossing was different from the marshy jungle where Yax had been raised and there were many new lessons to be learned about their changing world.

Some evenings, as they squatted by small fires started by spinning a fire stick in a piece of soft wood to spark dry moss tinder, the boy's teacher would burn incense made from the resin of the *copal* tree mixed with wood dust. Then they would pray and Naz-Hani would tell stories of Kukulkan, a fair-skinned god whose temperament was far more benevolent than most of the other gods revered by the Maya. Yax listened intently to the stories, wondering whether he would ever understand this great, white and bearded god who came down out of the clouds.

Naz-Hani told him, "Although Kukulkan has appeared before, he will someday come again. Most of the people in this land have long ago rejected his teachings of gentle kindness. Their priests would rather offer sacrifices and bloody offerings than show compassion to one another. I have learned that Kukulkan explained that his own blood sacrifice was the last blood offering necessary, but our clans are so steeped in their traditions they do not remember his teachings. I am saddened by our people in this thing, Yax Kan."

Naz-Hani admitted he was unsure about many of the teachings of Kukulkan, since most of his instructions to the people had long ago been lost. He tried to remember all he had ever learned to pass on to his young protégé, but there were parts which were clearly missing in the narrative. Over the centuries not all of the legends had been preserved and Naz-Hani mourned the loss of knowledge more than anything else. Even the reason for representing the god as a feathered serpent was now much misunderstood.

As many questions as answers were accumulated during these fireside sessions. Some questions were intentionally implanted by the kind old man, to whet Yax Kan's curiosity.

The priest clearly was preparing the boy to carry on his own life's quest for knowledge after he was gone. It had been his life's most important work to seek out any information about Kukulkan yet remaining among the people of the land, but there was much still unanswered, and he feared he was too elderly to seek much longer. He was confident that through Yax Kan, his life's pursuit would continue and not be in vain.

Naz-Hani had never been the type of shaman who would use pretense and intimidation to gain the respect of the villagers or visitors to their community. Rather, Naz-Hani relied on his actual knowledge and wisdom gained during his relatively long life to earn the respect of those he served. His love for his fellow Maya was evident in the way he lived.

Finally, after fifteen days, as they continued south, the landscape began to change again, becoming familiar; it was more like the home they had fled near the northern marshes, yet different. The air was moist once more, but the plant life had changed yet again. After a long and wearying journey, Naz-Hani finally told Yax they would come to Tonala, their destination, on the morrow. With a mixture of fear and curiosity, Yax tried to enter sleep, and when he finally slipped off, he dreamed of his home and parents in their village as it had been before, not as it was now, lying in ashes. On the rising of the sun he was anxious to be on the way, trusting his mentor not to lead him into danger.

4

Tonala

Upon entering Tonala, Naz-Hani sought out an acquaintance from long ago when he had come here on an earlier pilgrimage. This kindly friend, Seven Frog, proved to be their salvation. He was a skilled artisan, just prosperous enough to provide for them until they could build a hut of their own, and to protect his house guests from prying neighbors, who disliked strangers. Seven Frog was eager to hear the story of their journey and to renew acquaintance with his old friend, Naz-Hani.

Yax was only eleven years when his parents and sister, Natana, were captured and presumed sacrificed by what Naz-Hani told him later was a marauding group of Chontal-speaking Zapotecs. Over the next ten years in his new home of Tonala, Yax learned many other things of great importance which helped to satisfy his hunger for knowledge. Still he harbored a great emptiness inside from not yet 'feeling' the significance of this knowledge in his life. His body grew straight and strong, while his mind remained keen.

In Tonala, by the age of eighteen years, Yax was helping

to carve small stelae, or tree stones, which recorded ancient legends and prophecies through pictograms, so that the descendants of their people, and any immigrating tribes of the future, would know the truths left behind by the ancients. Naz-Hani instructed Yax to withhold his knowledge of glyph writing in Tonala, since they used few of them here and it might make him suspect to their priests.

The young scribe drew representations of the legends and prophecies on large deer skins which had been specially prepared through a secret tanning process, making them almost transparent and wonderfully smooth, and easy to draw upon with a stylus of hard charcoal.

Next, the arduous and painstaking art of carving the hard limestone of the stela was mastered. This was done in part with highly-prized hardened copper alloy chisels imported by traders from the land of the Inca far to the South. These tools were very valuable and rare, and if left out in the open the rain and the juices from rotting plants would cause pitting and soon dissolve the precious metal instruments.

The sap of one rare plant was also employed to soften the stone surface being carved. When left on the hard surface for a few suns, the hard stone or copper chisels could then be used on the now somewhat chalky exterior of the normally hard limestone. The stone would eventually harden again as it was washed with rain over time. The priests of Tonala provided the sap of this plant and would not confide in Yax which plant was used. One day he secretly followed them into the jungle and was nearly found out by one of them who had stopped to make water on the forest floor. He watched them harvest a particular plant from the array of vegetation in the southern coastal forest. Later experimentation assured him that this was the softening ingredient, and he remembered the plant so he could find it again, when needed.

Tonala was a renowned ceremonial center and many priests from other villages came there on feast days to join in rituals of fire, cornmeal and animal blood, performed between two large stone altars, one shaped like a jaguar, one like a crocodile. Both altars were perched on top of one of the pyramidal temples over a central staircase and ramp in the central plaza. Great feasts of venison, fowl, seafood, squash, corn, beans, and fruit of all varieties followed. The festivities sometimes lasted for weeks and the participants ate until they could eat no more. They then slept through both nights and days until they could begin feasting again.

During one of these feast times, Yax heard two shamans discussing some stelae in the older city of Izapa down the coast from Tonala. "Some of the tree-stones are taller than a man, with the most ornate carvings I have ever seen," said one.

"I remember some of the pillars are topped by balls as round as the moon…very difficult to carve into such a shape," the other remembered. "There were circular altars in front of nearly every tree-stone for offerings to the gods and their revered ancestors. One had a great bird upon it and another was carved into the likeness of a giant serpent head."

Upon hearing this, Yax went up to them, explained that he was a stone carver and ventured to ask them about the stories carved into these stelae, "Are they unlike the ones here in Tonala?"

"Oh yes!" answered one, "And much older, too."

He was invited to accompany the senior of the two to

Izapa on the following day, "I will welcome your assistance in understanding the tree-stones, young man." The priest noted the rippling muscles in the young stone carver's arms and no doubt also thought of how useful Yax would be in carrying supplies for the excursion.

Naz-Hani was too feeble to undertake another journey, but he encouraged Yax and as he bid him farewell, it was obvious that he was as excited as Yax about the excursion. He had never been to Izapa, he said, and wanted to hear about all Yax would find there. He knew Yax was no longer a child, but his caring heart was nevertheless fearful that he might come to harm.

Yax and the shaman, Shemitzah, traveled along the coast for three days, finally arriving in Izapa, where, as usual, the residents seemed reluctant to have strangers in their midst. A few small huts were scattered throughout a wooded area laying a little inland from the coast and some of the stone structures were beginning to show signs of neglect. Shemitzah, explained that this city had flourished in times past, but was now almost deserted with only some idle priests left who selfishly took advantage of the remaining clanspeople.

Izapa was a very old city; older than Tonala and other cities within a few days' journey, and there was much to be learned here. There was one old tree-stone, or stela, in Izapa which particularly puzzled Yax Kan. It depicted at least eight man-like figures and two other god-like characters, along with a *wakah chan*, or world tree, which was unusual in that it was not as stylized as he would have crafted it based upon others he had seen; rather this tree was more realistic. It had twelve roots, a grafting scar, and plentiful fruit in its branches. It held greater mystery for him because of the simple realism of its story. Although there were many symbolic representations on this stone, most Mayan carvings were far more abstract and ornate.

He could read its symbolism easily, but did not understand why he had not heard a story corresponding to these figures and their actions before. There was a royal couple instructing two others about eternal principles, and a fresh spring, as well as a stream of dirty water, some sort of rod extending toward the tree, and symbols for the afterlife and immortality, such as fish and humming birds. Yax Kan had the impression that this stone was part of the answer to questions he had about life's meaning. At the top of the stone was the jaguar symbol, which was used to indicate the importance of this story, and it seemed a good omen to Yax Kan, who bore the jaguar's mark. The puzzle of this stela remained in his heart when he and Shemitzah left Izapa to return home.

Yax Kan was tall for his people, almost five feet, nine inches, and his dark hair hung down below his strong jawline and was cut to taper down to touch the base of his neck. As Yax Kan grew in stature, he also grew in wisdom and skill. His abilities and store of knowledge had surpassed all other scribes and artisans in Tonala and the regions thereabout. Rather than exulting in his superiority, this merely increased his hunger for something more.

He wore a simple rough deerskin breechcloth and rawhide sandals strapped to his ankles. Without a shirt not only his strength was evident; the jaguar tooth and claw marks on his shoulder were conspicuous to all who saw him, but he

Tree of Life Stela in Izapa

did not concern himself with that. He was tired of hiding himself. Yax Kan's self-esteem was well-rooted in the value that Naz-Hani had bestowed upon him through respect, kindness and love, not on his outward appearance, or the opinions of strangers.

As they walked through Izapa and discussed what they had found there, the shaman Shemitzah marveled at the intelligence and understanding of the young man. He realized how much time and effort the renowned Naz-Hani had invested in Yax Kan's education. He also contemplated on what things the boy would accomplish in his lifetime. It would be interesting to follow the young man's activities in the future. Yax might learn something valuable one day.

In another place there was a stone carving depicting a bearded man in a boat of strange design, much larger than the dugouts he had seen. The boat was sailing easterly toward the sun glyph over the fish and waves representing the open sea. Yax wondered silently who this man was, *"Was he an ancestor or just a traveler who had come from another land?"*

Yax knew he was partly of the Maya people, but also descended from the Totonac, a group which had inherited blood, knowledge and many traditions from the ancient tribe known as the Olmeca, or rubber people. They were named after the rubber trees from which they made the hard, black rubber balls used in their religious 'games,' which had often ended in human sacrificial offerings to the gods. It was supposedly a great honor to be sent into the next life after having played in the ceremonial games—win or lose—at the whim of the ruler. Ominously, here in Izapa were the remains of such a ball court, as well. Yax Kan's people still mimicked this brutal pastime in the larger cities.

According to Naz-Hani, these ancient ones had once inhabited the area stretching from here in Izapa to many miles north of the White Mountain area about 2,000 *haab*, or long years of 365 *kin*, earlier. He explained that the Olmeca had passed on secrets of the sun, the moon, the planets and the stars to the Maya. As their successors the Maya had devised a precise mathematical and multi-dimensional model of the universe, and from this knowledge the Maya had prepared calendars and tables regarding the past, present and future.

Yax had no idea where the Olmeca had originally received their knowledge, but old Naz-Hani had taught him it was from the great god, Kukulkan or Plumed Serpent, himself. There were representations of Kukulkan in every city he had ever heard about, including here in Izapa. Although some shamans preferred paying homage to animal deities such as the bat god, the god of the night, or the jaguar god, the god of the forest, or to Chaac, the long-nosed god of rain, all of them recognized the white and bearded god, Kukulkan, shown as a plumed serpent in their oldest stonework. None ever tried to deny his existence, but some leaders had taken on his name and tried to exalt themselves to his divine station.

Yax parted company with Shemitzah as they returned to Tonala, and then went straight to Naz-Hani to share all that he had learned. Yax talked for many hours with only a few interruptions from the old one. They both were excited by this new store of knowledge and possible answers to some of their questions about the origins of their people and traditions. Naz-Hani fit this information into stories he had been gleaning for many years, but still could not make a picture complete enough to clear the mists of forgetfulness from the many hundreds of years of his people's legends. Further searching would be necessary to learn the truths they sought.

5

A Farewell

Shortly after returning from Izapa, Yax was called for by Naz-Hani to the old shaman's deathbed. As Yax entered the small hut, the heady smell of *copal* incense burning reminded him of many sessions with Naz-Hani teaching him spiritual precepts. He hurried to his side and found his old mentor looking pale and as though he was suffering greatly.

With his head propped up on a stone headrest and gazing at Yax through the haze of incense smoke, Naz-Hani spoke, "Yax Kan Balam, my adopted grandson, together we have probed the traditions of our people, and have often found them wanting in purpose and truth. We both know there is some underlying thread of knowledge, lost over time by overly-ambitious rulers and too-zealous priests. I challenge you to continue our search for these truths. Long ago, I taught you that the most important missing precepts were related to Kukulkan, who was the only god in the Maya religious beliefs offering peace and brotherhood to our people, but this too has been buried by false legends and shrouded by mystery and superstition."

"Yax, here is the black jaguar pelt that your father gave me long ago, after saving you from the jaws of the great beast. I am no longer certain there is any jaguar god; I only know you were preserved as though for some great purpose. You must continue on the quest for the truth in all things. I know you will find what we have both been seeking. Perhaps, I will learn new truths when I pass into the underworld of Xibalba, after the death I feel coming upon me. We will talk again someday about what we have both found in our lives here in the Upper Kingdom, upon the face of this world. I feel cold now and must say goodbye, but hear me, Yax Kan, I will do all I can to help you from the other side. I feel assured my spirit will not die with this old body."

"Grandfather, you cannot die yet!" Yax cried. "There is still much for us to learn together. Let me prepare the concoction of the nine sacred plants, and it will give you the strength to remain in this world." Yax clearly did not desire to lose his dear mentor and only family.

Naz-Hani gazed directly at him through the haze. "No, Grandson, it is not right to stay beyond one's time, and I know in my heart this is mine. It would be a mockery to use the mixture of nine at a time like this. You will be able to search farther afield with me gone, than with me here, and besides, I hunger to learn the lessons of the otherworld. You must continue our search for what is real in this world."

Naz-Hani's voice weakened and his trembling grip on Yax Kan's hand relaxed. Yax placed the great black fur over the old man's small frame to warm and comfort him in his final moments. He had been father, mother and clan to him for most of his life. Yax already mourned for his teacher in his heart.

MARK OF THE JAGUAR

"Know that the one true God cares for you, Yax Kan!" The dying shaman's voice was clear and strong, and surprised the young scribe. Then with a great sigh, Naz-Hani was gone. His grip tightened once and then his hand fell from Yax Kan's grasp as though it were a stone.

Yax was outwardly stoic, but inside his spirit grieved and wept. Seven Frog, who had been standing by the door to their hut, put his hand on Yax Kan's shoulder to gesture his compassion and support, and then he left to make preparations for the funeral.

Yax went to his workshop to prepare a fine funerary carving to be placed in Naz-Hani's grave. He carved a jaguar from yellow jasper with eyes of inset black obsidian, and memorial glyphs on all four haunches. This offering was given out of respect, not because Yax believed it would accompany Naz-Hani on his spirit journey to Xibalba.

It was many days before Yax ventured out of their hut after they had put Naz-Hani's remains in a stone tomb under the ground next to the hut. The townspeople had grown to love and respect the great shaman, and mourned his passing by ceremonially breaking pottery, smoking *mai* leaves and burning *copal* incense.

The old man had been unable to impart his entire vast store of knowledge to Yax, which left the young man pondering, "How did we come by this knowledge? Why was it given to men, particularly my own tribe and ancestors?" He wondered what the legends contained that could be used to guide his life, and whether he would live to see the fulfillment of the prophetic, dream-like stories he had been taught. He had accepted the open challenge given by Naz-Hani at his dying long before it was given to him, and he rededicated himself to seeking and discerning these lost truths.

Although an artist, craftsman, scribe and shaman, Yax found he had received a better education regarding Maya religious legends and futuristic revelations than the young temple acolytes of his age. These aspiring priests, in their youthful arrogance, were willing to lower themselves to speak with him only because of his extraordinary skill in the sacred work of his stone carvings. They condescendingly asked him many questions because his artwork depicted so intricately the mysteries of the past, present and future of the entire known world from beginning to end. Some stories known to this young prodigy, they had never before heard.

On his part, Yax was too familiar with the local priests of Tonala to believe they had great supernatural powers, or that they were seers. Although he knew the kings of the land claimed godhood itself, he had never seen much real evidence that this was true. He had been taught by Naz-Hani this unbelief was something he could never admit to others or he was more likely to be selected for blood sacrifice. However, as a seeker of truth, Yax needed more than claims and stories to satisfy his searching mind. This was one reason he had neither sought nor made a close friend in Tonala before or after the passing of Naz-Hani.

He was unimpressed by masks, elaborate costumes of jades, shells, feathers and furs, or of breastplates, helmets and physical prowess. His was not the mind or spirit of a warrior, or even a religious zealot; rather he was more akin to the scholars and scribes of other times and places.

Many legends related by Naz-Hani referred to a great city

by a great lake, far to the North, Teotihuacan, birthplace of the gods, a city even further north than Oaxaca, which lay South of the Zapotec temple of the white mountain. He knew this great city contained even greater temples and great pyramids, enlarged every sacred calendar round of fifty-two years, when all things demanded renewal and a new skin of stone and cement was applied. He felt sure what old Naz-Hani had described as the 'Avenue of the Sun' would hold a record preserved in stone that would reveal all he must learn, the knowledge about origins for which he yearned.

Now that Naz-Hani was gone, Yax longed for a companion with whom he could truly share his insights and feelings. He was unsure whether such a person existed in the restricted, almost enslaved society in which his people dwelt. The common people were constantly being indentured by local ruling classes, the *ahauob* and *cahalob*, to build and rebuild the massive temples and pyramids. Outwardly these leaders built these structures to revere the pantheon of Maya deities, but in reality they were monuments to the myopic and egotistical rulers. Their earlier communal system of equitable agricultural labor had been expanded into unjust and enforced servitude by the elite rulers and the burden on the people was nearly unbearable.

The young men were conscripted as needed to serve as soldiers, and trained for battle with no consideration of innate skills or personal aspirations. It seemed most young men had ceased to consider that they might entertain desires to make personal choices in their own lives. Minds became enslaved before bodies, and their lives were so predetermined, they imagined warfare was their choice, not their forced destiny. Of course, the known alternatives seemed even more unsavory. Most of them could only consider lives as slaves, sacrificial victims, or priests in a filthy brotherhood of bloodletting, unless they had served a rare apprenticeship to a tradesman. Those lazy but cunning ones with perverted ambitions became such priests.

To a great extent battles were stylized confrontations, with the lives of a few being forfeited in a kind of deadly game as leaders traded warriors with other groups to be taken captive and used for human sacrifice. The swords in the *Mayab* were gruesome weapons with sharpened pieces of obsidian along their edges. Their stone war clubs were as likely to maim as to kill. In recent years, though, war had been bloodier, and weapons like the *atlatl*, previously used only to take game, were also used to kill enemies. Secret brotherhoods were formed to allow murder for power or wealth within one's own city to go unpunished. These organized criminals belonged to an evil group that had endured for centuries in their darkened, hidden chambers, and the originators were long forgotten.

The lives of the lower-caste women were especially held to be of negligible value, and Yax could not understand how men could treat other beings with such disregard.

Yax seemed to be an enigma in his time, unable to accept the mores of the society around him. He had indeed been fortunate, considering his parents had been common villagers. He had learned shamanic skills and had become an artisan and scribe, considered of great value to the rulers and priests. They looked upon Yax as a lifetime servant, of course, but he was allowed much autonomy in exercising his craft.

6

Adventure

Yax was now a man and yearned for adventure, but even more for answers that he could not find in Tonala. After much planning and preparation—and telling no one, not even Seven Frog—Yax slipped out of the village early one morning, unnoticed, to journey toward Teotihuacan, the city of the ancients far to the north.

He traveled through the coastal jungle for many days until reaching a broad stone-and- concrete road, called a *sacbe*, the trade route that ran north and south. He continued north on this road, and after pacing himself for most of one day he found a place to rest, so weary from the first leg of his journey that he slept the rest of the sunlight and all night through without thought of finding and preparing food.

Cold and hungry, Yax awoke so early in the morning that a few of the brightest stars still shone in the brightening sky. He had been traveling for an entire moon cycle, and he thought he was still far from his destination of Teotihuacan. How far, he was not sure. As he began rekindling the banked coals under the outcropping of limestone where he had spent the night, he let his thoughts wander back over the events that had demanded this journey.

Fortunately, his education had not been limited to religion, medicine and rock-carving, because while contemplating his past and future, he used his curved and decorated spear-thrower, to hunt and kill a pachybara, a large rodent, for his morning meal. As it cooked over his small fire, his appetite was whetted by the lowland morning air. He wolfed down the greasy meat with relish and afterward ate two wild figs and chewed some dried herbs that would enhance his energy for the long trek ahead.

On a rise, gazing into the distance at the unending jungle stretching out toward his goal, Yax was grateful for the seemingly endless trade route, which allowed him to pass through the dense foliage so quickly. Each day he could easily cover about twenty miles wearing sandals made of tough peccary hide and carrying a light woven hemp pack. He always took a short afternoon nap to escape the heat of mid-day.

Yax hefted his pack and began the easy jog that he could maintain for hours. *"Will I find the answers I seek when I reach my destination?"* he silently mused. *"Surely the ancients would have left some clue to the source of their sacred knowledge in the great city of pyramids. Did the gods walk among them or visit their kings and priests?"* His mind seldom rested.

As the sun began to sink again, he came to a rocky haven where he could spend another night. A brief hunt with his dart throwing stick brought down two small waterfowl for his evening meal and he set to spinning his fire stick with a small bow to light his cooking fire. After eating one of the birds, he let the other smoke beside the coals. He lay down under the light deerskin blanket from his pack and enjoyed the deep slumber of those who work both body and mind each day.

The next morning he saw travelers coming toward him in the distance on the long straight road, and for safety's sake he hid in the jungle next to the road to let them pass. They had no doubt seen him as well, but at such a distance that they would be unable to see exactly where he had slipped into the jungle if he were very careful.

Lone travelers could be easily overcome and many thought that any stranger was an enemy worthy of death. He had undertaken this journey on his own, and without a protective token from the nearest 'Keeper of the Mat' or some other noble; at best he would be taken into slavery, if caught. His one valuable possession, the black jaguar skin given to him by Naz-Hani would certainly be taken from him to be worn by one of royal birth.

As he waited for the group to pass, Yax peered through the dense foliage of the jungle trying to discern through the morning mist what was happening in a small clearing about fifteen yards away. He heard noises that had a vague familiarity. They were not voices, at least not human voices, but quiet sounds that seemed to come from some living creature. As he crept forward, careful not to snap a twig or vine underfoot that would give away his presence, the mist gradually cleared and he beheld a primal struggle.

A huge boa constrictor was crushing the final weak breath and the last of life's spark out of a juvenile, ebony-colored tapir. The long-nosed creature's final movements were very slight as it met unconsciousness and then death. After a few minutes of stillness, the great reptile slowly began to uncoil from its now lifeless prey, and started the laborious process of unhinging its lower jaw and sliding its gaping mouth over the snout of the limp animal in order to engulf it.

Then, in an instant, without warning of sight or sound, and before the boa could begin to respond, the tapir was snatched out of the huge snake's mouth by the largest she-jaguar Yax had ever seen! Yax held his breath. In a single bound the jaguar lifted the heavy carcass into the buttresses of a mangrove tree next to a swampy stream. It hissed once as it released the tapir onto its perch, and then began tearing at the soft underbelly to feast on the tender organs within.

The slavering she-cat looked up once, seeming to peer directly into Yax Kan's eyes, but then went back to her juicy repast. She must have weighed as much as two men. Yax shuddered and felt a tingling in the scars on his shoulder caused so long ago by one of her kind. He reminisced only momentarily on his childhood experience as he turned to go.

Yax was grateful that he had been downwind or the jaguar might have chosen to take him for her meal. He thought it unusual to see a big cat hunting during the daytime; she must have had barren hunts in recent nights.

The snake had already slithered into the jungle in search of other game. It seemed to Yax that the serpent was hardly perturbed by the loss of its kill. As he had often observed in nature, animals quickly accept the whim of fate and continue on with the cycle of their lives, content with the lot that nature bestowed. He decided that he should probably do the same, but that did not slake his insatiable desire to learn all that he could in this life.

Noiselessly, he slipped back the way he had come, thankful for the insight that he had gleaned from this voyeuristic experience. Once again on the stone highway, he began his steady jog which, except for his brief nap at mid-day, he would maintain until almost nightfall. The pace allowed him plenty of time for reflection, even as his senses automatically remained alert for the dangers he accepted as an unavoidable part of his life.

As the sun set over the forest, Yax settled in the branches of a tall *ceiba* tree, satisfying his hunger with provisions of smoked meat and fruit from his pack. He quickly fell into the sleep of clear-conscienced youth. His dreams were of a kindly father figure who was white-robed and wise. This person was pointing at the carved figures on the tree-stone in Izapa and explaining their meaning. He also showed him a beautiful city by the sea and told him stories of the one god, but by sunrise his memory of the dream was unclear, and in the press of preparing for another day of travel it soon slipped from his mind.

"Perhaps today I will reach Teotihuacan," he thought.

7

Discovery

One day after his mid-day nap, as Yax topped a low hill on his trek, he was surprised to see a young couple traveling toward him. The young woman was carrying a small child and a few belongings. The man carried a large load on his back with a *mecapal*, or tumpline, around his forehead. A scraggly tan dog was on their heels as they hurried along. Though he usually stayed out of sight of travelers, Yax felt no fear of this man, barely older than himself, or of his little family.

"Hail, stranger!" the man called out.

Yax raised his hand in greeting, and they were soon standing face to face. "Where do you go with your family in such a hurry?" Yax questioned.

"It is not where we travel to, but what we hurry away from, that concerns us," the young father answered, as he rested his pack on the stone highway. "And it would be well for you to be cautious as well, unless you wish to end up as slaves in the mines of the Zapotecs."

"Zapotecs!" At once, Yax was attentive and angry. "They

are the ones who took my parents and sister to be sacrificed when I was only a child," he said bitterly. "Are we near a Zapotec city?"

"No, we are near their mines, but I can't believe that they would kill able-bodied people. They take most captives to be used as slaves, not for sacrifices. When was your family taken, and from where?" The young man seemed to be interested, even though he nervously kept watch behind himself on the road for possible pursuers.

"I am Yax Kan. My parents were taken from me, and I escaped, nearly ten years past in a village near Comalcalco. I thought surely that my family would have been sacrificed to the gods by the blood-thirsty Zapotecs!"

"I am Zomer, and I tell you they would only have killed your parents if they tried to escape or were armed, unless, of course they were of the elite class." It was clear from the expression in his eyes that Zomer did not think Yax looked like royalty. He had been able to tell by his simple dress that he was not a Zapotec.

Yax was so preoccupied he didn't notice the potential slight. His mind was in a confusion of anger and hope. "If my family is not dead, where might they be?"

"It is most likely that they would be working for the 'Zaps' in their mine over those hills to the northeast which lie south of their city of Oaxaca and the Temple of the White Mountain further north. We have traveled swiftly and carefully since our own village was plundered and clansmen taken. We had wrongly supposed we were too important to them in growing food for their soldiers and slaves, to be taken to work in the mines. They have always raided further away in the past, but they are either getting lazy or desperate because they came yesterday late in the afternoon and took everyone and everything they could. I and my family barely escaped because we were down by the streamside looking for willows to weave fish baskets when we heard them and hid in the reeds."

This was almost more than Yax could bear. His emotions ran wild within him. For ten years he had believed that his family was dead. Now he suddenly found that they may not only be alive, but close by. He told Zomer that he must try to find and help them. He noticed the young mother held fear in her eyes, and knew that he must not hinder these people from their flight. The baby boy in her arms must not grow up without parents as Yax had. It did not seem probable that another child would be fortunate enough to have a 'Naz-Hani' near at hand to raise him.

"Thank you for your information and warning, but I see that you must be swift in your flight. Go now, and may the great god, Kukulkan, protect you!"

"Yax Kan, thank you for your blessing; it gives me hope that anyone cares for another in this world of ours. I may be able to do you one more service before we separate. At the village near the mines, where I have often packed the harvest from our fields, there is a good man named Sasak Kukum, meaning White Feather, who is a master metalsmith. If you see him, you will know he is not a 'Zap' because of his height and because of the burn scar on his left cheek where molten metal splashed on his face many years ago. If you ask for his help discreetly he will not fail you, because he too despises the horrid Zapotecs. Go in safety, Yax Kan."

With a wave of his hand, Yax watched them for a moment as they passed over the hilltop he had just descended. It was early yet and the sun had not risen high, but Yax feared that he could not stay on the road and continue in the direction from which Zomer had come. He left the road and found that the forest was dryer and sparser here. Yax decided to travel directly through the trees toward the hills Zomer had indicated, hoping he might learn more as he went. He wisely avoided any trail that looked like more than a game trail, and even then he was careful not to leave signs of his passage.

"How old would my parents be now?" he pondered as he went, *"And if they are slaves, is my sister kept with them?"* His chest was light with the new hope that they might be alive, but tight with fear that he might lose them again if he was not very careful and clever.

It took hours of walking through the low hills before he could see that he was nearer to the higher hills of his destination. Then as he approached those hills he smelled the smoke of cooking fires, but not the aroma of roasting meat. *"They must only feed the slaves corn mush,"* he thought. Then in an opening in the brush he saw movement in a scattered village; children and very old men and women were each engaged in their own tasks preparing dinner for the stronger adults who would be returning near dusk from the mines.

Another smell met his senses, an acrid odor that was unfamiliar and certainly not coming from the wood and foodstuffs of cooking fires. He crept cautiously from tree to tree, keeping low to the ground, peering through the oncoming dusk at everything visible in the settlement.

Yax began to see warriors swaggering in the midst of the

people, evidently loosely guarding these poor slaves, as they brandished straight swords and curved cimeters with terrible teeth of obsidian along their edges. The broken inhabitants of this cheerless place flinched when the soldiers walked near them, averting their eyes and striving not to bring the Zapotec's wrath upon themselves. Yax had never felt this way toward other living beings, but in his heart he wanted to avenge these poor, terrorized people, as well as his lost family, and strike these strutting quetzals, wearing their fancy battle clothes.

Holding himself in check because he knew that he must, Yax waited until they had passed. He almost moved on, and would have missed what he was looking for, had he not suddenly smelled again the hot, bitter fumes of a few moments before. He looked for the place where this smoke originated, and saw one open hut with a bench and stool. Upon the stool sat a man who appeared to be neither a warrior nor a slave. A light-skinned, lanky fellow with his hair pulled back and bound so that a tail hung down his spine. Yax silently moved closer to the edge of the settlement. He thought he saw a lighter patch of skin on one cheek. This must be the man that Zomer had described to him, Sasak Kukum, the metal master. Yellow smoke spewed out of a small kiln-like structure by the man's fire where he was melting some kind of ore.

Yax settled down under some shrubbery and chewed on some parched kernels of *maiz* to await complete darkness before approaching the metalsmith's hut. It seemed like many hours, but eventually the slaves had returned and gone into their various quarters to eat and sleep. Many slept in hammocks hung near their huts, but their sleep might have been the sleep of death, for no one stirred. In their captivity they had evidently learned to take advantage of every opportunity to rest, so they would not be beaten by their taskmasters for moving too slowly or making mistakes born of exhaustion, as they worked throughout the daylight hours.

Moving stealthily through the moonless night toward the dwelling, barely visible in the starlight falling within the shadow of the hills, Yax silently approached Sasak Kukum's hut. Fearful of being heard, he tapped the doorpost lightly, hoping that the man inside would not be fearful or cry out an alarm.

"What is it?" a deep voice quietly answered his tapping.

"A stranger, alone, come to find you because a man named Zomer told me you might help me," Yax whispered.

"I know Zomer. Come in quickly then, and we will speak," Sasak answered.

Once Yax had pulled aside the door flap and entered, he saw that the room was dimly lit by a small oil lamp. "Are you the metalsmith, Sasak Kukum?" Yax asked, but seeing the whitened scar on his cheek, he knew the answer. He guessed that the man was about ten years his senior, and thirty years was considered a very mature age among the people of the Maya.

"Assuredly, and this is my humble lodging. Call me 'Sak'. Who are you and what do you need of me?"

Yax felt relief that what he had guessed was now affirmed. "My name is Yax Kan. I am seeking my parents and a sister who were taken by the Zapotecs many years ago. I thought them dead, but then I heard about these mines from Zomer as he was escaping from his village, ravaged by the slavers, and hoped I might find them yet alive, and somehow am able to help them."

"Even if they are alive, how do you propose to help them, boy? Are you a god that you can fly them out of the lands of the Zapotecs?" Sak's words were tinged with sarcasm, but not malice.

"I do not know how I will help them, only that I must try. Perhaps this is the reason I was preserved from the grasp of the jaguar as a small child, and perhaps with the help of whatever god looks over me, I will find a way." Yax Kan's voice quavered with emotion, but was also wrought with conviction.

Sak gazed intensely at Yax for a few moments. "I see that you are sincere, Yax Kan, but if I help you, I may be put to death, myself. Although I am not treated like a slave, this is Zapotec domain, and I am not immune to their wrath. They need me at present, because although they have the simple knowledge needed to work soft gold, I hold the answers as to how to smelt and work silver, ziff, *tumbaga*, copper and bronze, which knowledge I brought with me from the land far southward. Sit here on my sleeping mat and tell me about your family. Most of the Maya I have met would forget about their family members after a few years, and certainly would not risk captivity or death to save them unless they commanded an army of warriors to shield them, such as the rulers of the great cities to the south."

"I have no army, Sak, but I believe that an individual has much ability on his own, and may find ways to do things which armies cannot." Yax was thoughtful as he responded, and most of all he was hopeful that this man before him would help him despite his protest. Yax went on to tell Sak his story. He spoke softly of the raid taking his parents and twin sister, the flight southward with Naz-Hani, learning the ways of the shaman and the scribe, Naz-Hani's death, and finally, Yax Kan's intended journey to the great city of Teotihuacan.

"It certainly sounds like your friend, Naz-Hani, was right when he said you have a special destiny. I have never met one so young who has learned so much, and declares such lofty goals. So now you want to save your family from the Zaps, ay?"

Yax only nodded his assent as he gazed steadily into Sak's clear eyes in the lamplight.

"Well, young one, I have learned much also, and I may help you even though I know better. You see the Zapotecs are the enemies of my heart, as well, and I have never found a proper way to redress the ruthlessness that I see around me every day. Perhaps helping you will give my conscience rest from the constant guilt of being a favored stranger in this village of the damned."

Sak continued talking long into the night about what they could do first to discover if Yax Kan's family were actually alive and working in these mines. He explained that the main product of this particular mine was not metal, but lime, which had many uses, which included being an ingredient in their cement mortar and roads, and as a flavoring for their meat. Many trees were burned to heat the rocks, which cracked at high temperature and were then crushed into the useful substance. They both slept lightly until the early dawn, when they arose to see what they could learn. They stealthily climbed to the crest of a small hill following a narrow footpath.

"Here, Yax Kan, climb up this tall tree above the trail where the slaves will pass on their way to the mine. See if after all these years you can even recognize your family, if you are fortunate enough to see them. I will stay nearby to protect our retreat and await the outcome of your vigil. Do not come down until you are sure all of the guards have passed."

As instructed Yax climbed to a high branch heavy with leaves as a cloak against discovery, and Sak went off a little way to wait and keep watch. Soon the slaves began passing below and a little in front of the tree where Yax was hidden. Nearly thirty had passed and he was beginning to feel disappointment at his inability to find his family and worried that even if they passed by, he might not be able to recognize them by merging his childhood memory with the raggedness of these poor folks.

"What will I do if they are not here, now that I have this new hope in my breast?" Yax silently asked himself.

Finally he recognized his parents on the trail below! His now gray-haired father was carrying a small carved wooden adze, and walking beside him was his wife, carrying empty woven sacks over her stooped back. They looked better than he had expected, perhaps since they had always relied on each other they were somehow buoyed up. Following them was a beautiful but weary-looking young woman with long black hair. She carried the strap of a water bag over one shoulder. If he had not seen his parents first, he would not have recognized his sister, Natana, who had shared their mother's womb with him. Yax Kan's heart was so full he could hardly bear to remain still until they had passed. He wanted to call out their names and rush down to embrace them. Tears filled his eyes and he bit down on his lip as he watched his parents and sister pass out of sight down the trail, unaware that they had been observed by their lost son and brother.

It seemed like forever before the line of slaves and Zapotec guards had passed out of sight, so that he could climb down from his perch. Before he even thought about looking for Sak, the kind metalsmith appeared before him.

"They were there, Sak!" Yax blurted out in a loud whisper, "I saw them—my parents and my sister! We must help them!"

"Of course that is what we must do, Yax, but how? It will be tricky just getting you back out of the area undetected, but with three others, it seems impossible. They will be missed, where you will not." Sak's dour expression indicated his concern.

"I only know that I must do something. I cannot ask you to risk your life further, Sak, but I must try to help them, even though I may fail."

"No, Yax, I have had time to think about my own life and safety while you sat up in that tree. Life has no meaning unless it is used to help others. I know it is not a popular belief, but it is mine. I will help you, but we will need your jaguar god to guide us."

"It is Kukulkan, the kindly god of the feathered-serpent that I rely upon, Sak, not an animal or underworld god. I don't know why, but I feel that he will assist those who are also caring toward others. We must pray until we find a way." Tears formed in Yax Kan's dark eyes once more, but determination lit his countenance.

Sak felt his heart warm with compassion toward this courageous, young stranger, and he put his hand on Yax Kan's shoulder as they crept silently back to Sak's hut in the village, past the unsuspecting guards. There they sat silently praying and meditating while hoping for some useful idea or inspiration.

After many hours, Sak broke the silence with a gasp of insight. "Of course!" he cried. "It will almost be easy!"

"Tell me!" Yax pleaded.

Sak smiled with confidence as he explained the plan to Yax. "Four days from today a group of slaves will be taking a load of lime north to Oaxaca. I am to follow behind them with some of the metal ingots that I have been smelting from the rare ores found in this area. I am supposed to train some craftsmen there on the working of various metals into tools and jewelry, but I would love to do otherwise and never give the secrets of metal to these evil people. Your family will have to come along as the slaves I choose to carry my ingots, and supplies. There are not many and it will not be too difficult. Alone, you will be able to follow us carefully at a distance. I had forgotten that the chief guard, Alligator Turtle, had told me to choose slaves to assist me in carrying, hunting, cooking and so forth. It is the perfect opportunity!"

"But won't there be guards with you on this journey, Sak?" Yax asked with a worried brow.

"Yes, but with your help we can dispatch them a few miles up the *sacbe*," Sak said without concern.

"Sak! Must we kill them?"

"How else will we escape, Yax?"

"Surely there must be a way to overcome them without killing them," Yax answered. "Let's think about it some more. We have time before we must be hidden near the village entrance to follow my family to their dwelling tonight when they return from their work."

They lapsed again into considering the problem. After a short arc of the sun overhead, Yax said, almost to himself, "Why not? It seems only right."

"What are you talking about, Yax Kan?" Sak asked.

"Well, my parents and sister are slaves to the Zapotec, right?"

"Yes, of course. So?"

"Why not overcome the guards and make them bear our burdens while we escape?" Yax Kan answered with a grin.

"Yax, it would be just, but these men are not farmers or hunters. They are soldiers who have been trained in warfare."

"Nevertheless, they will be our temporary slaves if we are well prepared to help them see the wisdom of it." Yax Kan's assuredness made Sak feel a little more hopeful, but not much.

"Well, go ahead and explain your plan to me. I certainly want to feel as confident as you seem to be."

Then Yax confided in his new friend the ideas that had formed in his mind. When he concluded, Sak responded with little more than a wry smile. It was time for Yax to conceal himself at the top of the path from the mine to the village entrance and follow Yax Kan's parents and sister to their dwelling and prepare them for their escape. Sak was going about his business and did not need to hide.

When they did appear, it was surprisingly easy to follow them. They cut off on a path that circled around the main village to a hut that, although secluded, could not easily be escaped due to its position next to a deep ravine. The only approach was on the path past the village guards. Had the guards been less overconfident, Yax would not have been able to follow. Sak on the other hand went openly ahead on the trail, telling one guard that he was going to appraise the condition of these slaves for helping him on his journey to Oaxaca. The guard knew Sak, and admired his knowledge of metal, but was also jealous of his favored status. Nevertheless, he knew better than to argue with the plans of Alligator Turtle, his superior.

During their discussion, Yax easily slipped by in the trees behind the back of the careless guard whose attention was focused on the metalsmith. Sak had placed himself so that the guard would have to look away from Yax Kan's route of passage.

As Sak approached the hut, Natana was just fetching some firewood from a stack behind their dwelling. Although Natana was well past the time when she would normally have married, the Zaps would not allow it. They did not want to breed slaves, only capture them as needed; babies came often enough to the existing couples without promoting it among the younger slaves. Usually, the masters found it beneficial to let those couples they captured stay together, though. It seemed to keep them more docile and complacent.

Sak startled Natana with his approach. "Do not fear, girl. I mean you no harm. My name is Sasak Kukum and I wish to speak to your parents."

From his hiding place in the trees Yax saw that Natana's eyes were full of fear. She may be unwed, but she had not escaped abuse by the heartless guards in the past, and as he saw the alarm in her eyes Yax Kan's heart ached at the thought of how she had been forced to live these many years. He remained hidden until receiving Sak's signal, as they had planned.

As Sak followed her to the hut, Ramarkiah came out of the entrance. His eyes were unusually intense for a slave, but the look of subservience that had impressed itself on his countenance was still heart-rending for Yax.

"What do you want, Sasak Kukum?" Ramarkiah asked.

"I'm glad you know me, friend. May I come into your hut for a moment to speak to you?" Being asked permission by one favored by the Zaps and whom he had seen walking freely through the village left Ramarkiah perplexed, but he motioned for him to enter. Once inside, the hut could barely hold four people. There were scant belongings, mostly items gathered from the forest for minimal comfort or as tools.

"I know who you are, Sasak Kukum, and know that you work for the Zapotecs," Ramarkiah said with careful disdain.

"Ramarkiah, I understand your distrust of me, and I know that you were taken as slaves over ten years ago. Is that right?" Sak asked.

"I am not sure, but it must have been nearly that. Why do you ask?" Ramarkiah replied.

"Did the Zaps take all of your family in that raid?" Sak asked, hoping that the derogative nickname for the Zapotecs would help to put Ramarkiah at ease, and it seemed to.

"As you see, my wife and daughter are here with me." Ramarkiah was puzzled now.

"And you had no other children?" Sak continued to probe.

"I had one son, Yax Kan, but the Zapotecs must have killed him, because he was not taken with us." Hurt showed in the older man's eyes as he remembered that which he would rather not dwell upon.

"Ramarkiah, your son is still alive! He thought you were dead, as well. I have befriended him, but we must be very careful because the Zaps do not know he is here."

All three family members' eyes were now round as the moon and shining with tears of wonder. They could not believe what they were being told. Then Sak went to the entrance to the hut and signaled to Yax.

As Yax stooped to enter the low hut, his mother gave out an unbelieving moan, from deep within her breast. His father sat looking at the man who had been a boy. His twin, however, jumped up and threw her arms around Yax Kan's neck, overjoyed at the reunion with her womb-mate. In a moment all four were embracing each other in tears and crooning to each other words of endearment and astonishment.

It was quickly decided that Yax would be safer staying there and explaining their plan, while Sak should return to his own hut, lest the guards become concerned at his absence. He would pass the message to the chief guard that he had found suitable slaves for his journey. Sak and Yax would meet later the following morning after the workers had gone to the mines.

That night Yax Kan's small family realized that even in the most difficult circumstances, one can still feel great joy and relief. How wonderful it was to realize that loved ones lost had not been lost forever.

Yax learned that his father had not wanted to risk the lives of his wife and daughter by trying to escape, just as his captors had hoped. But now with a son miraculously restored as a strong and vibrant man, Ramarkiah believed the impossible could happen! When Yax presented the plan, there was little hesitation in any of their hearts, all brimming over with love for Yax.

He talked far into the night telling them of his life with Naz-Hani until the old man's death, and of his journey. He shared with them all that he had learned, and all that he hoped yet to learn. On their part, there was little to tell but drudgery, pain and hopelessness. Finally, hope had returned to their hearts, and it seemed worth the possible consequences to trust in their son and his unlikely ally in performing yet another miracle—their escape!

8

Escape!

Over the next three days, Yax could hardly eat as the fear and anticipation knotted his insides. It seemed that in an instant his joy at finding his family had turned to pain as he had witnessed the indignity they had suffered for so many years. The day of their departure arrived, with the conspirators yet unable to clarify all the details together since three of them had been working in the mine. Early in the morning a guard fetched the family of slaves going along as servants on this trip to Oaxaca. Sak had everything packed and ready for the journey, and Yax had gone ahead before dawn to a rendezvous place described to him by Sak. No words were wasted as they loaded heavy packs on the backs of the three 'camels.' No one knew where the derogatory term for slaves had originated. It was an ancient part of their language for someone carrying a heavy load on his back.

Sak led the way up the trail with the three slaves behind him and two guards in the rear. One of the warriors was an older man with a pot belly; the other was younger, but constantly complaining and wearing a sour expression. Their eyes were small and mean-looking after years acting as cruel taskmasters over enslaved laborers. It was still early, but the sun shone down with a heat that weakened anyone laboring under its fervent rays. The main group of slaves with bundles of lime loaded on their backs had left earlier and was miles ahead of them.

As the group traveled, they passed through large barren areas where all of the trees had been cut down to provide wood for heating the lime. At midday they again reached an area where the forest was untouched and could provide some shade. They were only about five miles from the mining village, but as was customary, they stopped for a rest and something to eat. The time had arrived that Sak and Yax had agreed upon to take action.

"Say, men," Sak opened his small sack of supplies. "I just learned how to brew this excellent herbal drink that quenches the thirst better than any I have ever tried. Do you want some?" The guards watched as Sak lifted the bag to his mouth to take a drink with some dripping down his chin. "As gold is bright, that is really delicious!" Sak exclaimed. He held the skin bag out to them.

Even though the family had been warned to act naturally and not pay much attention, their eyes riveted on their guards, waiting for a response.

"Anything is better than this bitter water from the well near the mines." The fat guard dropped his water skin to hang by his side. "I can't wait to get to Oaxaca and drink some clear spring water. And a few other things that are good to drink, too, ay, Mazco!" The thinner guard, Mazco, grinned and reached for the bag, taking it right to his mouth.

Yax had prepared the brew to taste refreshing, with wild mint, anise and other more potent herbs. Sak had held his tongue against the mouth of the bag lest he actually drink any of the powerful stuff.

The paunchy Ka'wun, or coyote, grabbed for the bag and nearly finished it off in his greed before handing it back to Sak. "That is good, Sasak. We shall have to make it regularly when we get back to the village, but as Mazco says, there will be better things to drink in Oaxaca." He winked at his comrade.

They all rested in a shady spot until the hottest part of the day was past, and they could then continue their journey. It should take less than three days to get to Oaxaca, they both thought, as the two guards drifted into a deep slumber with help from the drugged brew. They had tied the slaves together with short ropes and attached the rope end to Ka'wun's ankle so that they could rest without worrying about the weaker slaves escaping.

When both guards were sleeping soundly, with Ka'wun snoring loudly, Sak walked over to them and tried to awaken them. When he realized that they were not going to wake up very easily, he and the others moved in quickly to tie the guards up with the leg ropes. Yax came out of hiding in the forest and helped them by gagging both men carefully so they could not yell out to any other Zapotecs who might come within range of hearing.

Though worried, Ramarkiah, remembered facing fierce animals fearlessly, long ago when he had been hunting as a free man. He exulted in once more doing something of his own free will, and not because he was commanded. They tied the guards for walking as Sak had witnessed the Zaps do to the strongest and most determined captives they had brought to the mines, with a hemp rope between their legs and around their necks. One tug on this rope brought the bravest man to his knees, fighting against pain in his groin and struggling to breathe. Then they sat down to wait until the drug dissipated which Yax had put in the brew they so greedily drank. It was a potent dose of a decoction Naz-Hani had taught him to make to help the sick to sleep when they were in too much pain. Yax Kan's education was not wasted, and the guards were feeling no pain!

When the guards groggily awoke they were amazed at their predicament. Sak and Yax then burdened the two with the packs carried by the three former slaves, and made them march in front of Sak and the others. The escapees had agreed to head northeasterly away from both the mines and their presumed destination of Oaxaca.

They traveled warily at first, but after two suns had passed, they felt they were far enough away that they could talk in normal voices. The two warriors cursed at them, but were kept weakened by not giving them too much food and water, and Yax held firmly to the two ropes attached to his charges, which easily reminded them of who the master was now.

It would be many days before the group was missed and they had been careful to hide any tracks which would give away their direction of travel, even setting some false trails along the way to elude any search parties. They had buried the guards' long *macanas* with sharp edged flints imbedded along the edge of narrowly carved hardwood, and kept only their more practical obsidian knives. Ramarkiah, who had fashioned a throwing stick similar but less decorative than the one carried by his son, reveled in once more bringing in game for the evening fire. His and Nahomi's faces radiated with the happiness of reuniting with their son and their pride that he had rescued them. Natana's expression held that and more. She gazed at Sak fondly, and her looks were returned with growing ardor. It was evident to all of them that Natana and Sak were falling in love. Yax and his parents were joyous that at last Natana could consider becoming a wife to such a good man.

After traveling nearly twelve days, Yax had to tell his family something that was very difficult for him. He waited until they knew from talking to a few families in small settlements along the way that they were nearing his clan's territory near Comalcalco.

"Father, I must tell you something, and I hope you will understand. I found you unexpectedly, and my joy is full that you, Mother and Natana are alive and free again. Surely my prayers have been answered, but I have to continue the quest that I began, to find the true god that is yet not understood by me. I promised Naz-Hani that I would do this thing, but I promise you I will return and tell you of my discoveries. Leaving you now is one of the hardest things I have ever done, but I know that I must."

Ramarkiah and Nahomi looked at their son and were unable to speak. They wanted him to be happy, but they did not expect to have to part from him so soon. Natana was also visibly upset and Sak put his arm around her in comfort.

"Yax, I see now that I needed you to free me from my old life as much as did your family," Sak said. "Though I have known you only a short while, I will ever be in your debt. Here, my friend, take these pieces of gold; they are very valuable and may help you at some point in your journey." Sak handed three large gold nuggets to Yax.

"We will meet again, brother," Yax said to Sak as he gave him and Natana a hug. "And, to you my parents, I pledge that I will return to share with you what I may learn."

His mother held him in her arms for a long time. She was not a woman of many words, but her love for her children was strong. She and her husband would have argued further with Yax about leaving them, but both sensed a mature man's resolve in this thing he must do, so they held back any objections.

Ramarkiah look into his grown son's eyes and uttered a father's blessing upon him in a hunter's words, "Be safe on the trail and at night. Take heed of that which grows to harm a man and befriend that which lives to help him, my son."

The Zapotec soldiers, tied to a nearby tree, breathed out some empty threats toward Yax as he walked away from the group, but most of their bravado had left them long ago, before their gags had finally been removed. Sak had told Yax that he would release the soldiers without weapons or shoes when they had reached a suitable point in their journey and he could be sure of their departure. Sak did not think they would go back to Oaxaca, surely to face a punishment of death or worse for their failure. They might try to gain employment as mercenaries in some city-state in the Yucatan, but he did not care. He had only spared their lives at Yax Kan's persuasion, but the surly warriors were as yet unaware of Yax Kan's intercession on their behalf, and would no doubt be ungrateful even if they knew.

Yax moved swiftly north, not following the trails that they had just traveled along. His heart was full of happiness because he had found his family, and full of anticipation of the journey ahead. He walked for nearly fifteen days before he turned west and came again to the paved *sacbe* running northward toward Teotihuacan. He skirted several guard posts through Zapotec country and was able to evade detection as he continued on his journey.

9

Teotihuacan, City of the Ancients

ate one evening, Yax began to pass small peasant huts, similar to his home as a child, but with sod roofs rather than thatch. His passage did not arouse much curiosity from those who had much to do to eke out their existence from this harsh land. As he came over a small rise in the flat landscape, the massive pyramids and high mountains suddenly appeared in the distance. His heart raced with the thrilling realization that he might shortly gain answers to his questions.

It soon became clear that the pyramids, because of their great size, appeared to be closer than they actually were. He decided to camp for the night and began to look for a suitable site. He was no longer surrounded by dense jungle, but was in a flat land of swamp and lakes. The night before he had smoked some of the meat from an armadillo he had caught for dinner and roasted in its own armored shell. He ate that rather than hunt again and have the need for a cooking fire which could attract unnecessary attention in the midst of the scattered settlements.

As he chewed the smoked armadillo meat he passed a

stone quarry that had not been used for many years, and decided that he could safely stay on one of the upper sheltered shelves cut into the limestone. The rock was gray and dusty from the grime of disuse, and the bottom of the quarry was filled with stagnant green water. It was warm enough that he need only use his jaguar skin for a ground cover to be comfortable for the night. He fell into an anxious slumber with some sadness that though he could see his destination, he did not reach it.

When morning arrived, Yax was so eager to be on his way that he took no time to eat and was on the road at first light. This time, although the pyramids were clearly visible on the horizon, he did not fool himself that they were very close. His pace was brisk and he did not stop until he saw a fellow traveler coming toward him on the road, a very large man with a dejected appearance.

"Tell me friend, if you will, how long will it take me to reach the great pyramids in the distance?" Yax inquired.

"Why does a man so young go to the place of the dead?" the older man replied with a look of concern in his eye.

"I know of it as the Birthplace of the Gods, and I hope that I can find answers to the questions of my heart in a place called the 'Avenue of the Sun'."

The man still frowned, but was not rude to Yax. "You are still a long way from Teotihuacan and cannot reach it until past mid-day if you are fast indeed. Though you seem anxious to go there and have hope that you will find answers, let me warn you that it is a dying and evil city. You called me friend, and because of that and because of your inexperience I would give you more than you ask of me. Since the coming of the Tolteca to this place many in the city will call you 'friend' also, but they are not to be trusted. They have cheated me and stolen from me, and I feel lucky to be leaving alive. What you call the 'Avenue of the Sun' once was known by that name since it runs past the Pyramid of the Sun, but is now called the 'Avenue of the Dead' because of the great blood sacrifices made there. If you go there, there is only one person that I would advise you to seek out, and even that with great caution.

"There is an earthenware shop next to the central plaza with the sign of a dwarf over the entrance. This shop is owned by an honest little man with a big heart, Lemnoch Double Reed. Go there first, without drawing attention to yourself, and you may find what you are seeking. At least you will not gain a lump on your head, or worse, and have your pack stolen."

"Thank you for your advice, friend. I will heed it, for I discern that you are an honest man. What name do you go by?" Yax asked in sincere gratitude.

"My name is Zaconiuh, but it is rarely spoken. I am known to my few friends as 'Big Zero', and zero is what I have to my name after spending three years as a merchant in that worthless place! Be careful, boy, it is probably the last place you should go to seek for answers!" With that said, the forlorn Zaconiuh, turned from Yax and tramped south along the broad dirt road, his shoulders sagging from more than the weight of the small pack on his back.

As Yax watched him go, he decided to move more slowly, rather than rush, so that he might get to town after dusk, and more easily slip into the potter's shop unseen by unfriendly eyes. He sat under a tree and chewed on a piece of smoked meat and some dried berries from his pack. It was the last of his provisions and the land this near the city did not appear to promise anything more for his sustenance.

He traveled on until the sun was high in the sky and then he found a small stream where he could drink and rest in the shade of a rocky prominence until the heat of the afternoon had passed.

10

The Potter's Daughter

In mid-afternoon Yax cautiously continued his journey. He was unable to avoid being seen by those traveling on the dusty road, but remembering the warning he had received by Zaconiuh, he did not invite conversation with any who looked his way. The sky was dusky red as he entered the center of the city. After some wandering through the streets, he found the square that was the trading center of Teotihuacan.

He noticed that some of the stalls were closed, but appeared to be occupied since lights still flickered inside. He smelled the unfamiliar oils in their lamps. His eyes searched the lintels of the small stone, palm-roofed enclosures until he found one with the dwarf symbol that Zaconiuh had described. Slipping along the darkest side of the square, he came close enough to peer into the shop to see who was present. Yax saw a very short man with broad shoulders and bowed legs, standing next to a girl, sitting at a narrow plank table covered with small unpainted clay pots.

He stepped into the shop so quietly that he clearly startled the man and girl. "What is it? Who's this then, a stranger?" the little man exclaimed in an anxious voice.

"Do not be alarmed. I have come here at the recommendation of one Zaconiuh, whom I met on the road today," Yax declared, uncertain as to his welcome. "Are you Lemnoch?"

"That's me, sure enough. Zaconiuh? Oh, you mean Big Zero! Yes, you could have met him today as he left the city early. He bid me farewell as he was leaving. Well, if Big Zero told you to come here, then you must be alright. Besides, now that I see you in the lamplight, I feel more at ease. You look honest, and you're not dressed like a warrior. You're not too dangerous, now, are you?" A wry grin crossed the man's swarthy features at his own jest.

"Father, why are you so rude? Can't you see this man is weary and hungry? Come in and sit while we finish our work. My father means no harm; it is only his way of getting to know you. What is your name?" the young woman asked.

In truth, as Yax gazed into her dark, shining eyes, he was not at all sure he remembered his name. This young woman was one of the first ever to address him directly, and easily the most beautiful he had ever seen. Her long hair was glossy and bright, and her skin glowed like a golden figurine. His tongue seemed attached to the roof of his mouth and he could not even stutter for endless moments.

"Ya...Yax Kan," he finally mumbled in response to her patient waiting. Then more clearly, but slowly, "My name is Yax Kan."

"Welcome, Yax Kan, the timorous. There, you see, I have my father's rudeness upon me, too. I'm sorry. My name is

Tutoma. If you like, when we are finished here, you may come to our home for evening meal. You appear to be a stranger in need of our hospitality."

After speaking, Tutoma graced him with the most radiant smile ever smiled, he was certain. Yax sat down on a rough wooden stool by the back wall of their workshop and watched with admiration while they finished painting the pieces they had begun. He recognized some traditional Mayan designs on the work, but kept silent, only partly out of shyness. He did not yet know how these straightforward folk might react to questions about religion, and he fervently wanted them to like him, especially this young woman, Tutoma.

After clearing out the small booth, they led Yax out of the more populated area of Teotihuacan to a humble home at the base of a small hillock at the edge of the city. There was no one else in the adobe hut, and he soon understood from their explanations that Lemnoch was a widower and Tutoma was his only daughter.

They had a simple meal of corn cake and beans cooked with peppers and a spice that Yax thought he recognized— and liked very much. He could hardly eat though with Tutoma smiling and talking and moving gracefully about the house, everything about her fascinated Yax. He was clearly infatuated, but neither the daughter nor her father seemed to take much notice.

What they learned from Yax was that he was a scribe and craftsman who had journeyed from far south of Teotihuacan. What Yax learned was that they, like Zaconiuh, were considering leaving the city of Teotihuacan, and finding a new home, as life was very difficult in this time of tribal segregation on the outskirts of the larger cities. Finally, Lemnoch suggested that it was time to sleep and offered Yax shelter for the night in a small lean-to where some few crude wooden gardening tools were stored.

Yax thanked him and after finally untying his tongue enough to also say good evening to Tutoma, he went out with his pack and spread his sleeping mat on the ground under one end of the shed. He did not fall into sleep right away, but lay there trying to remember what it was he had come to Teotihuacan to do. He knew that he would remember by morning, but right now it was too delicious just thinking about his new acquaintance, the lovely, smiling Tutoma.

Early the next morning, as the turkey gobbler in the yard was about to proclaim, Yax was awakened by Lemnoch's touch on his arm. "Yax Kan, what will you be doing today? We are going to the shop soon, and you must have some plan?"

Since Tutoma was in the house and not in sight, Yax could speak easily to Lemnoch, "I need your help, Lemnoch. I must view the sacred writings on the walls of your city, especially on the Avenue of the Sun. Will you help me?"

"The Avenue of the Sun? Oh, you mean the path of the priests on their sacred festival days, and during funerals. Well, today is not a day of much portent. You should be able to see the walls for yourself, but there is not much writing there, mostly pictures. I have never known the malevolent priests of Teotihuacan to use glyphs for their religious drawings. They have more powerful ways to express themselves, most often due to their displeasure." Lemnoch was serious now, not the jovial host he had been last night.

"Zaconiuh told me that I might not be safe walking alone in your city. How will I find my way, and who will guide me?" Yax asked as he waved Lemnoch's red-faced ducks away.

"Well, if you need a guard, I can send Tutoma with you. She could talk any attackers into the ground." Lemnoch almost regained his cheery demeanor with his joke. "To be serious, even though you seem fit, it may not be possible to protect you, if you make yourself too visible to the rancid ones. They are easily disturbed and always looking for a rabbit to skin."

"A rabbit?" Yax asked in perplexity.

"That's father's way of saying that the priests flay anyone they don't like, and some that they do. You should stay far away from them, Yax Kan." Tutoma had walked up to them without Yax noticing. She was even more beautiful than the night before, but now Yax was involved in his chief pursuit and not so easily distracted. Also, the apprehensive tone in her voice and serious fearfulness in her eyes released Yax from his infatuated state long enough to discuss the matters at hand.

"I have come too far not to ask the questions that brought me to this place. Surely there is someone who is knowledgeable and not so easily provoked?"

Lemnoch fiddled with his bundle while considering Yax Kan's question. He seemed to have something to offer, but looked doubtful about the wisdom of the proposal he might make.

"I know one of the priests better than the others, and he is not so mean-hearted...but he is still one of them! I am not sure how he would respond to your questioning."

"You must help me, Lemnoch. I have nowhere else to turn and know of no other person in this great city." Yax pled with his eyes as well as his voice.

Light suddenly appeared in Lemnoch's face. "I may have just thought of a plan to help both of us, Yax. Didn't you tell us last night that you were a craftsman in Izapa?"

"Yes, I am a scribe, rock carver and modeler in stucco. Why?"

"Well, modeling stucco is not so different from making pots and urns of clay. Why don't you help me make some new and useful designs for my shop, and we will see if we can find a way to help you meet old Pulque Breath, the priest I know. Better a valued apprentice than a stranger. What think you, boy?"

Yax affirmed this with a vigorous nod of his head and said, "I will gladly work for you, Lemnoch, especially if it will help me find some way to ask my questions of one who is knowledgeable, priest or not."

"Good, then I must hurry to the shop. By the time I arrive it will be past my usual time to open and I have customers coming early. Tutoma will stay and work with you today, and show you where our clay and tools are. The plan will work if you will create some elegant and usefully designed objects for me to sell." When he finished speaking, the kindly little man headed toward the city.

Yax looked over at Tutoma and she smiled coyly as she said, "Well, it looks as though I have either an apprentice or a teacher. Come to the clay pit and we shall find out which it is."

They began working right away with the roles of instructor

and student seeming to reverse with each lesson. Tutoma was expert at forming the clay vessels, but Yax easily modeled the surface of each with beautifully intricate designs that he had used for years on the temples and stelae of Tonala. Wisely, he was careful not to use any sacred symbols or written glyphs that might offend the religious sensibilities of local believers by being different from their own.

"Here, Tutoma," Yax said, "This is the design of a butterfly's wings that I have used before. How do you like it? And here we can use the leaf design from the sapodilla tree found in the Southern forests."

"Oh, yes, Yax Kan! They are very nice, and it is fun to have some new designs. I was tired of the ones we have used for years," Tutoma replied with a lovely warmth in her voice.

As for Yax, he was as close to being intoxicated as he had ever been, simply from being in her presence. They worked all through the daylight and accomplished much, finally baking the vessels in a small kiln in the yard of the house. Often during their work their hands brushed each other's with an exciting effect. Yax thought Tutoma smelled like a rare flower, but he knew it was actually the pigment she was using on her pots, made a few days earlier from some bright red hibiscus blossoms and some crushed red annatto seeds, the same spice she used in cooking beans.

As Yax watched Tutoma work the clay, he realized he had never seen anyone so beautiful. The slight curve of her nose and the angle of her eyes entranced him. Her movements were not only feminine, but she had a childlike grace and guilelessness that warmed his heart. He realized that she reminded him of his mother taking care of the hearth and home of his childhood, nearly forgotten. His heart swelled as he felt himself falling in love with this young woman of sixteen.

As for Tutoma, she could hardly look at Yax without quickly turning her head and blushing for he was unabashedly watching her every movement, even though he continued working all the while.

Wood for the kiln fire was scarce because of Teotihuacan's overpopulation in the recent past. Even though the number of residents was rapidly declining, the damage to the countryside had been great, and the land would need years to recover. The remaining people knew this, but they did not know what else they could do to survive. Tutoma and Yax spent quite a while gathering the scant resource before they could bake their pottery in the rock kiln.

That evening when Lemnoch returned, they had a large, new inventory for him to inspect. "This is wonderful, my children!" he exclaimed. "See how much you have done and what intricate patterns you have used. We will certainly get the attention of Smoking Squirrel, the priest I call Pulque Breath. He comes by nearly every week to buy pots for the kitchen of the priests. I will charge him according to the great worth of such beautiful work."

Yax was much more talkative now, asking Lemnoch all of the questions that Tutoma had been unable to answer, but the potter was not much help. Yax also shared much about himself and his family, including the adventure when they were so recently found and rescued.

Lemnoch assured Yax that as an apprentice and nominal resident of the city now, he would legitimately be able to carefully ask Smoking Squirrel his questions without drawing undue attention to himself.

The next morning the three of them packed the pottery in woven sacks to carry it to the stall in the marketplace. After unloading, they began painting. This too, was something Yax was skilled in doing, and Tutoma praised him until he blushed through his sun-darkened skin.

Lemnoch smiled at Tutoma and Yax while they happily worked on his wares. *"There are times in Teotihuacan when it is not so pleasant,"* the potter thought, *"Let the children enjoy whatever they can in life."*

11

Avenue of the Dead

It was three days later when the priest finally appeared. He was wizened and scrawny, except that his belly protruded as though he had swallowed a melon whole. And, surely enough, Yax noticed a mildly alcoholic exhalation wafting from his mouth.

"Ho, Double Reed, you have something new here. New designs and a new helper! Has the city grown so much that your daughter was not sufficient help? Has business increased so greatly?" the priest wheezed out.

"No, holy one, but it is good to have something new to offer my old loyal customers, such as yourself. Surely, the priests of the Temple of Quetzalcoatl would enjoy something different to look upon at their meal times. Am I wrong, old friend?" Lemnoch baited his sales hook with a straight face.

"Well, you know, Lemnoch, we need only that which is needful and nothing more...but it is pleasant to share new things. Our patron, the feathered serpent, is a wise god and he wants us to enjoy simple pleasures in life. But who is your new apprentice, or is he the new master? His designs are very practiced, it seems."

This was not the direction that Lemnoch wanted the conversation to go right now, but he feared the priest enough that he dared not evade this inquiry about Yax altogether. "Yax Kan is an artisan sent to us from far South by an old friend who has left Teotihuacan, as many others have before him. He has agreed to work for my shop until he decides what other endeavors may be available to him. Now, did you want to buy something today?"

"How much for that pitcher with the jaguar design? I broke our old pitcher yesterday, and must replace it." Smoking Squirrel acquiesced.

"Only fifty cacao beans for you, my neighbor. For others it would be much more."

"Fifty cacao beans! For that I could buy the live ocelot in a bamboo cage at the other end of the marketplace. Surely, you meant to say twenty cacao beans?" The old priest bartered well.

"No, I meant fifty beans," Lemnoch continued, "But today it is so good to see you that I will lower it to forty."

"Forty beans is the price of four pitchers without embellishment. Surely you don't want me to waste the resources of the temple, do you? I will give you thirty, but only because, as you said, I am an old and loyal customer."

Lemnoch smiled inwardly, as this was the price he had hoped for. He would have taken twenty. "Well, I know I will be able to get much more for others like it, but as you say, you are one of my most regular patrons, so let it be done."

As the priest counted out the beans and put the pitcher

in his sisal basket, he looked again upon Yax, whose bare shoulder displayed the four parallel claw marks left by the jaguar. "That is quite a scar on your shoulder, boy. How did that happen?"

This might be the only chance he had to converse with the priest, Yax thought. "I was injured by a jaguar when I was a very small child, sir, but my father saved my life."

"Ooh my, very unusual to be in the grasp of a holy cat and escape with your life. You are very fortunate indeed!"

"Yes, sir, that is what the shaman in our village thought, also, but I have always given thanks that my father was there to protect me. He was a great hunter in our village."

"Be that as it may, you were smiled upon. The jaguar priests in the Great Way have a small temple that may interest you. It has life-size murals of their jaguar god, and they would thrill to see your scars. Perhaps you were preserved for some special purpose that they can discern." Smoking Squirrel smiled a knowing smile, since the purposes of the jaguar priests could be less appealing than this stranger might realize. Tutoma and Lemnoch frowned at each other behind Yax Kan's back.

"It is not the jaguar god that I would choose as my patron, mighty one," Yax flattered. "I am more interested in the Great Kukulkan, the one you call Quetzalcoatl, and would ask you about him and other matters concerning the ancient ones."

"You know somewhat of the history of Teotihuacan, do you? The Old Ones were mostly killed in great battles amongst themselves, finally leaving behind only their king, and now we use their city and the older temples to worship the gods they revered before us." The priest spoke almost as a skeptic. "But whatever questions you have, I will gladly answer, since I have chosen to spend my life serving Quetzalcoatl, as you noted that we now call him. Walk me back to the temple and as we talk, I will show you the great pyramids and other sights, even the mural of the jaguar, if you like."

Yax looked at Lemnoch, who nodded his assent. "Thank you, sir, I will gladly come with you, and appreciate your willingness to help me find answers to my humble questions."

As they walked away together, had Yax been looking, he would have seen a fearful cloud pass over Tutoma's face. She surely felt in her heart, as did most of the citizen's of Teotihuacan, a mortal fear of the temple priests. Anyone could be chosen for sacrifice. As a young virgin, she was particularly vulnerable, and could no doubt identify with the danger. Lemnoch watched her face and easily discerned that she had already developed strong feelings for the sincere young man who had so recently come into their lives. For both their sakes it was important that Yax Kan's life would be preserved. Soon, he must take his endangered daughter far from here. Like Big Zero, they too must leave this place.

As soon as the priest and Yax left the shop, Yax began his questions, "Who were the Ancient Ones? Where did they come from? How did they know so much about the heavens and the history of the world? And did Kukulkan appear and talk to them?"

"Hold up there, young man. Where do all of these questions come from? I have never heard such questions, let alone answered them. I will do my best, if you will let me think about one answer before requesting another." In truth,

Smoking Squirrel was flattered by the opportunity to display his knowledge. He was not very advanced in the ranks of his brotherhood, but that did not mean he had never listened to the oral traditions, or been inattentive at the ceremonial celebrations.

"First, it appears that you give credit to the Old Ones for everything we know. Your Maya forefathers and mine gave us a wealth of knowledge from our own ancient ancestors. We have only gained part of our wisdom from the Old Ones."

"After the Old Ones were killed in the great battles, they were followed by a group from the south known as Ammonites, who came here for sanctuary, refusing to take up arms according to the oaths of their fathers. They worshipped in these great temples you see, and gave important symbols of power to visiting priests and kings. With no defensive system they were eventually taken over by our forefathers. Now we use their city and their temples to worship the gods they revered before us." The priest seemed to speak as though he was a skeptic.

"Kukulkan, or Quetzalcoatl, the white and bearded one, appeared to our forefathers after the Ancients were gone, and as far as the past is concerned, our histories have melded together. It is difficult to tell which is which. You see the Olmeca, Tolteca and the Maya, and other tribes further south and further north, all shared blood from the same stock, the original parents of all the earth, the fathers from across the sea, and then our common forefathers." The old priest studied the young man.

"What is it that you are really seeking, Yax Kan? I perceive that you are more serious than I supposed, and more learned.

What do you ultimately hope to learn?" Smoking Squirrel said in a serious tone, and then waited for a response as he stroked his round belly with a brown, wrinkled hand.

"It is just that we know so much, but we know so little…I know that doesn't make sense. The priests of Tonala thought I was presumptuous even to think about such things, but I feel compelled to know. Why do we have so much information about the creation, stars, planets, numbers and the calendar, but so little knowledge of who Kukulkan really is? Did he really appear to men, or not?"

The old priest answered slowly. Being honored as a savant was a new treat for Smoking Squirrel, and he wanted to enjoy the moment, "Yes, but we have long ago lost much of the information about a land called Bountiful. Kukulkan appeared there and told the people about his blood sacrifice, so that is what we do today to appease him and the other gods. I serve in his very temple."

At first, Yax did not want to contradict the old priest's beliefs where they were in conflict with his own, "But surely there are written records kept on stone walls or tree stones, or on scrolls of skin or bark, that tell us exactly what he said?"

"No, there were no records of the event allowed except those kept by twelve high priests chosen by Kukulkan. He commanded them to keep correct records on metal plates, golden ones that would never rust or tarnish, but those have been long lost, as well. We were told that too many records and recording scribes could cause confusion and untruths. It has been more than a five hundred years since his coming and we have only oral traditions to base our teachings upon."

Yax Kan's face fell as he realized that what he sought was

no longer common knowledge even here, in the ceremonial center of Teotihuacan. "My old mentor, Naz-Hani, now dead, told me just the opposite. He said that Kukulkan had instructed the people no longer to sacrifice by the shedding of blood. Was he mistaken in what he told me?"

"Yax Kan, that is a great sacrilege here in Teotihuacan, to deny the sacred blood-letting! It is well that your old shaman is now dead and not here, speaking such things. And be careful who hears you! I can only tell you some of what I have learned after over twenty years in the order of Quetzalcoatl. Blood-sacrifice is the practice of priests and kings from here in Teotihuacan clear down to the city of Chichen, a long journey from here, far down in the Yucatan. The Zapotecs and Mixtecs, also practice these rites. With so many doing the same thing, how could it be otherwise? We believe in the Great Spirit, Yax Kan, but we also believe that the way we worship is the correct way!"

Yax was surprised at the outburst, and realized that he had been careless in asking his unorthodox questions so directly and so hastily of someone he had just met. He nodded his head and shrugged as if in agreement, and then followed Smoking Squirrel to the Temple of Quetzalcoatl and the Pyramids of the Sun and the Moon. Looking up at such huge structures, he was awed by the amount of work and knowledge it had taken to build them. They were taller than a great *ceiba* tree in his home to the south, and broader at the base than the great rivers he had seen. The stones were fitted together differently than in the temples familiar to him. Dark bloodstains ran down the steps of the immense Pyramid of the Sun. Yax shuddered to think of so much death and pain.

As the sun fell lower in the sky, Yax excused himself to go back to Lemnoch's stall. Smoking Squirrel invited him to stay the night at the temple, but was not very persuasive. He told Yax that he had grown fond of him and feared for him among his peers, especially as he might become a sacrificial offering.

By the time Yax returned to the stall of Lemnoch, the potter and his daughter were already packing their wares to go home for the night. They seemed genuinely relieved to see him and asked many questions about his time with the priest, but he could see that some fear was gnawing at their centers. When he told them that the priest had invited him to stay at the temple of Kukulkan, they visibly blanched.

"What is it, my friends? What is the fear in your hearts? Smoking Squirrel was kind to me, and I am sure he meant me no harm."

"It is not what the old priest meant that worries us, Yax. It is what his brethren may decide if he tells them about you. You are an unusual young man, and they seek those who are unusual in any way. You must flee Teotihuacan! You must leave in the morning and not come back to the city!" Lemnoch did not express these statements with joy in his voice. He did not want to see this fine young man leave him or his daughter.

"Even though I am not sure that you are right, Lemnoch, I have learned all that I can here. I hate to leave your family, but it appears that I must. Would you consider coming with me? Zaconiuh said that the city is dying, and with your skills you could easily make a livelihood in another city far from here." Yax let his eyes lift to Tutoma as he made his appeal.

"It seems that it is time for us to go, as well. Tutoma is in danger also," Lemnoch said. "But we must not follow you too closely. The priests may decide to send temple guards to find us. You must leave first, and we will follow within ten days or so. I do not think there are any portentous ceremonies that are imminent, we will be safe until then."

"How will I find you? Will we meet again? Do you know where you will go?" Yax worried his questions out in rapid succession.

"We will go to the city where Zaconiuh went, a place called Lamanai, on a river close to the sea to the south. It is a very long journey, but Zaconiuh said that it is a good place to live and near the sea-traders' route." Lemnoch's voice was a little dreamy, as though he had often dreamed of this journey, and was only waiting for some force outside of himself to give him permission to take his only child and go there. "I know others who will go with us. A large group is always safer when traveling on the trade routes."

"It is good. I will eventually journey there to meet you, my friends, and I will try to find the answers I seek along the way, answers so important that I do not think life worth living without them. If the stars shine favorably upon me, I will meet you there someday."

The next morning, after taking Tutoma's hand to his cheek and gazing long into her teary eyes, he departed. He was not sorry he had come, for he had met Tutoma and her father, and he had also learned a little more, and added some important pieces to the puzzle in his heart. They exchanged vows to meet again in Lamanai.

12

Beneath the Pyramid of the Sun

A fter Yax had gone about two miles from the house of Lemnoch, he saw ahead of him on the *sacbe* a group of temple guards who had stopped some travelers and were questioning them. He had just decided to get off the cement road and try to find a hiding place, when the guards looked back toward Teotihuacan and saw him.

"Hey, you there! We want to talk to you!" One of them yelled and they began to jog toward him.

In fear, he turned back toward the city and ran. They yelled at him to stop, but he only ran faster. He was still in excellent condition from his long journey and he had no trouble staying ahead of the guards with their weapons and heavy leather armor, but as he approached the city he feared that he had no place to go. It would be too dangerous for those who might assist him to go to Lemnoch's stall in the market, and he knew of no other place in the city.

Yax ran through the main part of the city, now out of sight of the guards, and continued toward the pyramids and temples, hoping to find a hiding place. As he ran past the

Temple of Quetzalcoatl, he thought he saw a familiar form. Yes, there toward the opposite side of the temple square was the bulky form of Smoking Squirrel. Not knowing whether he was friend or foe in this situation, Yax jumped behind a stone wall. It was not soon enough though. The old priest had seen him and he walked over to Yax Kan's hiding place.

"Ho, young Yax! What are you doing here?" the rotund priest inquired. "Surely Lemnoch has opened his stall and needs your assistance this early in the day."

"O worthy one, please help me! I am being chased by temple guards, and I have no one else to turn to. Will you help me?" Fear was obvious in Yax Kan's voice as he risked everything rather than lie to this apparently friendly acquaintance.

Once again, Smoking Squirrel, a priest of lowly position among his brethren, swelled with the pride that comes from being in an important situation so unfamiliar in his menial life. Without thinking of the consequences of his actions, Smoking Squirrel whispered, "Come, boy, follow me. I will help you."

They ran toward the rear of the great Temple of the Sun, Yax following closely behind Smoking Squirrel. As if by a miracle, they climbed unseen into an opening in the east wall about twenty feet above the base and down a secret stairwell that led into a subterranean tunnel below the base of the great pyramid.

"Follow quickly. I must hide you for the rest of the day, and come back later to help you escape the city," the old man panted out as they ran. "I am afraid I foolishly told some of the Jaguar priests about your scars, and they have sent their temple guards to find you. Fortunately, I did not tell them that you were a friend of the potter in the market."

Within a few yards it would have been darker than night except for some small oil lamps set on ledges in the passageway. Along the sides of the tunnel, Yax could make out large slabs of dark stone that supported the ceiling. As they went further past a widened area, he saw what looked instead like cement supports every few feet with rock and mud walls in between. Although it was dry in the tunnel, it had a rank smell that Yax could not identify. The wall seemed to close in on him.

They turned northerly until they came to a dead end, a chamber with four hollows on each side of a central circular room. Narrow skins hung down as partial doors in front of each of the alcoves. In one of the rooms there were pottery vessels filled with water, grain and hard dried corn patties. In another, where two pottery lamps burned, Yax could see an altar with a carved jade mask lying upon it.

"What is this place, Smoking Squirrel? What will they do with me?" Yax was suddenly fearful, even wary of his protector.

"Do not fear, Yax Kan, now that I have brought you here, no guard will dare to follow," Smoking Squirrel wheezed. "The high priests who are allowed entrance here are not due to come again for many days. I keep the lamps trimmed and I stock it with food and water for them when they are done with their fasting and praying on a holy day. It is also a place of secret refuge for the priests of Kukulkan, in case of emergency. I must not stay here for I have duties elsewhere and will be missed, but I will return tonight to lead you out of the city. It was not my intent that those weasels in jaguar skins should have you for an offering, but I also did not think to endanger my own life by the telling of a story. I should know better in my old age!"

"Thank you, sire. I do not know why you are helping me, but I believe you will be helped in return for having done so," Yax said. "My adoptive grandfather, the shaman I have told you about, taught me that we are helped according to that which we have given in our turn. I will wait patiently, and not endanger you further." Yax settled down next to the jars of food and water, in a dark part of the cave-like room with his small pack still over his shoulder, to wait for the old priest to return. Somehow he felt that he could trust the old man. *Pulque Breath he may be, but a friend in time of need, just the same, thought Yax.*

Hours later, Yax awoke, startled by a sound that brought him out of his dozing with a jolt. Where was he? What had he heard? Then he remembered, and realized it was footsteps in the tunnel. He started to rise, thinking it was Smoking Squirrel, but before saying anything or coming out of the shadows, he heard a voice, someone muttering to himself, and it was not Smoking Squirrel!

"I ought to make the old man do this himself, but he would probably faint at the thought of carrying anything this heavy! High priest Wan-zac told me the old fool had grain and water, but no *metate* to grind the corn down here, and it will be my turn next to come down here to fast. I had better not rely on his memory or physical ability if I wish to grind dry corn when I shed my blood to mix fresh *tutiwah* to end my fast." The man was standing within ten feet of Yax's hiding place as he set the heavy grinding stone on the ground in the front of the store room.

"Maybe I should check to see if there is still food and water here, too. No telling what Smoking Squirrel has forgotten," the man said. The grumbling hulk of a priest moved a few feet toward the back of the alcove where Yax crouched with his heart pounding. "Well, I see enough sealed pots here to feed the entire priesthood of Teotihuacan, I'm sure they can't all be empty." With that the priest turned and walked away.

Hiding in the shadows, Yax was sitting on his heels in a cold sweat, breathing in short, quiet gasps. If the priest had seen him, he might not have gotten away. Yax had noticed a wicked-looking obsidian knife in his sash, and he had no desire to face the priest even though he was younger and perhaps stronger and more agile than the man. Besides, the priest might possibly have run out yelling for others if he had detected the intruder. If he had noticed Yax, but was wily enough to ignore him and continue talking to himself as he walked away from him, then Yax could be trapped here like a rabbit in a shallow hole. He could only wait and pray to Kukulkan that he would be safe until Smoking Squirrel returned.

Now time passed very slowly. Yax could not rest, and fearfully waited in the darkness, shivering from leaning on the cold stone. It was dusty in the tunnel and there were insects, rodents and bats that Yax could hear squeaking and skittering around in the cave-like rooms. The weight of the massive pyramid above him threatened to engulf his very being.

He heard footsteps again, but this time he also heard a

familiar voice, "Yax Kan, it is only me. Do not be afraid. There you are. Now, didn't I tell you that I would be back and you would be safe?" old Smoking Squirrel asked.

"Smoking Squirrel, there was another priest here a few moments ago, but I'm fairly sure he did not see me." Yax described what had happened, and he could see the fear rising in the old priest's half-lit features.

"We must hurry!" the old one said. "You are probably right about not being seen or an alarm would have been given, but we must not be trapped here in the secret tunnel."

"My life would be worthless," the old priest mumbled softly to himself. "If the others knew I had desecrated this sacred place to hide this young stranger. I don't even know why I did it myself. It's as though his life must be preserved and Quetzalcoatl himself wants him to escape. I'm not sure of that, but I am sure that we must hurry and be very careful."

Smoking Squirrel ran as swiftly as his old frame and the dark, narrow passageway would allow, to the stairway that led up into the night, now darker than the dimly lit tunnel behind them. They crept up the stairs and peered out into the darkened space behind the Sun Pyramid. They turned south and traveled past the courtyard of the Temple of Quetzalcoatl. The night was still and the moonlight was dimmed by the thousands of smoking fires burning in the city of just under fifty thousand residents. Rather than turning toward the main avenue the way Yax had come, they went further behind the temple to a narrow path winding between stunted trees.

"Here, Yax Kan. This is the path to the eastern gate." Smoking Squirrel whispered close to his ear. "Go there and wait until just before morning, when the rays of the Sun God are nearly peeking over the horizon. The guards will be sleeping by then and you can slip through. Follow the path that forks to the east until you come to the great lake south of the city. If you follow its shoreline around to the southwest you will meet the trade road far beyond where the jaguar priests' guards may still be posted. Although I don't know why I have helped you, it makes me feel good in my heart, boy. I wish you well." With that said the old priest slipped away into the darkness toward the sanctuary of his sleeping quarters. Yax found the way to the east fork of the path in the dim light of pre-dawn. He traveled to the trade road and then upon it for many days, before the fear of being followed and captured finally subsided in the drum of his heart. The rainy season had begun and Yax was wet more often than dry. As he journeyed further South the rain was more constant. The dripping of water became an ever present sound in the sparse jungle. Even though the rain kept the mosquitoes and other pests under cover, he longed for the comfort of a dry shelter and a fire, while he found what comfort he could upon the trail. Although he was soaked, he was only chilled temporarily in the cool of the morning just before the light of a warm, new day.

13

Opposition

The next afternoon the rain had finally stopped and Yax dozed fitfully in the mid-day heat. Realizing that his mind was too full to sleep, he began to meditate upon the purpose of his danger-filled quest. It came into his heart to ask Kukulkan, sincerely, what he should do next to find out the truth about him. Praying silently, he felt darkness surround him, as if sent to distract him from his petition.

He had heard a jaguar grunt in the nearby forest and remembered tales that old Naz-Hani had told him about shamans claiming to transform themselves into were-jaguars by night. His mind wandered as he imagined the existence of such creatures in a jungle area such as this. . .

Suddenly a beautiful, golden she-jaguar appeared at his feet! Yax froze with terror. The majestic animal padded carefully up past his legs, her legs straddling his body, to the point where she peered directly into his eyes and he could feel the musky warmth of her breath on his face. She was surely the most wondrous creature he had ever beheld. Her feline grace was evident in her movements and the vitality of her black-spotted golden coat, loosely stretched over flowing sinews. A rumbling sound came from deep within her chest. Yax was transfixed now less with terror than with awe.

Then, as if by magic, she was transfigured into the most ravishingly beautiful woman he had ever seen, with yellow eyes aflame and flowing golden-brown tresses. Regardless of her seductive vivaciousness, a feeling of terrible diabolic design came over him which filled him with abhorrence. This feline woman wanted to thwart him, to distract him from his quest if she could. As if sensing his loathing, the feral creature was instantly transformed back into a cat with vicious teeth and claws. She snarled in his face…

He awoke, alone and shivering, lying in the clearing below a large allspice tree where he had stretched out to rest in its branches. His fall from the tree must have caused his startled awakening, but it had been a soft landing and he was not hurt. His body was chilled, even in the heat of the early afternoon, and fatigued rather than rested. Shuddering at the apparition he had beheld, he wondered why this dark vision came to him now, after learning so much. This dream was surely not from Kukulkan. Perhaps there were gods of evil, as described by the priests of the Maya, though long ago they had been regarded by Yax as not worthy of his worship. Perhaps they fought against the benevolent Kukulkan and wished to frustrate any attempt to understand him by turning a man's heart toward carnal desire and superstitious fears.

Shivering from feelings between despair and fear, he continued pleading for guidance. The thought kept arising in his mind, as if from outside himself, that he was wasting his time and would never find the answers he had sought for so long.

He was despondent and worried that he might never succeed, feeling as though he should abandon his quest, a feeling that was encouraged by an unknown dark presence. As if in answer to his prayers, he remembered Naz-Hani's exclamation on his deathbed, "Know that the one god knows of you, Yax Kan!" He continued praying with that remembrance in his heart. A small voice echoed in the recesses of his mind and he prayed earnestly that he would be able to understand the voice. Then he heard it clearly in his consciousness, "Yax Kan, your search is approved of the Lord. You must continue with steadfastness and patience to seek the truth about Kukulkan. There is more that you must learn. Be of good cheer and you will be preserved from the enemy of righteousness. You will be given the knowledge which you seek."

Later that night while Yax sat pondering the words and his dream by a small fire, bats flew overhead, squeaking in a pitch at the edge of his range of hearing. Great night moths and wood roaches flew about illuminated by the flames of his campfire. He was startled when a bat swooped down and grabbed a night moth right out of the air in front of his face; then Yax silently laughed at his own fright. Soon the fire died down and he was asleep.

Yax dreamed once more that night, this time about a kindly man standing by a beautiful white temple near the bluest of seas. Most of the dream was gone from consciousness when he awoke, but he spent the next day pondering about a society of people who could live, work and help one another without constant war and bloodshed. A group of people whom Yax imagined would worship the most powerful god, a benevolent deity, wanting only happiness for those he had created.

14

Captured!

*T*raveling out of the forest and down from the Chiapas highlands into the northwest edge of the southern lowlands, Yax was surprised by a small band of Maya warriors. He tried to turn and run, but found that he was already surrounded. Yax decided it was useless to try to fight so many, and knew he was poorly trained for such a battle. Since he offered no resistance they simply took his belongings and hunting weapons, roughly bound his hands and pushed him ahead of them. He watched for a chance to escape, but none came.

The warriors were not painted or dressed for formal warfare, but they carried lances with long obsidian points, deadly macanas and heavy stone maces. Yax learned from their conversation that they were not being led by a *macom*, or important military chief. They had been sent out on a scouting mission looking for likely sacrificial victims from the small surrounding settlements. As he listened to them talk, they joked that he would make a good offering to the Jaguar God of the Underworld, especially since he bore the easily recognizable tooth and claw marks on his shoulder and back of the great jungle cat. He had remained silent and for some reason they had not asked him any questions, probably thinking that he was just a local hunter who could be used to appease their god-king in his holy needs.

They paraded him past the residents of a large city with beautiful and intricately designed temples. Then they took him up a broad stairway into the central palace of Palenque. There in the throne room, their king, Kan Balam, or Snake-Jaguar, sat in full royal regalia. As was the custom among Maya royalty, his chiseled features had been unnaturally enhanced by his mother binding a board on his forehead and hanging a stone in front of his nose when he was a child, thus giving him a high, sloping forehead and slightly crossed eyes, thought handsome and better to peer into the world of the spirits. The lord of the city wore a cape of golden jaguar fur clasped with a jade hook, a headdress of iridescent green quetzal feathers, fine fur and leather, and he held a lustrous jade-headed manikin scepter in his right hand. Quetzal feathers were so rare and prized that it was unlawful to kill one of the beautiful birds and only royalty were allowed to wear or display their feathers, carefully plucked from the live birds before their release, and green jade was the most precious of gems, more precious than gold.

As the king gazed closely at the young captive, he noticed much more than his soldiers had. He saw the almost permanent ink stains on his hands, bound in front of his body, and the callous on his left thumb where he held a chisel while carving stone.

Kan Balam rose from his white stone throne covered

with soft furs and spoke directly to Yax Kan, "Where is your home village, captive?"

Before Yax could answer, he was thrust down by the soldier at his side so that he lay stretched prostrate before the throne. When he had regained his breath, he said, "Noble King of Palenque, I journeyed here from far off Teotihuacan on a quest required of me by the gods. I once had a home village, but that was long ago, and it no longer exists."

"Oh, you have been sent by the gods, have you?" The sarcasm was clear in his tone, but there was concern in the great ruler's heart, "Do they speak to you through the trees, or the animals, or perhaps the breeze that so rarely moves the leaves in the jungle? I asked you your home village, captive! If you do not answer directly this time, I will have your tongue cut out!" The king's eyes flashed as he snarled at his captive.

"Oh, great Keeper of the Mat," Yax cried out, "I was born in a village near Comalcalco to the north, but was taken from there as a small boy. I was raised far South in Tonala, where I learned the art of writing and carving in stone. I spoke truly of having last come from Teotihuacan on a quest, but the gods do not speak directly to me, except from the legends of the past, and the stone trees and murals that I have studied." Yax did not wish to reveal the most sacred personal experience he had received on the trail, in a dream and a voice in his heart.

Somewhat placated, Kan Balam said, "So you are a wandering scribe, eh? My warriors tell me you also bear the mark of the jaguar. Turn yourself so I may view it. How did that come about?"

Yax sensed that his answer to this question could either

Yax Kan meets the great King Kan Balam

mark him as a sacrificial victim or free him from their bondage. As it happened it did neither. "It is true that I was marked by a black jaguar as a child, but the jaguar gave up its life, that I might live, or so said the shaman who raised me up and taught me of his ways. Your warriors have taken my pack with the skin of the great cat which was slain by my father."

The royal Kan Balam seemed more interested in this captive than his minions could understand. Usually, he carelessly pronounced their sacrificial fate with hardly a glance, but something about this captive had caught his interest. The monarch of Palenque sat on his platform throne of polished green serpentine contemplating the prisoner.

"Remove his bindings and leave us!" he commanded, "And leave the captive's belongings!" This was more than unusual, this was almost unthinkable, but the men knew better than to raise an eyebrow, let alone question their demigod. They backed out of the stone chamber of the throne with their eyes downcast, leaving Yax on the floor, his pack beside him.

"Come forward and kneel before me, boy!" Only an elderly priest remained, squatting against the far wall of the chamber, tending a brazier of burning incense.

With quaking legs, Yax slowly arose to a kneeling position and then crawled the few steps forward to the feet of the king. Although he had seen such rulers at a distance in ceremonies, he had never before been in the close presence of one so powerful. As he lifted his eyes, he saw that Kan Balam had a split big toe on his left foot touching the stone floor. Yax gave no indication that he had noticed, but knelt there shaking, more from the fear in his heart than from the cold stone beneath him.

Kan Balam was nearly fifty years of age, and had the high forehead and long curved nose of royalty. He had reigned in his dead father's stead less than two years. Makin Pakal, or 'Lord Sun-Shield', had been a powerful ruler and had built remarkably innovative structures to attest to his greatness, including the corbel-vaulted throne chamber where they now sat. Kan Balam had long been contemplating how he could match his father's pre-eminence among the god-kings of all of the city-states in the *Mayab*. Lord Pakal had been placed on the throne by his powerful mother, Lady Zac-Kuk, when he was only twelve and he had ruled for nearly seventy years, while his son, Kan Balam, waited on the father's death to inherit the kingdom. No more time could be wasted before he assumed not just the power, but also the glory and deification to be derived from his progenitor's name.

He could afford to leave no doubts in the hearts of his people, which might be kindled by the knowledge that his kingly lineage was unusual in that it contained two great matriarchs, who had both declared their sons to be the next sovereigns of their realm, counter to their matrilineal reigns.

Kan Balam's own self-doubts continued to haunt him. He had felt little of the divine in himself since his informal accession to the throne. He had been fasting for many suns, and blood-letting from his sacred parts to release the *chu-lal*, or sacred life force, and then eating of the holy *tutiwah* before asking the gods, especially his namesakes, the jaguar and serpent gods, for a way to truly inherit his father's greatness. Now, this boy has been given into his hands, marked by his namesake, Balam, the jaguar god, and having the sacred abilities of writing and carving on stone. Surely, this must be an answer to his supplication.

"What name have you, boy?" The king's tone had softened and was almost paternal.

"Yax Kan, your greatness." The ruler was startled that the boy also bore part of his own name, Kan, the serpent.

"Do you truly know how to carve stone?"

"Yes, great one."

"Yax Kan, would you like to preserve your life to see another sunrise?"

"Truly, O king!"

"Tell me more of your skill and experience then, and I shall decide if you have some usefulness in my domain."

Yax spoke at length to the king throughout the remainder of the day, and Kan Balam condescended to allow him to sit cross-legged on a small leather mat and have some water and corn cake brought by the priest, while he told his story. He had not had a long life, but it had not been uninteresting, especially to a prince who had been unable to travel much distance from Palenque in his lifetime, fearful that he would not be available should his father die and one of his brothers let ambition overcome fear, and claim the throne for himself. Even less opportunity arose as king to go further than another nearby city-state for royal state visits or to take captives for sacrifice, just as members of those city-states came to his domain on occasion. Their ritualistic warfare was only normal for the times.

As Yax related his great interest in the ancient stories behind the carvings and murals he had seen on his journey thus far, Kan Balam was impressed that this young man was surely the one he needed to assure his own place among the gods of the afterworld. The king would start by glorifying his father and thus bring his father's glory upon himself.

"It is well, Yax Kan. You can be of use to me with your skills, and you may even find the answer to your own quest in the gods and ancestors of Palenque. We have many craftsmen here, but you must have some singular quality that would have the gods deliver you to me in the time of my inquiry. Old Hun'tul will take you to the quarters of the craftsmen and will make secure for you the assistance of the others at my command, who have similar skills. Go now until the rising sun. I have further to discuss with you about the task I will require."

Following the priest, Hun'tul, Yax was once again struck by his uncanny good fortune in being yet alive after an audience with such a powerful man. No, he still did not believe Kan Balam was a god, but he knew better than to let his personal beliefs interfere with his instincts for self-preservation.

Yax would do as he was required, but he did not feel that his quest would be fulfilled in Palenque. Deep within he felt that something was drawing him to continue beyond this place, but he would accept this unavoidable delay in order to learn what was here for him to learn. He thought of the great serpent he had watched in the woods, patient in his acceptance of the fact that his dinner had only been delayed. He also thought of his family recently rescued from slavery in the mines of the Zapotecs and now waiting for their second reunion. He hoped they could also endure with patience. He had already gleaned some valuable information and felt that he was being led and protected so that he could learn even more before his mission was fulfilled.

Surely there was something better in the after-life for himself and the humble people he had known than to end up in Xibalba, the underworld filled with only death and decay, with no hope for escape after death. With each speck of knowledge came further questions regarding the purpose of life, and each bit of information also strengthened his resolve to continue because it proved what Naz-Hani had taught him, that there was always more to be learned.

15

The Assignment

*T*he next morning after a sumptuous meal of wild berries, baked corn cake and wild turkey eggs, he was summoned to the king's presence. This time, however, he was taken to a large, shady, thatched building that was much less formidable than the throne chamber had been. Kan Balam waited impatiently to begin their discussion again. "I am happy to see you rested and well, Yax Kan," the king began. "We have much to do and the time is short. My father, the great Pakal, died more than twenty *uinals* ago and still his spirit cannot rest, or pass to me his blessing and the secrets of immortality. This is because I have not yet fulfilled my duty as a royal son. He lies in an unfinished tomb, and do you know why? Because my worthless craftsmen are unable to devise a suitable embellishment for the stone covering his resting place! Before he died he began instructing his workers in the design of the chamber and stone sarcophagus wherein would reside his remains at death. According to those instructions our ancestors are shown on the sides of his tomb with his mother, Lady Zac-Kuk, and his great-grandmother, Lady

Kanal-Ikal, each shown twice to ensure their preemininence. He died before his instructions were completed and the door to eternity that is placed over his body remains to be carved in a manner unlike anything that has ever been crafted before. It must be finished before my formal accession to the throne. This will be your task. What think you?"

Yax was surprised, but also pleased that he was being asked to do something physical, and not some impossible magical task the potential of which might have been inferred by the tooth and claw marks on his shoulder, or by some other mystical omen that had come to the king in his dreams the previous night.

He was confident in his ability to carve stone, and in the knowledge of the Maya beliefs in the next life, given to him by Naz-Hani. He barely recognized the names of the gods of these residents of Palenque which he had seen carved on the walls of the city's buildings, but their attributes had evolved from those many deities with which he was familiar. He expressed to the king his willingness to undertake the task with a humble demeanor, since he had the wisdom not to attempt to over-impress the ruler of this city-state of approximately 20,000 Maya.

Kan Balam then continued to speak for many hours telling him what he expected in the carving of the sepulchral stone cover. It must depict great power in Pakal; power that it was clear had been endowed upon his heir. It must also represent all of the gods of the Maya pantheon and much mystery, as well. Only those who are given the key should be able to see all that lies within the secrets of the carving. This would be the way to sacred power that he, the living king, must wield.

As a final gesture of confidence, Kan Balam gave Yax a tiny golden jaguar cub that had been brought in by hunters only this morning after they had killed its mother. It appeared to be another omen and would be a suitable associate for this intelligent young man. No doubt 'Snake Jaguar' felt that the jaguar god would be sure that Yax followed his instructions, as well. Yax held the kitten usually reserved for royal companionship, not knowing what to think, but not daring to question the ruler of Palenque.

The young scribe walked to his quarters carrying his new four-legged companion with images dancing in his creative mind. He needed materials and tools to begin. The other craftsmen were so relieved that the pressure to create an impossible perfection had been lifted from their backs that they were more than willing to assist him. First, he needed hardened charcoal styluses and finely prepared skins to draft his creation. Chisels of hardened wood, stone and tempered copper would all be used, as well. He also needed the life fluids of many different kinds of plants to act as fixatives and transfer agents to aid in preparing drawings and to cut the lifeless stone above the already entombed and moldering body of Pakal.

The others understood most of the materials that were needed, but had to be given extra instructions as to the special preparation of the skins so that they would have the transparent quality essential to the task. Also, none of them had ever before heard of the plant extract that could soften stone and they were somewhat in awe of young Yax Kan's knowledge. He would need to go himself looking for that plant when the time of need arrived, and hope that it was available here, since it was nearly two hundred long-runs south to Tonala. If necessary, he would travel south to obtain the plant himself, although most assuredly with armed escorts.

The Temple of Many Inscriptions had been built under the direct supervision of Pakal, for his own burial chamber. After actually seeing the tomb lid over Pakal's body, Yax assigned two of the other servants to begin smoothing the surface from its rough hewn state. They worked for many hours using volcanic stone and a paste made with crushed obsidian and milkweed sap to scour the surface into a smooth face ready to be carved. Meanwhile, Yax measured the lid and had the large processed skins glued and sewn together with a very narrow overlap until they matched the size of the immense stone, which was twenty-seven hands long.

The burial chamber was deep in the middle of the Temple of Many Inscriptions. The light in the tomb was poor and many torches were kept burning by slaves, while the smoke found its way up a long narrow stairway. Other slaves stationed in the entrance at the top of the pyramid took turns continually pumping on skin bellows whenever there were men working below, to replace the stale air in the tomb with fresh air flowing through a stone pipe built into the wall along the stairway.

In the evenings Yax found comfort in watching the small jaguar kitten growing each day under the care of a servant assigned to the task by order of Kan Balam. Yax and the bright-eyed kitten with short, pointed ears played and bonded. The size of its head and feet attested to its future growth into a very large jaguar. Its pelt had small dark spots unlike the spots it would acquire in maturity with dark circles around a lighter brown center. It slept by his side at night, comforted by his heartbeat, as it had been by the heartbeat of its mother.

The young scribe's thoughts were full of memories of the sweet Tutoma, and he often day-dreamed between necessary tasks in fulfilling his new king's assignment. His longing to be with her was greater than he would have expected, having little previous experience with beautiful young women.

Yax personally spent many days drawing the intricate design on two sets of skins, both the size of the tomb lid, or the 'door to eternity,' as Kan Balam believed. The second drawing he made in secret. The main motif of the drawing, a 'Tree of Life' with corn god symbols and the quetzal bird roosting in the top was slightly like the stela he had seen in ancient Izapa. He also showed Pakal emerging from Xibalba to be raised into the upper world of the gods.

Finally, he went to the priest, Hun'tul, and requested an audience with the great ruler. Hun'tul had been huddled in one corner or another watching him throughout most of the time he was working, and hurried off, seeming glad to be able to report anything to his king.

As he came before Kan Balam, Yax wondered once again if the work that he had done would be elaborate enough to impress the one who had commissioned it. He had personally prayed to the great god, Kukulkan, that he would be able to preserve his own life and yet somehow be of service to Him. Although he did not hear a voice in his mind, he did feel peace in his heart that he would be preserved in this great undertaking.

He spread one of the rolled skins out on the expansive

stone floor of the king's throne room, near the door opening so that the light would be sufficient to illuminate the details of the work. The drawing was not as ornate as others Yax had seen in the area, but it contained many of the same themes as other carvings he had studied in Palenque.

The *Wakah chan*, or world tree, was central to the drawing, which in Palenque was called *Na-Te'-K'an*, or precious first tree. There was a human figure near its base that was clearly Lord Pakal, since it displayed a clubbed right foot and split left big toe which Yax had learned were also traits of the dead king Pakal. At the top of the tree was the quetzal bird, representing both Ehacatl, god of the wind and first born of the gods, and also Kukulkan, god of heaven and earth. At its base was a composite god of the underworld, part Chaac, the rain god, and part Tonatiuh, the sun god. As well, there was a border that appeared to be glyphic in nature, but did not at first seem to express anything, much different from the kingly lineage displayed along the sides of the coffin. Yax waited for the king to absorb what was drawn before explaining anything about the draft.

Kan Balam was at first perplexed, then he began smoldering and yelling in a loud voice, "Is this a child's drawing that you bring to me? This simple life tree and serpent, a sky band and this quetzal with its curved feathers, even with my father escaping the jaws of Xibalba! Do you think that I have commissioned you that you may waste my time and the time of my other servants? For this have I spared your life?"

"No, great Kan Balam; it is more than at first you see, sire! Please let me explain to you the purpose for what seems like a simple design."

"I see what I see, Yax Kan! What more is there?"

"In one of our talks you asked me to create a sacred mystery, your highness. This drawing before you is more than it appears. The rest of its secrets are not apparent to the searcher or the common thinker, because the final carving will be on immovable stone and these drawings will be destroyed. Only you will know the true meaning of the design."

A thoughtful expression came into the king's features. He waved all others outside, and then with great deliberateness, motioned to old Hun'tul to follow them. With obvious hurt showing in his eyes, Hun'tul obeyed. The old shaman had been the king's personal tutor since his youth, and privy to all his doings. He clearly did not enjoy being sent from him at a time of possibly great import.

The king turned to Yax, "Show me the key, then, and it must be more than clever or I will use your flayed skin to cover the tomb of my pet ocelot!"

"Please, oh king! You must understand that the simplicity of the design is to deceive others into thinking that what is first seen is all there is to see. A complex picture would draw the study of the curious mind, but the simple image will be taken at face value and given no more thought. First, let me show you the border."

Yax rolled out the other identical drawing and then flipped the skin over, displaying a mirror image of the first. It had been simple to complete the second drawing since he had only to trace the one from the other after treating the skins so the lines could be seen through them. He laid the one with its edge adjacent to the other's identical side, and the king gasped. Together they made completed glyphs and pictograms, where before they were only indistinguishable markings! Then Yax put the other edges together and the same was true of them. They told the story of the world and its gods. The creative periods were designated and there were other pictograms related to mythic legends of the past.

Yax had truly put much of his learning into this drawing of simple appearance. He overlaid a dotted "X" shaped symbol in the center of one border over its counterpart and the crossing lines of the reversed drawings depicted a magnificent jaguar head, which had been totally indiscernible until the drawings were turned and put together. The king was visibly impressed. Surely this secret would ensure that inordinate magical power would come to the one whose name included that of the jaguar: Kan Balam!

Finally, Yax put the noses facing each other of the two identical, but reversed drawings of the great Pakal. It was as though Pakal was looking into the eyes of Kan Balam, his son and successor. Kan Balam's eyes widened in recognition; the hovering image of the Bat God of the underworld appeared as the overlay pressed against the original. It seemed to fly out at the king with supernatural vitality! Truly this would bring him all the power and majesty of his great father, Pakal, directly from the underworld, and it would give him the secret he needed to feel secure in his exalted station. He looked at Yax Kan and smiled.

"Yax Kan, it was at first my intent that none but you and I should see the secret key so that after I understood it, I would end your life and be the only living person to know the secret." Yax Kan's eyes widened with a sudden understanding of what should have been obvious. "Do not fear! I have had a change of heart. It would be an inauspicious choice before the gods to whom you have shown veneration, for me to harm you. You may choose anything in my kingdom and I will give it to you as reward, but you must continue to be one of my *cahalob* and promise never to reveal the secret you have given to me. It will be the basis for my power from the gods!

Knowing that it would be unwise to show the king his true feelings, Yax thanked him and told him he would like to think about his reward. Sadly, the king had not offered the one thing that he wished for -- his freedom to continue on his personal quest.

The drawing was simply a piece of artwork to Yax, symbolic of unliving gods created by man to imitate living creatures, things unknown pretending to be known. He also knew what the drawing was not, because he knew it was not created by divine guidance, but born of necessity and desperate human invention, no matter how unique.

Pakal's tomb lid in Palenque

Pakal's tomb lid (Jaguar god overlay)

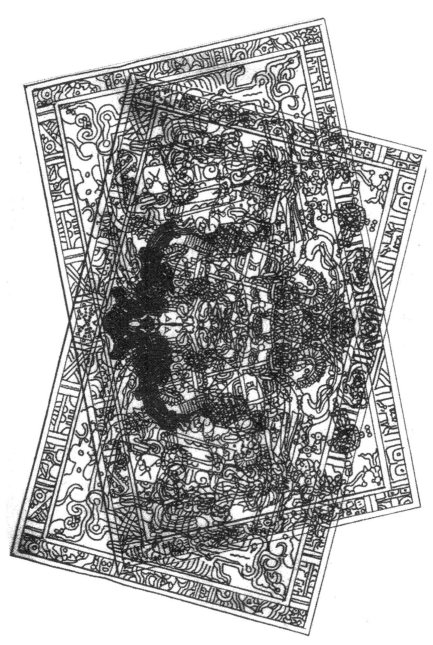

Pakal's Tomb Lid (Bat god overlay)

Yax had located the plant necessary to make the solution to soften the stone and the next morning he began the arduous task of carving the face of the 'door to eternity.' If only he could simply walk through such a door to get the answers to his own questions. He shuddered as he realized that death was one way to enter that door to get his answers. This was not an alternative he was ready to face. Certainly it was the last way for anyone to find such answers. How close he had come to that entry at the hand of the king, he would never truly know.

The carving of the great tomb cover took another 6 months with Yax and his assistants working from dawn to dusk, but Yax was able to delegate much of the rough stone-carving within the outline which he traced on the stone surface. Whenever he could, he wandered through the corridors of the great buildings looking for answers in the murals and carvings of those who preceded him in Palenque, being careful first to evade the inquisitive, old Hun'tul. Yax once found a mural of Maya people with light-skinned servants and wondered at its significance. Did their light skin have something to do with the light-skinned god, Kukulkan?

He also watched the many slaves and stone masons working to move great stones from the quarry using low, flat carts made with heavy stone wheels. In the *Mayab* wheels were used only for the building of sacred temples and objects; the lower classes being forbidden to use them for commerce or agriculture. Once a holy edifice was completed a sacred fire was built and the holy wheels were burned and then crushed as a sacrifice to the king-deity of that particular structure. It was even unlawful for a depiction of the sacred wheel to be made in murals, stucco reliefs or carvings. Oddly, no one seemed to care if wheels were used on a child's toy, the only other place Yax had ever seen them.

When the tomb carving was finished, Kan Balam required that Yax show him the secret of the lid again using the translucent skin drawing as an overlay. The duplicate skin was then ceremonially burned in many long strips in a stone censer on top of the temple. After long hours of study, Kan Balam realized that another overlay could be made anyway, so he decided he might as well keep this original in his treasury. No one would think to turn it over and place it on the tomb lid in mirror image. Only he would know the secret, magical power of the tomb!

16

Liberation

*e*arly in the morning Kan Balam activated his own portal to the Otherworld by shedding his own blood through a sacred blood-letting ritual. It was believed by his people that he was also in the process of generating celestial energies to assure abundance in their agricultural endeavors, their main community-sustaining activity. They came bearing gifts of precious gemstones and metals, the honey of bees, cacao beans, and garlands of bright flowers and parrot feathers as tribute to offer their king. The air was heavy with incense smoke and the perfume of thousands of jungle flowers plucked by palace slaves for the occasion.

The great king, Snake-Jaguar, had waited upon the perfect alignment of the stars and the planets, especially the planet Venus, to assure success. He planned every minute of the day to elaborately display his personal power through manikin scepter, flapstaff and basket-staff rituals, and especially the link to his sacred patrilineage. There must be no doubt that he was destined to be the *ahau* of all *ahauob*, the lord of lords and keeper of the sacred mat.

His grandmother's power had come to him not only through her son Pakal, but through the matrilineal lineage of her daughter, Pakal's sister-wife, who was also Kan Balam's mother. The king burned the blood-soaked mulberry bark paper in a basin on the stone altar to create a pillar of smoke, conjuring up a vision-serpent, which would assure the people that his reign was the will of the gods. Kan Balam exulted in his drugged, pain-induced trance-state that led him to believe he was actually seeing a great dream-serpent in the smoke. He felt that at last he could expect his people to worship him as they had his father. And to think, he owed much of this success to a simple scribe.

Later, after his mind had returned to this world and the mid-day banquet was finished, he was pondering this fortunate occurrence again. He called for Yax to appear before him that he might learn of his desired reward.

Yax entered the private chambers of the monarch with trepidation. Why was he being called to him now, after what Kan Balam would consider his greatest moment? Why not call his more notable *cahalob*? Had he reconsidered and decided that he must send Yax to the next world to preserve his secrets in this one? Yax Kan's heart was fearful and unsure.

"Yax Kan! My young gift from the gods, how are you? I have remembered my promise to give you anything in my kingdom. Have you made a decision? A princess for your wife perhaps? Or your weight in gold and jade?"

The king was clearly in a cheerful mood—that was good. Sudden relief played across Yax Kan's features. "My lord, I have no desire for riches, and am not yet ready to choose a mate. My needs are simple, but I fear they are beyond hope."

Yax determined to be honest with the ruler and hope for the best.

"Nothing is beyond hope, my young scholar, not while you are a friend of Kan Balam, *Ahau* of *Ahauob*. What is it you desire that you think is beyond my power?"

Yax hesitated as he carefully considered his words. "You remember, O King, when we first met; I was brought before you as a captive by your warriors? You will recollect that I was taken captive in the forest quite a distance from your city. You may also recall that when you asked me about myself, I told you that I was on a quest.

The great king nodded slightly for Yax to continue.

"Majesty, you have treated me with great mercy, consideration and hospitality in return for my humble talents in finishing the tomb of your father, the Great Pakal. I am grateful to you and wish to simply be allowed to continue that which I was seeking before we met. I can only be happy when I have found the answers I seek. If I have served you faithfully in my task, mighty Snake-Jaguar, I would ask only to be trusted to be set free with your blessing. Once I was called Yax Kan Balam by my adoptive father, a shaman of much wisdom, because I had been spared by the jaguar god. Now as your ostensible namesake, I would request this one favor."

It was clear from Kan Balam's silence that he was not very pleased with Yax Kan's desire. "I intended to require that you stay with me, so that I might assure your silence. As I think about it, I realize that it would only assure your immediate punishment if the secrets were ever divulged. I have grown to admire you like a favorite son, Yax Kan. It will be difficult to let you go, but if that is your greatest wish, it will be so. Will you swear with a sacred oath that you will not disclose our secret?"

Yax Kan's eyes were shining, "Oh, yes, my king! I do swear. I have no wish to discuss the matter, and no one would know to ask me outside of this city, the only place where I am known as your servant. Thank you, great king!"

"Well then, you may depart as soon as you wish after my accession ceremony is completed this evening. Farewell, Yax Kan Balam, marked by the jaguar god!" With that the king turned to his sleeping chamber and Yax departed with an exultant heart. He had worried he might be put to death, but instead he was being set free!

Old Hun'tul was waiting for him outside of the royal residence and casually asked him where he was going. Still elated, Yax told him that the king had agreed to let him leave the city and continue on his journey. The old priest seemed relieved at the news, probably thinking that perhaps now he would be taken back into the ruler's full confidence.

"Where do you journey, Cahal Yax Kan?" It was the first time Hun'tul had ever personally questioned him without the command of the king, or had used this honorific title.

"I am unsure, Wise One, but I am willing to travel to the end of the Yucatan, to the great city Chichen, to find the answers to my quest."

"And what quest is that?" Hun'tul persisted.

"I seek the truth about Kukulkan, the Fair One of legends. Do you know something to help me in my search?" Yax turned the question well, but a surprise awaited him.

"I remember that when the last true followers of the white

and bearded god were taken into the otherworld, there were three of them who could not die. At least I remember the tale told by my grandfather. Kukulkan took them away because the people would not listen to their teachings. Now only death awaits those who seek him openly in Chichen, or any of the other places where Kukulkan's priests reside, unless you are very careful.

"You have made my Lord Kan Balam very happy with your carving and I warn you out of duty to him. The gentle Kukulkan of legend has long been gone from this world and can only help you in the next. Do not rush to join him there—you are still young!" With that warning ringing in the air Hun'tul walked into the outer room of the palace to wait on the bidding of his pupil and king.

Yax considered the old shaman's words as he packed his few belongings and spent one last night in Palenque, waiting for the dawn to light his way north along the trade route toward Chichen. The jaguar kitten had grown into a doting cub that followed Yax whenever allowed. He had named him Wi'tzin, meaning 'little brother,' and Yax anticipated that they would have many adventures together.

Although anxious to continue his quest, his heart yearned to travel to Lamanai where he hoped to find Tutoma and her father safely waiting for him.   He had never before experienced this kind of longing and he was a little bemused by his feelings.

Later that night a great feast was held to honor the newly crowned *ahau* of Palenque. The food was rich and delicious with every delicacy the kingdom could provide. There were dance performances and mock battles fought to celebrate the occasion, and Yax was honored at one point by the new king, who announced that Yax would be leaving on a journey to please the gods on the morrow. All were amazed at the release of this servant of their king.

After only a few days Yax left the lowland forest and passed into a dense low jungle on either side of the *sacbe*. He traveled for almost a full moon cycle through the grand Yucatan. Although he desired to go to Lamanai to find Tutoma, he felt compelled instead to travel northward toward Chichen. He passed through the city of Calakmul, an ancient place, reduced to the dwelling of an illiterate society which had ceased to make records even of their own kings. Their ignorance and lack of direction worried Yax, for if it could happen to such a great city, he could foresee it happening in all of the *Mayab*. There were many cities along the route, but he avoided any more contact than was necessary to cautiously acquire a few supplies which he was unable to obtain in the jungle. He listened for useful information in the small settlements, keeping his ears alert and unobtrusively reading any carved glyphs he found in each of the many communities of the heavily populated land. The larger cities were being abandoned by the citizens seeking the freer life in the small villages. As always, his questions were multiplied, rather than their answers.

Upon reaching a small village called Ichpaatun on the eastern shore of the Yucatan peninsula, on a bay so large he thought it was the sea itself, he traveled north for what seemed forever along the shore of that bay. The grey stone along the shore was dead coral that cut at his sandals, and he soon learned from Wi'tzin's example to avoid walking on it, the cat preferring the sand or vegetation whenever possible. Yax snared large Iguanas coming out of their holes or caught them while they were swimming, and roasted them over small fires on the beach for the two of them. The white meat was delicious, though a little stringy. However, upon learning from a fisherman that they were worshipped locally, he no longer captured them. Occasionally, he was able to spear a fish for their supper with a spear he fashioned from prongs of bamboo.

Once he ran out of fresh water and went inland almost two days, until he found a natural well, called a *cenote*. Here he climbed down into the limestone cave surrounding the well to fill his drinking gourd, careful not to disturb the bats and scorpions that clung to the wall and ceiling.

Clouds of biting flies attacked him in the daytime, and when they flew off to rest, swarms of bloodthirsty mosquitoes took their place through the night. Fortunately, he knew the plants to use to protect his skin from both. Each evening he heard the sounds of the steaming jungle increase as the light faded, and nocturnal predators awoke and began to search for their meals.

As he traveled he saw snakes dangling from hanging lianas, watching him with cold, emotionless eyes. Once by a waterhole he disturbed a flock of butterflies that arose in a cloud of moving color, iridescent gems seeking the lovely jungle flowers all around them. Wi'tzin chased after them, bounding into the air and making Yax laugh. Yax felt like a young child again, dazzled by the beauty and life around him.

Traveling over an inland *sacbe*, he arrived at the city of Chichen with a hope that was not to be fulfilled. Here once more was a temple dedicated to Kukulkan that should hold the desired answers to the questions of his heart. A stone depiction of the feathered serpent appeared to slither down the stairway in its shadow as the sun set. His questions were to be answered with few words being spoken, but as always he gleaned something to lead him on.

17

The Ritual

Yax watched with horror from the shadows of the great Temple of Kukulkan, as the long-skirted *nacom* and his assistant priests with their filthy, blood-matted hair, cleared the blood and offal from the altar only minutes after sacrificing a captive warrior to Chaac, the rain god. He heard them make insulting remarks about the cowardice of the young man because of his screaming during the bloody rite. They called it the "holy death" and screamed in his face that worthy victims did not cry out as their beating hearts were cut from their breasts with obsidian blades. Their current victim had been a prisoner taken in a recent battle. His body had been painted blue, and he was then forced to play in the sacred ball game. Yax learned that the young warrior had courageously chosen death over a lifetime of slavery; even if he had escaped, his own clan would disown him as a coward if he tried to return home.

Yax shuddered with revulsion as he saw the *nacom* place the victim's heart in the shallow bowl of the Chac-Mool, an altar in the form of a reclining warrior, and then cry out to Chaac that he might be appeased by the gruesome offering and allow the sun to shine and the rain to fall for another calendar round of fifty-two *haab*. Burning censers were sending pungent clouds of *copal* smoke snaking up into the evening sky.

Finally a prayer was offered by the chief priest, the '*yahau kak*' or lord of fire, as he held a ceremonial bone-handled obsidian knife high above his head; the prayer was direct and to the point. "Oh Great Chaac, god of the clouds," he chanted, "I implore you to give life to the great city of Chichen. I give to you now, O lord of the sky, this heart and sacred corn meal mixed with the life-blood of our sacrificial offering, and I ask you for life for our city in return. Let the rain fall upon the places where seed is sown and life will be born again. Therefore, O Chaac, when I beseech the clouds to give up their rain, let them follow my command, because I will have the power from you as a priest and Lord of the Sun-god, Kukulkan, to command them. . . With that power, O Clouds, I now command you to bring sustenance to the people of the world below."

Yax was appalled at the arrogance of this priest. This was the first time Yax had seen this gory rite for himself and he was sickened and disgusted by the brutality and insensitivity of it. He realized that this was how he had always thought his parents had died at the hands of the Zapotecs, who he knew practiced a similar rite. He was not happy with the way it made him feel about the temples and priests of Chichen. *"Would these filthy priests remain bravely silent in 'holiness' if their hearts were extracted with obsidian blades? Did the gods truly continue to demand the lives of many people to be appeased?"* he wondered.

Naz-Hani had long ago told Yax that his own clan's ancestors had been given strict instructions from Kukulkan, himself, to do away with all blood sacrifice of any kind, and they had begun making other offerings of fruit and grains to the priests of the temple, a portion of their gain, that was to be shared with the poor. Naz-Hani, however, was no longer alive and would not have been able to assert his will among the priests of Chichen, even if he were. There was no doubt they would be vindictive toward Yax should they learn of his abhorrence of their abominable rites, but something within him would not let him simply accept or forget what he had seen this night.

Earlier he had viewed the *cenote* where other human sacrifices had been made, according to his guide, the boy Ribnaki, who had been showing him the city. The boy had suddenly appeared at his side with a baby coati-mundi on his shoulder. Yax told Ribnaki he was traveling on a secret mission and had shown him the claw marks on his shoulder, as though he were a member of the jaguar clan. Yax thought that this tale was as close to the truth as any and harmed no one. The boy had been awed by the tokens of Yax' experience which had scarred his body, and had offered to be his covert guide for the price of only one cacao bean. It was too dangerous to bring Wi'tzin into Chichen, so he had left the young cat in a small but deep natural underground cave, too steep for him to climb out without help. Yax realized that he needed to teach his companion to remain out of sight without being tied or otherwise hindered, so that he would better be able to come to his aid, if needed.

That night in his camp Yax determined in his heart that

the knowledge he was seeking, and had continually prayed for in his heart, was not to be found in Chichen. At the rising of the new sun he would also rise and be on his way, southwest to the white-walled city by the sea that he had learned of earlier in the day at a booth in the marketplace, and which young Ribnaki had confirmed was only a full sun's run away. Even with all the knowledge of the priests at Chichen gleaned from their observatory and combined with their ancient lore, it was plain to see that they were not the followers of a loving god such as the one Yax sought.

He felt sure of his own belief because of feelings deep within and because he knew that the ancients had been given knowledge of an eternal nature to benefit man, even though it was now being perverted throughout the land. If the god of Chichen truly was Kukulkan, then that was not the god he was seeking. Somewhere there was an answer to his questions. Someone could tell him about the one true god, whether that god was Hunab-Ku, Itzamna, Kukulkan, or some other deity not yet known to Yax.

The events of his life flowed through his mind. First, he was preserved from certain death in the jaws of the great jaguar by his father. Next, he was preserved by Naz-Hani from the raiding Zapotecs, who took all of his family but himself. In Izapa he had seen the tree of life stela that had sparked his desire to learn about the quest for immortality through the teachings of a venerable ancestor. It was truly auspicious that he had been led to his parents and sister, and that he had been able to rescue them without bloodshed.

After meeting the beautiful Tutoma, he had been saved from the jaguar priests in Teotihuacan, and then from death by the soldiers and priests of Kan Balam in Palenque. Now, he had seen what it was like to be much less fortunate, witnessing the death of the young man who had just been sacrificed by the priests of Chichen. "Why am I being led and preserved?" This question burned silently in his heart and mind.

He remembered the presence of dark forces around him while dreaming of the jaguar woman, and wondered what evil force wanted to hinder him in his quest. He prayed silently in his mind, but this time not knowing to whom. "Help me find the truth!" he prayed over and over.

18

Temple of the Descending God

Yax moved quietly through the jungle along a *sacbe* that made travel possible through the dense jungle. He had risen very early, before the sun, to leave his camp near the detested city of human sacrifice. It was not yet noon when he found himself passing by the large city of Coba with its great temples and two large *cenotes*. He feared that these wells, as in Chichen, were used for other than a source of water. Careful not to be seen by the local citizens as he scouted the area, he decided to continue on to the white-walled city that Ribnaki had told him about, where more than one temple had been built to a god who had descended from the sky to visit his people.

As Yax looked out over the white sand and eastern sea near Tulum he was for the first time reminded of the view of the beaches near Tonala. This was the closest he had ever come to feeling homesick for that place which Naz-Hani and he had adopted as their home. This place was different from Tonala, as well.

There were large sea-going dugouts on the beach with

traders unloading goods which had been purchased by the merchants of this coastal city. Workers carried the loads up into the town from the beach each using forehead tumplines, called *mecapals*, to more easily carry the heavy loads on their backs. Yax thought he saw symbols on some of the canoes that might indicate they were from far away Xicalango; others he determined from listening, were from even further, a place called Caqueti near a river known as the Orinoco, across the southern sea.

The white temples above the marketplace beckoned to him as none had before. Even in Palenque with its Temple of the Tree of Life, or *Wakah chan*, he did not feel the same stirring of his spirit that he now felt looking upon this beautiful city.

There was no chac-mool or bloody altar apparent here for human sacrifice, such as he had seen in Chichen. There was no large *cenote* wherein hapless victims were cast to 'visit the underworld.' The priests' hair was not matted with filth and the blood of their offerings, neither were the beautiful temples or their steps in need of cleansing from human remains, nor were skulls lined up on a skull rack platform next to a ball court, all as he had seen in Chichen. Perhaps this was the place he longed for, where he could at last find the answers and peace of mind.

He had tethered Wi'tzin in the safety of a large hollow tree stump, leaving him a small swamp rabbit to dine on until he could return to retrieve him. The growing young cat grunted his displeasure at being left alone, but settled down to wait for his companion to return.

As was his custom he watched the townspeople from the outskirts of the community to be sure that his appearance would not set him apart, an outsider to be despised and captured. He noted that there was little sign of slaves, or of guards, other than those set on the corner towers of the courtyard walls allowing for advance warning of possible invaders.

The dialect of this people was different from that in Palenque, but not much different from that of Chichen and what he had gleaned from conversing with the boy, Ribnaki. All Maya spoke a language derived from an earlier tongue, but had he not traveled from place to place gradually and stayed at least a short while in each location he would not now be able to interpret the differences in such a short time. He must be careful not to say more than necessary or he might still give himself away as a foreigner, thought to be a spy. He did not want to risk capture, detainment and servitude, such as he had experienced in Palenque, or worse.

He also knew that all priests spoke another special language which was very ancient and not changed as much as the Mayan dialects over time. Yax was allowed the privilege of learning the sacred language from Naz-Hani due to his mentor's belief that Yax was to perform a sacred mission seeking knowledge about Kukulkan, but until he began his journey he had not known that all Maya priests spoke the same secret tongue, while using hand signs shown in the sacred glyphs to augment their meanings. Having listened closely to Naz-Hani's teachings and to the priests of Tonala, he was proficient in the priestly tongue.

Surreptitiously, Yax walked into town through a small crowd and came to the marketplace of the city. He sat on a low wall under a small avocado tree watching and listening for most of the day, and at mid-day eating a refreshing sweet papaya he purchased at one of the stalls. Yax was tiring of listening to the conversations of those passing by in the market though. He now felt sure he could pass as just another shopper in this city of thousands. As he was about to return to get Wi'tzin and make camp in the outskirts of the city, Yax unexpectedly detected the strain of one loudly whispered conversation in the priestly tongue.

"I tell you, I feel sure that the next coming of the great descending god to our land will be much like the first time he came here," said one of two priests huddled in conversation. "There will be many calamities on the earth—cities will be buried, mountains will rise from the sea, and the earth will shake as though it has been jarred from its course around the sun!"

"But how do you know this, Malochi?" asked the other priest hoarsely. "Where is it written? Have you had a dream or a vision in the temple?"

The silver-haired priest, Malochi, did not answer at once. He stopped walking and gazed over at the highest temple by the seaside cliffs in deep thought. Malochi squinted his eyes at the glare of the sun off the bright stone, then, carefully choosing his words, he began his answer, "Ragoth, I don't think it was a dream or a vision, but as I ponder the oral traditions of our creed, which we both studied as young acolytes, I hear, or rather feel, something deep within me that says it will be much the same when He comes again. Those who have been faithful to exactly what He taught will be preserved, but those who have knowingly perverted the sacred ways will be destroyed."

"Well, I am not so sure." said Ragoth. "I think we may have a great flood again as our astronomers tell us we had over three thousand years ago. This would surely be a just end to the wicked rulers and priests who have done so much evil."

Then Malochi continued, "There is something else that I feel is true, but I have not yet told you. I have been given to understand that it will not be by flood, but by fire that the world will be cleansed, and as we both know, it will be done by the one true god, the great Kukulkan." At this point the two had finished their shopping for fresh foods for the evening meal of the priests, and had turned to go back to the largest temple. As they did so, the older priest who had spoken noticed Yax. He had seen this young stranger as they had passed him earlier in the day. Now, as he caught Yax Kan's gaze, the priest turned directly toward him.

Yax was startled and his first reaction was that he should run, but the desire to flee left as quickly as it had come. The gaze of the old priest was kindly and not one to fear. He walked over to Yax where he was sitting on the end of the stone bench and spoke in the tongue of the common people.

"You are a visitor, and have come on a pilgrimage to seek guidance from our people, am I correct?"

Yax choked and then, clearing his throat, said, "Yes, but how do you know what I am doing or why I am here?" Too late, he realized that he had inadvertently answered in the priestly language and not in the peoples' tongue. Now it was the priests who were surprised.

"Are you also a priest from another temple, and if so, have you come to spy upon us?" said Ragoth.

"No," said Malochi before Yax could respond, "I discern that this young man is not a priest, but perhaps he should be, nor is he a spy. Am I right, young man?"

"I am not a priest, but was raised by a healing shaman and among the priests of a city far from here. I am on a journey, yet I hardly know what I seek, except that I need to learn the true reasons for my existence and why our ancestors passed on the stories of the gods, the stars and planets, and especially of the white and bearded god Kukulkan, known as the feathered-serpent. It is his teachings that I most desire to learn, but I fear that most of what he taught has been lost or distorted. Will you help me in my quest?"

The kind old Malochi put his hand on Yax Kan's shoulder and looked deeply into his eyes. "You may come with us into the residence of the priests. Eat with us and we will talk further. Perhaps we will be able to assist you more than we can understand. You may even have been sent to us by our God who descended from the sky, and perhaps it is you who will help us."

Elated and tingling with anticipation, Yax followed the two into the courtyard and over to a large ramada made of poles and palms, unlike the temples of pure white stone all around them. Long after the evening meal, the priests gathered with Malochi around the young newcomer and discussed the ancient beliefs of the Maya. Yax shared much with them that he had not felt comfortable sharing with any others on his journey, discerning only that it was right to teach and be taught by these humble men. They were amazed at his stories and his store of knowledge about the gods, glyphs and traditions of the *Mayab*.

He, in turn, learned that this city was not ruled by a king or queen, and that the priests were very protective toward their people. They were for the most part married men who had children to support. They fished with their fishing dugouts and gathered roots, nuts and fruit from the jungles just as the other people in the city did. They planted gardens of beans, squash and corn. They even hunted occasionally, sometimes accompanying the guards who earned their keep by hunting, watching for enemies and helping to protect their community. However, their safety was most effectively maintained by their status as an important coastal trade center.

He also learned that this city, formerly named Zama, from the word `zamal` or `morning,' and now commonly called Tulum, because of the wall surrounding the city center, did not pretend to be the spot where their God, the Son of the morning, had come down from the sky many generations before. Rather, a group of his followers had colonized Tulum, seeking to form a community to retain and follow his teachings of brotherhood and love. It was to him they prayed for rain, food, health, safety, knowledge, and all other blessings upon their families, and not to the many other deities of the other Maya groups.

Yet, they were unsure about what else they should be doing. They agreed that much had been lost over the centuries since His coming, and they could only look forward to the time when these teachings would be restored. Even the nearby cities of Chichen and Coba still practiced the shedding of blood with animal sacrifices, which these priests said they had long ago been taught should no longer be done by those who followed the one God of heaven and earth. Yax Kan's

heart thrilled when he heard them say they did not believe
in blood sacrifices, especially the perverted human sacrifices,
but he held his feelings in check, wanting to be sure that this
was really the truth he pursued.

They further told him that they did not believe that they
were actually true priests of the one God, since none had
been ordained by one who had the authority before them,
who was also a prophet, or far-seer, chosen by God to lead
them.

Yax retrieved Wi'tzin before dark and the young cat
created a joyful stir of excitement among the youngsters of
Tulum. He was pleased to note that they were not fearful from
ingrained superstition, but treated Wi'tzin with curiosity and
much respect.

The next morning Malochi and Ragoth took Yax on
a tour of the walled city which featured two watchtowers
at its corners, and showed him the temples that had been
erected nearly a century earlier. Most of them had carvings or
molded stucco representations of the feathered serpent god,
Kukulkan. Malochi explained that He was depicted in such a
way because the quetzal bird was their symbol of heaven and
the serpent that of the earth, and Kukulkan was the God of
both heaven and earth. This was what Yax had been taught
by his mentor, Naz-Hani, as well.

The large symbolic carvings in the stone lintels of the
temples were more glyphs than true pictures of their god, as
he descended to the earth, but he did have a beard, a robe,
an apron, and the symbol of the plumed serpent by his feet
to explain that this was indeed the great Kukulkan. One of
the figures also included a pictogram of the lotus blossom,

which signifies life after death. They told Yax that both Coba and Chichen had carvings with similar symbolism, but those cities did not believe that these figures depicted the visit of Kukulkan to earlier people. Some of the priests of Coba even taught that the carvings represented a diving honeybee, and worshipped it as a god.

There were both original and more recent murals painted on some of the walls, depicting Kukulkan teaching his followers. One of them particularly captured Yax Kan's attention and he studied it at length. It portrayed the God with three of His followers and it contained the glyph for endless life over the heads of all three, although it did not give their names. Evidently these three had been granted power over death. *"Is this the treasure I am seeking?"* he silently wondered.

They took him to a building that was a place to observe the sky, both by the light of the sun and of the moon. They explained how in the spring, on only one date, the sunlight fell upon a mark on a post in the center of the room. This was the date that their God had been born as a man into the world long ago, but they did not know when or where that had occurred.

The main temple was the most imposing building in Tulum and was built overlooking the city and the ocean. A broad stairway led to its upper level where there were three alcoves carved into the upper façade. Malochi explained that the one in the center contained a figure representing Itzamna, the creator and father of all, on Itzamna's right was another figure representing Kukulkan, the son of Itzamna, deliverer of mankind from Xibalba, and on his left side was an empty alcove representing the invisible spirit god. Yax Kan's heart swelled as he learned more of Kukulkan and his true place in the religion of the Maya.

Yax questioned them about the roughness of the structures, which had walls that seemed to slant inward on four sides. His new found friends told him that this was partly due to the fact that there were fewer craftsmen among them and no slaves were used to build these temples, as in other cities, however, it also created the illusion of reaching up to greet the descending God at His return. They had been built by their ancestors with their own hands out of devotion to this enigmatic deity, mostly unknown to his worshippers.

"The Descending God"

19

The Prayer and the Blessing

*L*ate that night when all were asleep, Yax's thoughts were full of the things he had learned from the priests of Tulum. Finally, he crept out of the long hut and walked in the starlit night through the garden in the compound until he came to a bench overlooking the sea. Here with the sound of the waves caressing the sandy shore, he knelt in humility and quietly articulated his first vocal prayer. Tears came to his eyes as he prayed with all of his heart to understand certain eternal precepts. What should he do? Who should he worship, and why could he not find the whole truth in all his travels? Was Kukulkan the true god that he sought, as Naz-Hani had believed?

With the first light of morning glistening on the sea, Yax remained kneeling by the stone bench, a prayer in his heart as he meditated. As he looked up, his chest filled with warmth and wonder. All at once he was assured in his heart and mind that he would receive the truth in its fullness. *"Perhaps sometime soon,"* he silently hoped.

Yax arose with a gladdened spirit, and as he walked toward

the northern compound walls he saw a man standing on the bluff overlooking the lower beach below the small building covering the *cenote*. He did not recognize him or his manner of dress as one of those he had met the night before, and his curiosity drew him toward the man. As he drew close, the stranger looked toward him and beckoned. Yax was amazed at the lightness of his skin and his unusual clothing. He wondered because the man nonetheless looked familiar to him. His demeanor and spirit were the kindest that Yax had ever perceived in another man.

The stranger began speaking as Yax approached, "Good morning, son, it is early and we seem to be the only ones awake. You have been up all night. What are you feeling right now?" He spoke in the sacred tongue of priests, but with a purity that was more felt than heard.

Yax was confused by what the man said. Surely he could not read his heart and know of his prayers, or what he had experienced. Perhaps the man had heard him praying and was merely inquiring out of curiosity. "I fear I am acting in a way that would bring concern to anyone," Yax answered. "Excuse my oddness, but I am a visitor not of this place, and often do not act as those around me."

The stranger smiled, "Yax Kan, you misunderstand me. I know who you are, and that you have been praying to the One True God. I truly want to hear what it is you are feeling in your heart."

Still uncertain and puzzled by the man's statement, but reassured by his apparent honesty, Yax answered without guile, "I am feeling the touch of that God in my heart, and a warmth and reassurance that my prayers will be answered."

"That is good, Yax Kan, and so they shall. I am one of three disciples who were allowed to tarry on the earth until the second coming of the Lord. I was here in this promised-land when we were visited by the Savior of the world, the God of both heaven and earth, whom you know as Kukulkan, a name given him by those who remember him only in part. They understand that Kukulkan was a chief priest and a sacrificial victim, but they have buried the truth by denying His uniqueness and his infinite sacrifice.

"I tell you now that the God you seek is Jehovah, who came to Earth as Jesus, the Christ, the son of the Father of the Heavens. You should no longer call him by the name Kukulkan, which has become an abominable false god, demanding the blood of mortals, powerless to atone for the sins of the people.

"Jesus Christ appeared to your ancestors almost six hundred years ago in the place called Bountiful, and chose twelve of us as special witnesses to serve as his disciples with authority endowed by him. You are one of very few in your time who has continually sought after truth and righteousness to such a great extent and I have therefore been sent to fulfill your desire to learn of the one true God of heaven and earth, the Son of the Father.

"Yax Kan, your sojourn is being rewarded due to your determination to seek the truth." The disciple came toward Yax and led him by the arm to a corner of the great temple overlooking the azure sea.

"Much of what the good men in this place have told you is true. However, they know even less than you do now. You must share with them the things which I will explain."

Then the man sat down by Yax and spoke to him for a long time about events long past, relating missing portions of the ancient stories that Yax had yearned to have explained to him. He spoke of sea voyages, prophets, judges, kings, robbers in secret combinations and battles, and gave a history of a portion of the peoples who had inhabited this land, and their ancestors from across the sea. He spoke of sacred principles such as prayer, the godhead, faith, repentance, baptism, resurrection and the spirit world. Some things Yax was commanded not to reveal, and some he could not express even had he so desired.

He further explained, "Yax Kan, your people, the Maya, have lost sight of the fact that all blessings emanate from the one true God. They are preoccupied with material possessions and believe that manmade gods will send them rain, fruitful crops and good health. Most of their priests have perverted the truth about the pure sacrifice of the Atonement made by God's Son into false and needless bloody rituals and unholy sacrifices, such as the one you witnessed in Chichen.

"They go into war thinking that the planets, stars and false stone idols can yield up victory to them. And they have lost the understanding that by failing to worship the one true God of Heaven and Earth, the God of Life Eternal, with the sacrifice of a broken heart and a contrite spirit, they must also inevitably fail in all other eternal endeavors."

"Both good and evil exist in the world, Yax Kan. Many of the obstacles placed in your way are given to strengthen you. Some were put there by the evil one, called Satan, who will continue to try you. You must be alert and resist Satan, but when you call upon God, your Heavenly Father, in the name of his Son, Jesus Christ, I promise that you will always be preserved."

Yax remembered his recent dream in the jungle and was reassured that he had been right in his feelings that it was from an evil being. The disciple explained that the dream was sent by Satan to discourage, tempt and mislead him. Yax suddenly realized that this was the man he had seen in the later dream by the sea, which dream was sent by God to give him encouragement on his journey.

"The temples in this city were built many years after the Son of God descended from heaven as a resurrected being to visit this land, but they were built in commemoration of his visit and thus some are dedicated to the Descending God. However, these people have only a semblance of knowledge of his coming because his teachings have been lost and perverted over time and throughout the land. The authority of the true priesthood has been lost due to the wickedness of your forefathers, but it will at some time be restored in this land of covenant many years in the future.

"Your mentor and adopted grandfather, Naz-Hani, is now learning of the true gospel in the world of the spirits, and would have you know of his happiness. He will receive many blessings due to his diligence in searching for truth during his life, and in his belief in God the Father, and His Son.

"The carved tree stone that you wondered about in Izapa was a depiction of a beautiful vision given to your forefathers, Lehi and Nephi. The story in this vision explains that there are those who will choose the right and hold to the rod of truth to gain access to the tree of eternal life, and others who will fall away because of their blindness due to the false precepts of men, symbolically shown as mists of darkness. These others mock those who have chosen the better part. This story represents the Plan of Happiness that all men must follow if they wish to return to dwell with their God.

"Jesus Christ came first to lands across the Great Sea to other descendants of your forefathers known as the Jews, and suffered and died for the sins of the world. He was tortured and wounded by men who could not recognize who he was, being blinded by their own iniquity, and at the prompting of the Wicked One, also called Lucifer. However, the Anointed One freely gave up his life and died to secure our resurrection and offer an eternity with his Father and himself.

"Upon his death, great destruction came upon this land through volcanoes, storms, floods and earthquakes, such as you have learned about in your journey. A period of utter darkness befell your people at that time. Then the Great Messiah, King of Heaven and Earth, rose from the dead and appeared unto his disciples in the Old World. Thereafter he descended out of heaven in this land as a witness to your ancestors that he lives and that he is the great Jehovah, capable of allowing all people to return to live with him and his Father. He showed them the wounds that he had suffered as he was nailed to and hung from a cross of wood, similar to the life tree you carved in stone in Palenque without understanding this fact. You also know of the glyph of the sacrificial rite that shows this wound in His hand, the origin of which has been forgotten by your people.

"He taught immersion baptism by water following faith and repentance, and another baptism by fire and the Holy Spirit. The warmth that you now feel in your breast is given to you by this Holy Spirit. Remember this feeling, because it will not be with you always in this life, but only on occasion as you stand in need. You must understand that although you cannot be cleansed by baptism now, since the authority to do so is not now available to man upon the earth, if you remain faithful to this knowledge, this work will be done for you by one of your descendants in a true, sanctified temple of the Lord as part of the restoration of all things prophesied by prophets throughout all time."

When the disciple finished speaking, he offered Yax one more thing. "I have come to give you a special blessing from your Father in Heaven. Would you like me to do that now?"

By this time, Yax could hear the townspeople preparing for their daily labors. His heart stirred within him. He feared that they would be interrupted. "Yes, I want to receive anything I can from our one true God. Will we be undisturbed long enough?"

His new mentor assured him that they would and told him to arise and follow him into another nearby temple by a side portal that Yax had not noticed. The room was well lit by the light of the morning sun from window holes in the stone wall. Yax saw that it was the same observatory that he had been shown earlier. He saw motes of dust floating in the shining rays of light. The disciple confirmed that on the anniversary of the birth of the Savior every year, the sun shone through one of these narrow windows and cast its light upon a mark on the center pole which had been put there based on knowledge gained by inspiration from one of the good men of this town long ago. Then he was directed to kneel on a woven mat near the center of the room. As Yax

Kan's body was warmed by the beams of light streaming in, the benevolent visitor placed his hands on Yax Kan's head.

"Yax Kan, I give you this blessing in the name of the Messiah and by the authority of the Holy Priesthood received from Him.

"Young Yax Kan, your Father in Heaven has been very mindful of you during your life's journey. He preserved you from the jaws of the great jaguar, from the Zapotec warriors, the wicked priests of Teotihuacan, the soldiers of Palenque, and from the hand of its misled king, Kan Balam, whose heart was softened when he might have murdered you to protect his futile secrets.

"From this time forward have faith that your Father in Heaven and His Son, the Redeemer of the World, are aware of your desires and will bless you as you continue to be an example of love, mercy, charity and compassion to your fellow Lamanites, for this is what a portion of your ancestors were called before they along with others became the Maya. And those old ones that you revere were once known as the Jaredites, who came from the old world to this promised land long before the father of the Lamanites. Their records left much of value to your people, but they too perished in their apostasy.

"Due to the apostasy of your forefathers, rather than relying on prayer, prophecy and guidance from the Holy Spirit, their rulers have relied on astrology to predict the future, and astronomy to tell them when to wage war. These astrologers are the false prophets of your time, Yax Kan. The true prophets of God have long since been rejected and driven away or killed because of this apostasy from the truth.

Not many generations in the future, those great city-states which rely on these false religions based on the stars and planets, rather than on the gospel of Jesus Christ, will all fail and their monuments will crumble to dust.

"They will trample under their feet the sacrifice of the Son of God by thinking that shedding their own blood or the blood of sacrificial victims can gain blessings and insure happiness in the afterlife, after the Greatest of All has allowed his own blood to be spilt for the sins of Man.

"You should travel soon to your promised reunion with that sweet and gentle young woman you plan to make your companion and the mother of your children, for this is a necessary part of the Father's plan for his own children. Thereby you will be a great influence for good and a blessing upon your family and this people, now and in generations to come, in their preparation for the final coming of our Lord, Jesus Christ. As he descended from heaven, so he ascended back after he had taught them his word, and so shall he descend again in glory. Judgments will come upon the heads of the wicked and blessings upon the righteous according to the desires of their hearts and also according to their deeds.

"Now, go forth my brother, and remember these things that you may look forward to the morning of the first resurrection. Have faith, enduring to the end, and you will have nothing to fear, for you will be protected from wickedness and the Evil One, as long as you show love to others and continue to have desires to do good. This blessing I pronounce upon you in the name of Jesus Christ. AMEN."

For the second time that morning tears streamed down Yax Kan's face, and he realized that they were tears of pure joy. He understood now! He exulted in the knowledge that there was one true God, and that he was important to that God, because he was one of his sons!

As his eyes cleared of the cleansing tears, he saw that the disciple of Christ had departed. Yax did not feel loss, because he was too full of joy. He hurried to the enclosure, where the good men of Tulum were sleeping, to tell them the good news. The one they had called Kukulkan was more than they dreamed! He could now tell them of the God that they worshipped without understanding, and of the meaning of the true priesthood. Surely they would exult as he did in the truth of all things!

20

Yax Kan's Legacy

t took many hours more than the disciple had taken for Yax to explain in his own humble words those beautiful teachings he had just received. He asked the men of Tulum to bring their wives and children together in the plaza after he told them the barest of facts about his encounter. Hours were then spent explaining to all that although they were unable to have the fullness of the teachings of Jesus Christ in this life, that they could yet learn more in the afterlife, and they could begin to prepare now. He helped them to know the truths that had been lost or perverted by their forbears, and they accepted what was said because they were humble people who could be touched by the Spirit that was present in this assembly.

After teaching them all he could, and remaining with the people of Tulum for nearly twenty days, he bid goodbye to Malochi and a few others who had shown him kindness, to begin another journey. From that time forward, for many years, the people of Tulum remembered the teachings of Yax Kan, whom they called 'The Wise One.' They celebrated by beginning the tradition that lasted longer than the memory of his teachings, painting the temples the blue of the sea and the red of the atoning blood of Christ.

Now that Yax was grown and had discovered the truths of eternity, he knew that he must do one other thing before settling down with a wife, though he hoped he knew who that wife would be. He must be sure that his parents and sister were well and that they would be near him in the future after he had secured a promise of the lifetime companionship of Tutoma. He remembered that the Nephite disciple had said he would be a blessing to his "family," so he felt an urgent desire and a heartfelt duty to share these new truths with them. His prayers brought confirmation of the Holy Spirit as to the rightness of his decision and, again, he was driven by a need to know of his family's well-being. First though, he would go to Lamanai to be sure Tutoma was safe.

21

Reunion in Lamanai

As Yax once again set out on the white road with his feline companion by his side, his heart was gladdened thinking of Tutoma and her father. He felt strongly that they would accept the teachings he would bring them and he looked forward to sharing these things with all he encountered.

"I will call upon the Holy Spirit and invite him to be my companion often!" Yax thought as he exultantly hurried toward Lamanai. He traveled south, retracing much of the path he had followed going northerly only days before, following directions given to him by the residents of Tulum. After passing the large bay, he dropped South to a river running through a dense jungle which he had been told led to the city of Lamanai.

Yax built a small dugout canoe by hollowing out the soft pith of a kapok tree as the people at Tulum had instructed him. It would not last more than a season or two, but would suffice for this journey. Although the young cat loved to swim, Wi'tzin required much coaxing and earnest reassurance before settling down in the dugout and accepting this strange new mode of travel.

They traveled for a few days with scarlet macaws and white-faced monkeys calling out warnings of their coming, while hopping about in the branches of the overhanging tamarind trees. The supa, cohune and coyol palms shaded the banks, and black mangrove trees crept out into the current.

People began to appear along the banks of the river waving in a friendly and curious manner. Yax felt comforted about the safety of Tutoma and her father by the congenial local atmosphere.

Great egrets and other water fowl were plentiful. One small black and red bird walked along on the lily pads, screeching at the always patient river crocodiles. Tiny bats clung to tree trunks reaching out over the water as they waited for night to come so they could feast on the plentiful insects flying over the river.

The young traveler could see the tops of tall temples ahead on the river and pulled to the river bank at a small inlet. Met by fishermen in dugouts carved from mahogany and other hardwoods, he was treated with the respect due a stranger in their midst and spoke to them in a dialect very similar to their own to ask about Tutoma and her father, Lemnoch. They were not familiar with the two, but when he mentioned 'Big Zero' they laughed and one of them pulled a young boy over and gave him instructions to guide Yax and his beautiful jaguar companion to the home of the merchant.

The reunion was warmer than Yax had hoped for. Tutoma ran innocently into his open arms from the clearing between several huts and bathed his shoulder with tears of happiness. "I thought I might never see you again!" she whispered as she clung to him.

Big Zaconiuh grasped Yax Kan's arms firmly in greeting and called into one of the huts. Soon the kind, diminutive Lemnoch was savoring the reunion as well. They were all amazed by the antics of Wi'tzin, who, though he had outgrown the name of kitten, was hopping around like one wanting to share in his friend's reunion.

Their quiet laughter and happiness continued into the evening as Yax described all that had happened to him in the many years since they had separated. They were amazed at his brushes with death, and with his many accomplishments, especially in Palenque. However, when he began to describe his experiences with the disciple of the one called Jesus Christ they were filled with reverence. Because of their trust in the integrity of Yax, they accepted all that he told them. Lemnoch was especially happy because his only child, Tutoma, was happy. He was very fond of Yax and clearly approved of their coming together.

Zaconiuh's skeptical merchant heart, although a good one, seemed reluctant to accept Yax Kan's teachings. Having come away disillusioned from the city of Teotihuacan, he was jaded and skeptical when it came to any religious beliefs. The priests of Teotihuacan had left him little desire to worship. It was to be some time before the Spirit of Truth could claim his conscience.

Yax asked about the name of this city. It sounded like the name "Lamanite" which his visitor had used to describe their ancestors, but was the local dialect's word for a 'submerged crocodile,' possibly the name of a prior king or ancestor in this place.

His friends were happy when they learned that he had come to Lamanai before going back to Comalcalco to see his family, but when Yax came to that part of his plans where he must soon leave them, a sorrowful look came over Tutoma that nearly broke his heart.

Lemnoch, upon seeing his daughter's sadness, diplomatically broke the silence that had fallen, "We will have a special feast first. You have enough time to rest and prepare before continuing on. We will leave you two to talk while we go and prepare everthing."

At last Yax and Tutoma were alone together. "Tutoma, I know we were together in Teo for only a short time, but I have been thinking of you so much over the past months. Would you accompany me on my journey?…As my new bride?" he asked.

Tutoma's brimming tears were turned to those of gladness, and she let Yax hold her in his arms in answer to his question. "Where else would I want to be but by your side?" she whispered.

Yax Kan's heart was so full he could barely contain his joy. He had never doubted his desire to marry Tutoma, but now that she had accepted he felt unprepared. Then looking at this lovely girl sitting next to him on the jaguar robe, he knew that it was his fondest wish. He never wanted to be parted from her again.

He also knew that he had finally received all that he had previously desired to learn in life, by learning that not only the one true God, the great Father of all, loved him, but that this beautiful young woman by his side loved him as well.

The next morning Yax and Tutoma climbed to the top of the highest temple and stood holding each other and looking out over the vast jungle, down the river and into the brightening sky. The mists came up in white clouds out of the rain forest as they planned their future together.

Part 2

YAX KAN AND THE SKULL OF DOOM

22

The Wedding

Jt was early summer and the sky was blue and cloudless with humid breezes from the recent rains of days past rising from the jungle. Mists arose from the nearby river, running brown from recent flooding upstream. The jungle was greener than green. The excited village women chattered incessantly as they dressed in their most beautiful clothing, and prepared their most delicious foods for the wedding of the beautiful Tutoma to her handsome suitor, this man of the jaguar mark, Yax Kan Balam, as they already called him. It was not a royal wedding or a banquet for a king, but to the young bride and her groom, it was to be a special day to remember forever. The men of the village were not as lively, but they were certainly looking forward to the expected wedding feast.

Lemnoch, would miss his only child dearly in her absence, but he knew that she would be happiest with the man she loved and that was the most important thing. He loved his only child more than she could understand.

As the father of the bride, Lemnoch provided most of the

foodstuffs. He was a successful maker of pottery in Lamanai, and could afford to provide the best for his only child. Also, dwarfs were believed to be special folk among these coastal Maya, and he did nothing to dissuade them of their belief.

Kechika Coc, a scribe to the King of Lamanai, had given them the necessary permission to marry. Tutoma's father promised the bride to Yax, and in the absence of Yax Kan's father, Zaconiuh would act as proxy and present the dowry for the bride. Yax remembered the gold nuggets that he had been given by the metalsmith, Sasak, who was by now like a brother, and gave one to Zaconiuh to allow him to buy gifts for Tutoma and her father worthy of such a prize. Zak had purchased blankets, hides, incense and grains to provide an admirable dowry.

Tutoma was prepared by the women of the village as though she were a favored local daughter. Since her own mother was not living, she selected a suitable substitute to present her to the groom, a woman called Pepem, who had befriended them and was named after the beautiful butterflies in the region. Pepem was a widow who seemed to have a soft spot in her heart for both Tutoma and for Lemnoch. The bride was first dressed in an embroidered *manta* made of finely woven linen; then they placed garlands of fresh flowers over her neck and hair.

Tutoma thought of her husband-to-be as she was led here and there for various preparations. She remembered their first meeting in the pottery shop in Teotihuacan, and their day preparing pottery with new designs of Yax Kan's creation. Her heart fluttered as she recalled running into his arms and having him hold her upon his arrival in Lamanai. If the villagers had been watching they may not have approved of her forwardness, since young women did not socialize with young men, but they gave no hint of disapproval on the following day. This young woman was no doubt looked upon differently because she had come to them from so far away, and did not dress, speak or act as the other young women acted. And the mothers of the village were especially welcoming of her when they learned that she was waiting for a young man from far away. This lifted the onus of competition from themselves and their daughters for the best local young men. Not that the young men had shown no interest, for they had, but they were not encouraged by Tutoma.

Now, as the time arrived for the wedding, Yax was brought to the center of the village by Zaconiuh, who grinned broadly at his part in the festivities. Yax was unfamiliar with the wedding ceremony of these people, but he would have walked through the central fire pit to marry Tutoma. Fortunately, that was not part of the ritual and as he walked into the central area, he saw her.

"She is more beautiful each day," he thought to himself.

Tutoma was not allowed to look toward Yax. It would not be proper for her to meet his eyes before the wedding ceremony. She was even expected to keep her back to him and step away if she knew he were near. Theirs was already a curious situation in Lamanai, so far from either of their homes. It was usual for the father of the bridegroom to select the bride for his son, but Yax Kan's father was far away. Since, as foreigners they had done other things that would normally not be allowed between a young man and young woman, such as eat meals together and have long family discussions, the locals gave them some latitude. The cultural mores of Teotihuacan were much more liberal than here in Lamanai, and this bride and groom were also a little older than was usual for marriage. Here it was common for the bride to be fourteen or fifteen years, and for the groom to be eighteen. Yax was a mature twenty-two years, and his bride approaching the seasoned age of eighteen.

This couple was clearly a special case. They had met before either came to the area. The parents of the groom were absent, and the bride had no living mother. Nevertheless, all who witnessed the wedding would attest that no two young people fit together more perfectly than these two.

The time arrived for the bride to be presented to the husband-to-be. The shaman that had been asked to bless the union of the two called out their names in a loud voice, and Pepem led Tutoma forward toward Yax, while she kept her eyes downcast. Zaconiuh had already brought Yax to the shaman's side and stepped back with a vociferous exclamation of the groom's intention to marry this day, and that he would attest to the groom's excellent abilities to provide, if anyone so required. As the shaman told the couple to kneel before him, Yax inhaled the scent of the flowers warmed by Tutoma's body. He shivered with the knowledge that she was to be his bride.

Tutoma was still trying to accept the fact that this handsome young man had traveled so far to rejoin her, and that he wanted her to be with him from this day forward. She felt safe and protected thinking about his strong arms and his calm, deep voice. He replaced her dreams of young womanhood with the reality of a sweet, strong relationship. She smiled inwardly at the thought of Yax forever by her side.

The old shaman, Kwiutul, sang a lengthy song about two forest birds that were bound together for life by their love for each other. He sang in a high, reedy voice that lilted up and down with each verse as he shook a rattle made of turtle shell to the cadence of his song. He then waved some long heron plumes over their heads and told them and everyone else present that they were husband and wife, and that they were to be faithful and true to one another. He told Tutoma that she should bear many children for Yax, that his clan would be strengthened. Yax was admonished to provide meat for the table and protection for his family. The smoke of the *copal* incense imparted to everyone a pungent reminder that this was a ceremony long to be remembered.

Normally in their society, the groom would live with the bride's family for three to six years after their marriage, but again this would not apply to the notably unusual and transient Yax. They would be leaving within the week on their journey to meet with and gain the approval of Yax Kan's clan.

Yax wore sandals and a humble loincloth, but as befitted his station as a scribe, he was allowed to wear as a cape the fur of the black jaguar, reserved for the elite of the Maya culture. He remembered that it had been given by his father, Ramarkiah, to Naz-Hani, who had cured it with great skill and special care. Yax remembered both of his 'fathers' during this great event in his life.

Finally, Yax stood and took Tutoma's hand as she arose, and they lovingly gazed into each other's eyes. To Yax, Tutoma seemed to be engulfed in luxuriant blossoms. He admired her long black tresses drifting over the flowers on her back like the east wind over the evening jungle. Hypnotized by her closeness, he almost forgot that it was his time to speak.

"We will go now to the bridal chamber, and your family will share their *maiz* with your new husband," he recited ceremonially.

"Yes, my husband," answered Tutoma, "We will keep this night sacred with our vows of faithfulness to each other."

Following Lemnoch and Pepem, the couple walked to the wedding hut, which had been cleaned and prepared for their wedding night. There would be one other unusual non-event in the village that night: usually the young men of a village would come by long after dark to roust the young couple and harass the new husband, but with Wi'tzin being an almost fully grown jaguar, none of the young men were brave enough to attempt to disturb the hut with the cat tethered to the front on a long enough leash to reach all of the way around the hut. When they were alone at last, the newlyweds embraced in loving tenderness.

Chapter 23

Stranger in Need

T he week that followed the wedding was full of joy, with long walks along the river, and endless conversations about the past and hoped-for future. Yax excitedly taught Tutoma everything that he had learned from Christ's disciple in Tulum, and her faith in her new husband allowed her to open her heart to all of the truths he unfolded about the plan of happiness that was based on the sacrifice of Jesus Christ, God's Son. They found that praying together gave them a calm and peace they had never before experienced; that their united faith was a greater power than the strength of either of them alone.

Word of Yax Kan's experience in Tulum had penetrated the outskirts of Lamanai into the huts and hearts of the humble peasants. None were foolish enough to share the message with those of the elite class within the stone and mortar walls of the more affluent homes on the plateau. Although Yax had been given much information, he did not claim to be authorized to preach or convert others to a new religion. This was an explanation of apostasy from the original beliefs about Kukulkan, not a new upstart of religious fervor. Since the king would have to be considered part of the apostate leadership, it would not be wise to share the teachings with him. If the king heard of this religious interest, he would certainly feel threatened.

While sitting in the shade of a full mahogany tree by the water one morning, discussing what they would need to buy and pack for their long journey north, they noticed a man in a dugout approaching them from the South on the river.

"*Ch'ocua!*" the man called out in greeting. "Can you tell me if this is Lamanai?"

"*Ch'ocua!*" Yax responded, "You have found the place you seek. May I help you?"

"I have come a long distance looking for a brave man that I have heard came to this place not too long ago. I understand that he has been blessed to receive information from the one true God, and has a jaguar companion to witness to his prowess. Can you help me find him?"

Yax felt a strange turmoil arise in his heart, but answered the man with a question, "Who are you? What is it you want with this man, stranger?"

"My name is Chi Kal and I am from the city of Lubaantun. My people are in dire need of divine help. They are being deceived by evil men, who pretend to be priests of god, but are only lazy tyrants who enslave others to do their bidding and feed their insatiable appetite. I heard of this man, Yax, from a trader named Zaconiuh downstream yesterday.

"I am Yax Kan," Yax said. "I do not know what you think I could do to help your people, though."

"Surely a man of God, who has been blessed so greatly,

could ask the Father God to destroy these evil priests. Is this not so?" Chi Kal asked expectantly.

"It is not as simple as you may suppose. The Father is a benevolent God, and does not meddle in the affairs of men in ways which would take away their free will. Why don't the people rebel and overthrow their oppressors?"

"They fear for their lives. The priests have a talisman, a crystal skull, that seems to give the priests the ability to predict the death of a man, and it shortly follows. I escaped after the skull predicted my death, so I know it is only their doing, because as you can see, I am still alive. Those that I left behind, though, are unable to overcome the fear brought on by the deaths of many of their friends and loved ones. You must help us, O Yax Kan Balam!"

"Come to our village and speak further to my friends and me, Chi Kal. We will hear you out, but I do not know what we can do," Yax answered.

Yax helped Chi Kal secure his dugout canoe on the beach by the mahogany tree, and they walked toward their hut, which was not far away. Lemnoch was moving some newly painted pots into his fire pit kiln and when he finished his work he came over to where Yax, Tutoma and Chi Kal were standing.

After a formal introduction and an explanation as to why Chi Kal had come to Lamanai, Yax said, "Chi Kal, explain to Lemnoch how you hope we can help with the plight of your people."

Tutoma brought some fruit and nuts from her food cache for their guest and themselves. Chi Kal explained about the wicked priests and their enslavement of his people using the crystal skull to plant fear in their hearts. He also said that many had died trying to get out from under the priests' evil dominance.

Turning to Lemnoch, Yax finally asked, "Do you have some advice for your new son, my father?"

"It is for you to decide, Yax Kan. You are the one who has had the experience with the one true God. We are only beginning to build our faith based on what you have told us. You must pray again and ask for His guidance on this matter," Lemnoch said.

"I believe you are right, Father Lemnoch. I must ask with an assurance in my heart that the Spirit of God will let me know what I should do, or what I should tell Chi Kal to do. Chi Kal, if you want my help, you must stay here with us until I have received an answer."

"I will be happy if you agree to do this thing," Chi Kal said. "and I desire to hear more about the great Father, and his son, Jesus Christ."

Yax stood and went over to Tutoma by their little hut, "Tutoma, I must find a place where I can be alone for a time and pray to my Father in Heaven. This may mean that we will have to postpone our journey to the north. Will you submit to this if it is the will of God?"

Tutoma took Yax Kan's hand and said, "Yax, you are the best man I have ever known. That you would even consider doing this for a stranger in need is wonderful to me. Truly you have been chosen to do great things. I will support whatever you decide, but I will also pray that you will be protected, whatever it is you must do."

"Thank you. You are a great blessing to me! I will go now

and be back as soon as I receive an answer to my prayer. If that has not happened by nightfall, I will return a little thereafter. Talk to your father and have him teach what he knows of Jesus Christ to Chi Kal. It will help Lemnoch to be strengthened in his own faith." Yax turned and walked toward a rise behind their little hut on the outer edge of the village.

The main stone structures of the latest phase of the city of Lamanai were being constructed on a low plateau just above the river valley, but this wooded rise was south of the construction area. He found a small clearing that had once been used for a campsite but was now overgrown with low grasses. A cool breeze rustled the canopy of the jungle trees, and the tropical birds and insects provided music as background for Yax Kan's prayers.

It seemed as though the sun had moved far along its path in the sky when Yax finally looked up from his silent petition. He had a feeling that he should pray out loud, as he had that morning not long ago in Tulum, so he again closed his eyes and as he continued to kneel, prayed aloud, "Father, I know I have been greatly favored to have received more understanding of thy great plan than I ever thought possible. I am so grateful for the wonderful things that have been given to me—preservation from dangers, knowledge of thy plan, a loving wife, wonderful friends and the deliverance of my family from the Zapotecs. Now I have come to thee again to ask for something more, but it is not for myself this time. I have come to ask for help for Chi Kal and his people who are being oppressed. What would you have me tell them to do? I feel that I should help, and I think I must go with Chi Kal to Lubaantun, but I would have thee confirm this before I act."

Yax closed his prayer and continued to kneel without speaking for quite a while. The jungle was completely quiet. No birds, insects or other creatures were making their common sounds.

At first, the answer was just a warm feeling in his heart. Then he felt a quiet, yet powerful assurance in his heart confirming that he should help these humble people who were under the evil thrall of false priests. The Spirit of God inspired him to prepare to go with Chi Kal and to take Tutoma and Wi'tzin with him. Yax knew that the Lord would watch over them as they went to help Chi Kal's people.

It was dusky, but the sun had not finished setting beyond the trees on when Yax walked back into the village. He felt humbled that he could ask of God and receive an answer. He had learned in recent weeks that it was important to make a decision first and then ask if it was the right decision, otherwise it would be much more difficult to get a clear answer.

First he went to tell Tutoma what they must do; then he went looking for Chi Kal to tell him that he would be going with him to Lubaantun. Yax asked him, "Tell me of the beliefs of this cult of priests your people fear. I must know all I can to determine our best course of action."

"Well, they worship the god, Huyub Caan, who they call 'the Heart of Heaven', and say that he speaks through the crystal skull to direct them. They drink *balche*, a potent brew of honey and grain, that they claim helps them to get in tune with the underworld where their god lives. Some of them file their teeth to points and paint their faces blue and black, making them look fearsome, and they scare the people of my village, especially the little children with terrible stories of what they call 'death by the visitation of Huyub Caan.'

"There is one who leads them as their High Priest. His name is Beleb Cho, or Nine Rat, and he is the most malevolent of them all. He has grown fat and lazy on the labors of others, and he has no compassion. If anyone displeases him, he has been known to send their entire family to work in the salt farms to the south under the guard of a few of his mercenaries. Lubaantun is a ceremonial center and keeps a neutral status by sending occasional tributes to the more powerful nearby city-states. It has no king, and it provides salt to traders from the north and west in exchange for many rich trade-goods which are hoarded by the priests." Chi Kal rubbed his chin trying to think of what else might be useful to tell his benefactor.

"What you have told me is important, Chi Kal. We may be able to use the salt trade as a way to gain entry into the temples," Yax said. "Have you ever been inside where they keep this crystal skull?"

"Oh no, Yax Kan! Only the High Priest and his attendants serve within the place they call the inner sanctuary. I know that dead priests have been buried there, though, and it is taught that their spirits speak from Xibalba to give instructions from the gods of the lower realms to the High Priest. The crystal skull is brought out on days of portent chosen by the chief astrologer, and I have seen it speak on those times from a distance in the crowd of villagers, when we are all commanded to appear at the square," Chi Kal shuddered at the remembrance.

"The skull is placed on an altar and it glows with an

unearthly light, especially its eyes. It is a little smaller than a man's head. Its jaw moves as though it is alive! I don't know what evil spirit they have working for them, but it is very horrible to observe. Not only that, but it usually predicts the doom of someone in the city. Sometimes it is because they have displeased the priests, but sometimes it seems that the skull and priests destroy someone simply to retain their dominance by instilling more fear in the hearts of the people. The risk of having a loved one killed is enough to keep the people from rebellion, so it does not require an army to guard the city, or the salt mine." Chi Kal looked at Yax with a hope and determination that Yax could not deny.

"Chi Kal," Yax said, "we will go back to Lubaantun with you tomorrow, if you will trust us. I have received an answer to my prayers and although I don't know how we will help, it will be given to us to know if we have faith in God and ask him what is right."

Since Yax and Tutoma were already packed for a journey, they need only unpack some things for the shorter journey south to Lubaantun, and they were ready to depart. Clearly Wi'tzin could sense that an adventure was to begin, and the animal padded back and forth on his tether, swatted at whoever passed by, and coughed in his excitement. Yax and Tutoma settled down for a restless night to await the dawn and the trek ahead.

24

The Cave

Nervous with anticipation, the three began their journey in two dugouts: the one Yax had made to come to Lamanai, and the one brought by Chi Kal. Rather than burden Chi Kal with a most unusual passenger, Yax asked Tutoma to ride with Chi Kal in his dugout, and he took Wi'tzin in his. Chi Kal was clearly happy with this situation, as he had not yet gotten comfortable with the young jaguar's presence. It was amazing how the cat seemed to obey Yax Kan's unspoken will. Having traveled in the dugout before, Wi'tzin did not hesitate to join Yax again in the small water craft.

The jungle seemed alive with the sounds of howler monkeys, great macaws and other brightly plumed birds, and it was difficult to talk or think with their continual noise. Arriving at a place in the river where it turned toward the sea, Chi Kal motioned them toward the river bank. A few small crocodiles skittered into the river as they approached and they pulled their dugouts out into the nearby vegetation in anticipation of their return to Lamanai, at least for Yax and

Tutoma. Chi Kal was unable to plan past their dealing with the priests of his city.

Wi'tzin faded into the jungle as soon as they landed, and Yax knew that he would follow them as they continued their journey. The cat often stayed behind or ran ahead, hunted and rested, at his own pleasure in their adventures. He was young but very powerful, and had been known to drop out of a tree and bring down a large pachybara or other prey with ease, crushing the animal's head in his powerful jaws. As far as Yax knew, Wi'tzin had never encountered another jaguar in their travels, but had no doubt smelled or heard them as he roamed the jungle. Yax kept him tethered in Lamanai for their security and to help the villagers overcome their fear of the great cat. Soon the jaguar had regular visitors in Lamanai who brought him scraps of entrails or other tidbits to befriend the golden creature of their legends. The hunters especially enjoyed associating with this live relative of those they had sometimes slain, although the young cat did not let them approach too closely or touch him. Only Yax was his companion.

As they journeyed with packs held on their backs by the ubiquitous *mecapal* straps across their foreheads, the three plotted what they would do. As tradition dictated, Tutoma did not speak directly to Chi Kal, but soon the man recognized her wisdom and intelligence, and began to welcome her suggestions made to Yax. It was about a three day journey to Lubaantun. They stopped once to make a rope, and for Yax to add certain herbs to his stores for various potions he might need on their journey.

The first night Yax made a fire with a bow and drill, and

then baked roots that Tutoma had brought from Lamanai for a filling dinner. The smoke from the fire kept the mosquitoes down, and because of their exertions, the three travelers rested better than they had the night before.

"So, what have we decided so far in our plans to help my people?" Chi Kal asked Yax.

"My plan is to introduce myself to the priests as a representative of Palenque, a place where I lived for some time, with a request to buy salt. Palenque is far enough away from Lubaantun that they may not have regular trade with them, and even if they do, I should be able to buy more salt, pretending that I simply wish to make a profit from it. I have gold that I can trade, or I may be able to trade rare spices with these false priests. I have some vanilla and cacao beans that they should relish," Yax said.

"Oh yes, Yax Kan!" Chi Kal exclaimed, "They covet all of those things, and will probably be happy to trade. The salt costs them nothing, since they use my people as slaves, who must also find or hunt their own food or starve when they are sent to mine the salt in the coastal marshes. They hold their loved ones for ransom to be sure they do not try to escape, and so they will desire to come back to their wretched domain. Then what will you do, Yax Kan?"

Yax responded slowly as he put his thoughts into words, "First, I will learn the secrets of the crystal skull, and the habits of these imposters. Then I will know how to use the information against them. You must go to your people in secret, and especially beware of any traitors in their midst. Go only to those you know can be trusted, and prepare them to act when we are ready and need their help. We will not need many, if as you say these priests and their temple guards have grown fat in their indolence. How many did you say there were that we will need to overcome?"

"There are only ten priests, Yax Kan, and probably twice that many guards, but some of them oversee the salt mines to the south. The guards are mostly mercenaries that were criminals cast out of other city-states, like Xunantunich, Copan and Quirigua. They are cold-hearted and would kill at the least provocation, but as you say, they have not fought a willing and able opponent for many days. There may be over one hundred servants, but few of them would take the side of the priests in battle or support them in a coup by their fellow citizens." Chi Kal sounded optimistic, getting into the spirit of their mission, and seemed to have great faith in Yax.

"That is good," Yax responded. "Then, of all the people in your city we will only need thirty or so of your most powerful men with clubs or hunting weapons to overcome the priests when the time is right. I will be sure that the odds are in our favor, and that there is a definite plan for them to follow, but they must trust me, and they must be trustworthy, or this will all be to no avail."

"It will be as you say, Yax Kan. We will be ready," Chi Kal answered gravely. "I think I know nearly that many brave men now, and as soon as we get to Lubaantun, I will talk to them and find the rest. You can rely on us, my new friend, because we have so much to gain and so little to lose."

Tutoma listened to the two men discuss the beginnings of a plan, and although she felt strongly that what they were doing was the right thing, she also could not help but fear for her new husband's safety. She was happy that she could be with him, rather than being left behind worrying about him, but what was to be her part in this plan? She pondered this question silently as she packed the leftovers from their simple evening meal.

The second day they traveled near a large settlement which Chi Kal told them was called Nim Li Punit. As was Yax Kan's custom on his journeys, they did not make themselves known to the people there, as they did not need any supplies and they did not want word of their coming to precede them to Lubaantun. However, Yax did climb up into a tall tree to view the city and saw numerous carved stelae, he hoped to come back to this place one day and study what was carved on them.

The howler monkeys announced their passage with their incessant deep, booming screams. They did the same for any men or feline predators, which were their common enemies in the jungle.

Chi Kal explained that Lubaantun means "place of the fallen rocks" and was so named because the land was unstable. It was not unusual for their stone structures to fall apart as the land subsided. Yax would later learn that the inhabitants had not used the corbelled arch common in Maya cities in building their stone homes and temples, nor did they use mortar between the stones, which further contributed to the propensity for buildings to collapse.

They finally came to their resting place on the last evening of their journey, a cave which Chi Kal called Hokeb Ha, near a waterway called Blue Creek. He explained that he had found sanctuary there on his first night of escape from Lubaantun, and it would be a good place for Tutoma to stay after the men left in the morning. The entry was covered with vines and it was almost invisible, but it was the opening to a much larger cave, and Chi Kal warned them not to be surprised by the swarm of fruit bats that would leave at dusk and return in the early dawn to the depths of the great cave, their daily resting place. As he had said, the squeaking swarm flew past them at dusk. Yax and Tutoma were fascinated by the bats' erratic flight patterns and their ability to dart about so swiftly without running into one another.

They did not make a fire that might attract attention by its light or smoke in the evening, but rather huddled together after a cold meal of dried meats and cashew fruit, trying to sleep on this night before their daring quest began. The elevation of Lubaantun was higher than Lamanai, and they camped on a long ridge overlooking the lowland valley carved out over centuries by the river below.

25

Lubaantun

A s the bats returned to their cave at dawn, the travelers awoke to their chittering. Yax reviewed the first phase of the plan with Chi Kal and Tutoma as they ate a light meal of cold corn patties. "It is important that Tutoma stay behind in the cave, far enough from the city to remain undiscovered. I will have Wi'tzin watch over her. He will be our surprise for the priests later on. Chi Kal, you must go gather your trusted allies, while I will be gaining the trust of this Beleb Cho and his imposter priests. If I can, I will meet you here late this evening, but if not I will be here as soon tomorrow as possible. Tutoma, you must have faith that Our Great Father would not have let me know by his Holy Spirit that we should both come here unless there was a way for us to succeed. I promise I will be back!" Yax gazed deeply into the eyes of his bride and felt her love and trust in him.

"Chi Kal, show me the way into the city before we separate to our tasks," Yax said. "Wi'tzin," he looked at the big cat with a smile of fondness, and pointed at his bride as he spoke.

"Stay and guard Tutoma without being seen until you feel that I need you; then come to me."

Wi'tzin chuffed his familiar note of understanding, and turned to pad silently into the nearby jungle. Yax knew that the cat had understood the gist of his instruction, and after one more loving glance toward Tutoma, he turned to leave.

There was heavy dew on the grasses of the jungle and the leaves as they brushed past, and they were both thoroughly soaked before they reached a well-worn path to the city. It was early enough that none of the residents had gotten this far out to encounter them. When they reached a point where Chi Kal could point to a landmark and give final directions to Yax, they grasped each other by the forearms to give reassurance and once more agreed to meet at the cave that evening.

Yax carried a pack with only the supplies that would be useful to a trader on a long journey, so that no suspicion would be aroused when he opened it to trade for salt. His leather tunic covered his shoulders so that his scars did not draw unwanted attention.

"If only my confidence in myself matched my confidence in the Lord," he thought. *"I will need to have enough faith in the Great God to have faith in my own abilities."* He checked a pouch at his waist to make sure the gold nugget and sleeping powders were secure. Soon, he walked with all the confidence he could muster into Lubaantun.

Two guards, stationed on the road at the entrance to the city square, questioned Yax, then let him pass, telling him where he to go to make a trade for salt. A little further into town, Yax found a corpulent old priest with greedy eyes and a narrow, hooked nose sitting behind a table with a line of people waiting to trade some home-grown vegetables, small game, or wooden carvings for a handful of salt wrapped in a leaf packet.

At first, the priest did not seem to notice Yax, and when Yax came before him in his turn in the queue he said with surprise, "Aya, *ch'ocua*, young traveler! What can I do for you?"

Yax held up his hand in a formal greeting and explained, "I have come from far Palenque, and was told that here in Lubaantun I could buy all the salt that I could carry. Is this so?"

"This is certainly the best place to buy salt in the entire known world," the fat priest bragged. "If you have enough to pay for it, you will surely be able to take all you can carry home with you. I have not seen you before. Have you taken the place of the regular trader from Palenque, then? It was not that long ago that he was here."

Anticipating that this might possibly be the case, Yax said, "No, I have not replaced him. Our city can use more salt than he brought back in his last journey, and I have a need to provide for my family as much as he does."

"I guess there is no harm in that. What did you say your name is?" the priest asked.

"I am Palak, and hope you will let me see your great religious city before I travel home. Kan Balam, our king, commissioned me to learn something of your religious ceremonies while I am here," Yax said. This was true, since before leaving Palenque, Kan Balam had told Yax that he hoped to see him again someday and hear of new things learned on his religious quest.

At the mention of the great city's ruler, the portly trader-priest lifted his eyebrows. "I had better take you to our leader, Beleb Cho. He will know how to help you better than I."

The stout priest slowly stood and waved away the others in line. "You will all have to come back when the sun is lower in the sky. I must take this important guest to the temple to meet our high priest!" He motioned to a young servant to pick up the trade payments and large leather bag of salt and then steered Yax toward the tallest of the temples.

Yax noticed the unusual construction of the temple. Like the other structures he had seen, this one was built of dressed blocks without mortar. They were made of black slate slabs and laid in an "in-and-out" design. Each tier was built with a batter, every second course protruding slightly beyond the course below. The corners were built in a rounded fashion that was unusual and seldom seen by Yax in his travels. On the top, the structure was of carved wood. This is where the glyphs appeared, rather than on stone steles. Yax realized the wooden structures were a way of building up a city quickly. The priests had desired to get into "business" as quickly as possible once deciding to start this ceremonial city, so they had done so using slave labor with no other leader to hinder their evil activities. He also saw a ball court not too far distant, and hoped beyond hope that its presence did not mean that the losers lost their lives, as in other cities. He also hoped that Chi Kal and his people would successfully overthrow the wicked priests and their cruel domination.

Again, they met a guard at the top, but since the priest led the way and Yax was unarmed, they were not challenged. They entered through a hanging skin door on one side. On a high stone bench sat Lubaantun's leader, Beleb Cho. He looked at Yax with squinting suspicion, and he waved away the servants who were serving him confections on elaborately carved wooden trays. Yax had thought the old trader-priest was fat, but Beleb Cho was truly obese. Rolls of fat fell beneath his chin and under his arms. He had grown this way on the backs and even the deaths of the common folk, and Yax needed to deal with him carefully to achieve his goals.

"What is this, Uxpeq? Who have you brought before me, and why?" the chief priest asked.

"Excellency, this man named Palak, comes from far Palenque to trade for salt, but that is not why I bring him to your blessed presence. He also says he has a commission from the king of his city, Kan Balam, the son of Lord Pakal, to learn of our religious ceremonies, and I thought you should be the one to decide how to help him, Sire." It was apparent that Old Uxpeq was acting as servile as possible, mostly to curry favor, but also to keep from having to make any incorrect decisions that might come back to trouble him at some future time.

"Well, well," said Beleb Cho, "We have been honored by an emissary sent by a great king, have we? I have heard of Kan Balam, son of the great Pakal."

After being in the presence of Kan Balam in his palace, guarded by dozens of armed warriors, and servants without number, and remembering the spirit of the humble priests of Tulum, Yax was hardly impressed with this charlatan whose very tone was impudent and full of pride. It was evident that the leader wanted to impress someone who could further his trade relations with a rich city-state.

"Of course, we want to help you learn of our religion, Palak," Beleb Cho continued. "We do not have a religious observance planned at the present, and it would be difficult to arrange one at this season, since the people of the city are heavily involved in the harvest of their crops. However, I will share with you our *sastun*, the talisman that the gods have given us to know their will."

This was what Yax had hoped for. He spoke subserviently, but with the confidence that would accompany a representative of the court of Kan Balam, "I know that such as you will tell and show me would be appreciated by my king. Thank you, excellency." Inwardly, Yax was repulsed by the indolent Beleb Cho, and it was difficult to pretend to respect him.

26

The Skull of Doom

Beleb Cho, or 'Nine Rat', led the way into the adjoining part of the temple structure, walking as though he was unused to such exertion. He turned to Yax, "Our friend, please wait here while I enter the sacred center place of this temple. I will bring out our sacred talisman so that you may view it. You must not handle it, though. It has been known to kill unsanctified people who dare to touch it."

Beleb Cho had called the talisman a *'sastun'* or seer stone. Yax knew of such objects carried by shamans, but his mentor, Naz-Hani, had not deigned to own such a stone, and he did not seek one. He believed it was better to listen to his heart than to consult an inanimate stone, no matter how special it might be.

"I will be most respectful of the object, Beleb Cho, and will do as you say," answered Yax. It only took a moment for Beleb Cho to go into the next room and return with a bundle in his arms—something wrapped in a soft animal skin. He set it upon an altar in the room and waved toward it after pulling down the wrapping of the skin. There upon the altar was a perfectly shaped crystal skull. It was indeed spellbinding, and Yax inhaled a gasp of air.

"O, your eminence, it is most intriguing! I have never seen such a thing. It appears to glow within and has the very shape of the skull of a man." Yax spoke genuninely for he never had beheld such an object in all of his travels. He had seen many skulls formed from clay or wood, even of jade, and he had seen the skulls of men after the earth had claimed their flesh. But never before had he seen one fashioned from a huge clear quartz crystal, nor had he ever seen such a cleverly carved likeness with the natural ridges over the eyes and the temples. It was so beautiful and ethereal, that Yax had to remind himself that it was being used wickedly. It had been described to him by Chi Kal, and Yax could see where the jaw was a separate piece that could cunningly be moved as though the skull spoke. Upon looking at the front of the skull, he saw the light of a torch reflect from the back of the skull right into the eye sockets and out into his own living eyes. How frightful it must be for the poor people of this city!

Beleb Cho stood unspeaking while the skull played its full effect upon the young trader. "This is the talisman of the great god, Huyub Caan, the heart of heaven," he said. "On those nights when the stars and moon are in proper alignment, Huyub Caan speaks to us through the skull. In fact, he speaks to the entire population of the city, to tell them what they should all be doing. It is because of this that we have built such a great city with the willing toil of so many to honor our god. Do you have any questions, Palak?" The rotund leader waited for Yax Kan's response.

Yax finally pulled his gaze from the radiance of the skull. "Yes, uh, yes, I would like to ask some questions," he stammered. "Where did this come from? How did you get it? Did Huyub Caan create this, or did you create it and then your god begin to speak through it?"

"My dear Palak, please give me a chance to answer one question at a time!" Beleb Cho stood waiting until he had Yax Kan's full attention. "How the skull was crafted is unknown to us. It came into our possession by trade, but through sacred channels from priests far to the South. It is a piece of heaven, taken from the third world in the sky and given to man below. Now you must come back into the other room so we may sit and be comfortable while I explain more to you about our great religion." Beleb Cho was evidently exhausted from standing up for so long and needed a cool drink to be brought by his servants before he could begin to speak, and to soothe himself with pride in his own voice.

Yax listened during much of the sun's journey that day to the vainglorious description of their false religion by the arrogant Beleb Cho. It was nearly dark when he was finally fed and shown to a cramped sleeping room in a large hut where he was to spend the night. As quickly and quietly as he could, Yax slipped out of the hut and hurried on a path through the brush to meet with Tutoma and Chi Kal back at the cave, bypassing the way of the main road to avoid the guard, though he was probably sleeping at his post. As he approached the small clearing below the cave, he was surprised to see torches ahead, and he crept carefully to a place where he could spy on whomever it was that was carelessly drawing attention. "*Surely, this cannot be Chi Kal or*

Tutoma. They would know better than to light a torch that might be noticed uphill in the city," he thought.

Yax sensed, more than saw, the presence of Wi'tzin by his side. The big cat was on alert and his tail twitched back and forth as he swept his glowing yellow eyes back and forth between Yax and the clearing. Suddenly Yax saw two men with torches coming along the path leading from the elevated entrance to the cave! *"Oh, no, Tutoma is between them!"* His heart fell and he nearly cried out in his fear and anger.

"Yax Kan!" A whisper came from behind him. "It is me, Chi Kal. Those are temple guards from the city, and they were here when I got here. I am afraid that I was wrong thinking that no one else came to this cave. Someone must have told the guards there was a woman in the cave and they have taken her captive."

Barely controlling his emotions, Yax whispered back, "Do not let them see us, Chi Kal! We will have a better chance of finding her lightly guarded after they take her to the city. Or we will free her when we free all your fellow citizens." Yax now had a personal reason to overcome Beleb Cho and his cohorts, as well as to liberate the poor people under their thumbs. His heart beat in his chest and he wanted to run after his sweetheart held by these evil men.

Yax finally looked down at Wi'tzin. What was that on his side? Was it blood? Yes. "Look, Chi Kal! Wi'tzin has been hurt. He must have tried to help Tutoma and been injured by a spear or an arrow. He has a shallow grazing wound along his ribs," said Yax as he gently touched the jaguar's wound and realized that it was the first time the cat had ever been harmed by a human. Wi'tzin had probably retreated in fear and shock. Yax soothed the cat as he watched the soldiers take Tutoma toward the city, no doubt to be interrogated by the high priest. He held himself back though his urge to rush after her was difficult to control.

The two men were about to follow the soldiers with Tutoma in custody, when Chi Kal silently seized Yax Kan's arm. "Wait," he whispered. "What's that moving through the brush on the other side of the cave?"

They saw two men come out of the jungle. One was very tall, and the other was exceptionally short.

"It is Lemnoch and Zaconiuh! Why are they here?" Yax quietly exclaimed.

Swiftly and quietly, so as not to alert the guards who had just left the clearing, Yax and Chi Kal hurried to intercept their friends before they made too much noise.

"Zak! Lemnoch!" Yax called in a low voice. "Careful! The enemy has just left this place and they might hear you. What are you doing here?"

Lemnoch hurried to keep up with Zak's long strides. "We don't really know why we are here, Yax." Lemnoch said. "I was praying some time after you left, and when I finished I had a strong feeling that I should follow you. I asked Zak if he was willing to accompany me, and being the good friend that he is, he agreed to come. Why are we being cautious, Yax? What has happened here?"

"Father Lemnoch, I am sorry to tell you this, but Tutoma has just been taken captive by the temple guards from Lubaantun. Perhaps the Holy Spirit prompted you to come so you could help us," Yax said quickly trying to keep his voice from trembling. A look of deep concern etched itself in Lemnoch's countenance.

"Chi Kal," said Yax, "You must stay here with these two tonight, and I must hurry to get back to the city so I can help Tutoma. Explain to them all that has happened, and I will be back as soon as I can to finish making preparations. Did all go well with your recruitment?"

"Yes, Yax Kan, but hurry! You must go while there is still some light in the sky, for you cannot use a torch, and you must see where they are taking Tutoma!"

Yax knew that Chi Kal was right, and he turned and raced along the path where the guards had gone. There was not even time to dress Wi'tzin's injury, and Yax knew the cat would not allow any other person to touch it. The young jaguar had gone into the jungle to lick its wound, and Yax could only pray that Tutoma, the jaguar, and the three men would all be well until he saw them each again.

Soon after Yax and Chi Kal had left the cave that morning, Tutoma explored the nearby jungle looking for herbs and foods. She had not seen Wi'tzin since she had been left alone, but knew the cat well enough now to trust that he was not far away. She came upon some crunchy roots and she tasted a small portion to be sure they were the plant she thought she recognized. They would add to her dinner, even if she had to eat alone, and she washed them in a trickling stream she crossed in her search. She smiled to herself as she thought of her new husband, whom she loved with all her heart, but then a frown crossed her brow as she remembered his dangerous mission. Tutoma said a silent prayer for his safety, as Yax had recently taught her, to the Father in the name of his Son.

She softly sang a sweet song of thanks as she climbed up to the mouth of the cave and then she thought she detected a sound unlike the noises of the jungle. It seemed to come from the cave above her. Tutoma wondered if Wi'tzin would have gone into the cave in her absence.

Suddenly a small, grey-haired man rushed out of the cave carrying two bundles, which Tutoma recognized as their own possessions. "Wait! What are you doing? You can't take those!" she cried after him as he jostled past her and ran into the jungle.

She must have surprised him. She ran into the cave to see what, if anything, the thief had left behind. *"If he had known I was alone, would he have hurt me? Will he come back?"* she wondered.

Chi Kal had left his pack behind, although Yax had taken most of his goods with him. She must have surprised the thief before he had gotten it all together in the two bundles he took. He had left one pack, but most of its contents were gone. There was Yax Kan's pack of medicinal herb bundles scattered on the floor of the cave, and a few other cooking utensils which the thief had missed,. There were also a few other things of little value, but useful to Tutoma—a drinking gourd, a piece of smoked fish and one of the three blankets they had brought, woven from long softened plant fibers. The thief had left the two packs and loaded his booty in the other two blankets, but why he did not take the packs and the head straps she did not know.

"Perhaps as a thief," she thought, *"he was so unused to working for a living that he had never learned to carry a heavy load on his back."*

She quickly packed what remained together hoping that she could leave before someone returned to their hiding place. She had to hide, but could not go far or Yax would be unable to find her when he returned. She went further back into the cave with the last of their belongings where she would be less noticed by any future intruder. Since she had the smoked fish, and had held onto the crisp roots as the thief ran past, she sat down and began to eat, thinking, *"Where was Wi'tzin? What good was the animal, if it could not even frighten away a little old man?"*

After she finished her modest meal Tutoma sat pondering. She had seen the remains of small fires, and a few bones on the floor of the cave when she first came there, but had thought they must have belonged to Chi Kal when he discovered the cave. She wondered if perhaps there had been other occupants in this cave and it had not been newly discovered by the little thief.

As it was getting late in the day, Tutoma began to hope that Yax would return soon; Chi Kal, as well, of course, but mostly Yax.

Voices came from the jungle. "Yax and Chi Kal were both coming!" she thought. As she crept back to the mouth of the cave to quickly peek out, she realized that the thief was not worried about being accused. Instead he had led others to her hiding place!

"There she is! In the cave up there!" the grey-haired man pointed at Tutoma, and directed the men that were with him. There was only one way up to or down from the cave.

Tutoma had not found any openings in the back of the cave that might lead elsewhere. She tried to run past the men as they advanced, but there was no time.

A golden streak rushed into the group and bowled several over, coming straight for the man grabbing for Tutoma. Wi'tzin jumped on the man and would probably have killed him except for the spear that tore along his ribs, thrown by one of the intruders whom he had missed knocking over in his rush to Tutoma's side.

Wi'tzin gave an unearthly growling yell unlike any Tutoma had ever before heard him utter. The cat seemed incapable of understanding what had happened. He was big, but he was still young and inexperienced in the ways of hunters, having always been protected by the presence of his companion throughout his short life. The bewildered animal ran into the jungle before another such wound could be inflicted.

Tutoma was hastily bound by her captors, even though they were spooked by the attack of the brawny jaguar. They pushed her in the direction that Yax and Chi Kal had gone earlier, and she could only hope they would see her as she was led toward the town. Wi'tzin must not have found the older man very threatening when the man came along, but the cat certainly came to help when the others appeared. Tutoma hoped he was still well enough to get to Yax and somehow lead her husband to her place of captivity.

As they left the clearing down from the cave and entered the jungle, Tutoma wondered if she saw someone hiding in the nearby jungle. *"Is that Yax?"* she silently hoped with all her heart. As her captors spoke among themselves, they revealed the fact that they were temple guards and that they would be taking her to the chief priest. She knew she could not say anything that would give away her husband's ruse as he pretended to be a trader from Palenque. She could only hope that he would find her and rescue her in Lubaantun.

27

The Plan

As Yax rushed to follow the group of temple guards that held the bound Tutoma in their grasp, his mind raced. He realized that it would look suspicious if he arrived at the temple, coming from the jungle at the same time and in the same direction as the group. He decided that he would have to sneak into the city as he had gone out, and come from somewhere within the immediate area of the place where he had been lodged, and make sure he was seen before he could approach the temple and see what was happening to Tutoma. The high priest would need a little time, hopefully, to decide what to do with her, and Yax fervently prayed as he ran that such would be the case. Even though it was nearly dark, he made good time as he moved in a circular direction to come out on the other side of the city.

Ixtan felt blessed that no one was about in the area where he entered Lubaantun's temple square. Yax decided to go directly to the main temple as though nothing was out of the ordinary, and act as though he simply could not sleep and was strolling about in the plaza. This was going to move his plans along a little more rapidly than he had anticipated. He only hoped that Chi Kal could rush his group when he gave them the word.

As Yax walked up the stairs of the temple, he was hailed by a temple guard above him, standing near the high priest's residence. "Hey, there! Where are you going? You are not allowed on those steps, stranger!" the guard yelled.

Yax acted as though he was not sure what he was being told, and continued up walking directly toward the guard, holding his hand by his ear. "What's that you are saying? I need a torch to find my way, and I only knew to ask the high priest where I could find the salt merchant I met earlier to ask him."

By the time they met, Yax and the guard stood on the level of the great altar. Yax pretended not to be paying much attention, but he noticed some things about the altar that were very interesting. He would have to think about them later, however, as the guard was dragging him by the arm away from it and up the farther side of the stairs.

"It is forbidden for any but the priests to approach the altar, stranger. You are fortunate that it is not a holy day, or you would be put to death for such a breach of propriety," the guard explained. "Come with me. I will take you to see if the high priest is available, but I do not think he is."

They approached the flap of the deerskin door on the same end where Yax had first entered the high priest's quarters. Yax could hear voices within.

"Halt, Corozco!" said the guard that stood sentry at the door. "Who is that with you?"

"It is the trader from the north, Zan Loc. He has come

to ask the high priest something. Do you think Beleb Cho will see him?"

"If he is willing to wait, he will probably spare a short time, but right now he is interrogating some vagrant found in a cave in the jungle," Zan Loc answered.

"We will wait right here then," the guard, Corozco, said. Then he turned to Yax. "What is your name again? I do not remember."

"It is Palak," Yax said with some hesitation. He was listening to the voices coming through the flap of the door so intensely that he almost did not remember his assumed name.

Now he could hear the bellicose voice of Beleb Cho raised in anger. "You must tell us what you were doing alone in that cave, or we will have no choice but to torture it out of you, woman!"

It was almost unbearable for Yax to just stand there while his wife was being threatened, and he feared she was frightened and possibly hurt. He quickly pulled back the flap of the door and slid unexpectedly past the sentry, who hastily followed, grabbing him and trying to pull him out.

"Hold, Zan Loc! What is this now? Is it Palak, the trader? I thought you had gone to your quarters. Come in. We are having a little fun with an uninvited stranger in our midst, but one that is very mysterious, it seems." Beleb Cho reclined on a couch covered with furs, while Tutoma was being held in a kneeling position in front of him.

She did not turn her head toward him, but Yax was sure she must know it was him who had entered the room. She knew his false name and his assumed business in the city. Yax realized that she was being careful not to recognize him. It broke his heart to see her so helpless and with tears staining her cheeks.

"I apologize for interrupting, Beleb Cho. I lost my way and when I saw your temple dwelling, I thought I would stop to ask for a torch. Where is this woman from, then?" Yax bluffed.

"I know not, but perhaps if we let her sit overnight in an animal cage it will loosen her tongue. What think you, Palak the trader?"

Old Beleb Cho gave Yax a look that made him uncomfortable. Did the rogue suspect that he was in some way connected to Tutoma? Yax did not know, but could only continue with his ruse.

"I think it would be prudent to treat such a beauty as though she were a princess until you find out otherwise. What if she is traveling with an emissary from some city you would want as an ally or a trade partner, even if she is a servant? Of course, I think like a merchant, so perhaps I am wrong." Yax paused in his speech to see the effect on Beleb Cho. Would he reconsider his treatment of his captive?

"Well, perhaps you are right. We may have been a little hasty after all. Where is the old reprobate that led you to her?" Beleb Cho asked the guard, while allowing a servant girl to feed him crunchy roasted locusts and chile peppers.

The small thief was pushed forward by a guard and stood with his head bowed before the high priest.

"Why did you inform us of her presence, anyway, old fool? Did you think you would earn some reward for bringing a trespasser to our attention?"

"N-n-no, your eminence. I was just doing my duty as a

citizen, sir," the old man stammered. "The girl was in that cave, and I thought it strange." He was clearly worried that he had made a grave mistake that could lead to his harm, rather than the expected compensation.

"And did you forget to tell us that you had stolen from her, citizen?" the high priest demanded in a sarcastic but threatening voice. His men had found the bundles hidden just past the clearing of the city and had brought the humble booty to the high priest's attention. "Well, get out of my sight before I cast you into a pit full of rats for not being completely forthright with me, old wretch!"

The old thief ran from the temple on feet more nimble than any would have thought possible. Beleb Cho laughed wickedly and again turned to Tutoma.

"Well, woman, it seems that the goddess Ixchel has smiled upon you tonight. You will sleep in the quarters of some of my servants, rather than in a cage! We will talk further on the morrow. Yach'ka, take this woman to your hut and do not let her out of your sight! And take these wretched bundles with you—my men tell me they are of little value."

Yax breathed a silent sigh of relief as Tutoma was led away by the servant woman, who had been attending the high priest. He caught Tutoma's relieved glance in his direction, but he dare not acknowledge it even with a nod. He assumed that Beleb Cho intended to permanently enslave Tutoma, or worse.

He and Beleb Cho talked a little more about the salt trade, and then Yax began to leave the high priest's chambers.

"Palak, are you sure you don't have some special interest in that young woman?" the high priest asked.

"No, of course not, other than the fact that she is very pretty and would be a good slave to cook for me on my way back to Palenque, perhaps. Why, what made you think I had any interest at all, your eminence?" Yax answered, fearing that something had given him away.

"I wondered if you might want her, my trader friend. I thought we might add her to the trade, since she is not a local and may have no one who will come forward to claim her."

The rancid old priest was merely exhibiting his usual greed. "*Good!*" Yax thought.

"Certainly, if I can afford such a trade, I would be interested. I will probably have to hire some help to carry the salt pack as well for she does not look as though she would hold up under much of a burden. We will have to see how much you wish to accept for the salt." Yax acted as disinterested as he could. He hoped soon to release Tutoma along with everyone else held in servitude under this selfish priest's dominion.

"Well, then. We will discuss it further in the morning. I am tired of all this wasted sleep over a worthless woman and an old thief. Good night, Palak!" the high priest said.

"Good evening, my great host." Yax said, nodding before turning and leaving the enclosure. Now he had only to be sure none of the temple guards were watching, so he could discover the women servants' quarters and try to speak to Tutoma. He headed for his quarters and—once he was sure he was unwatched—he turned onto a side street and began searching for Tutoma.

As Yax worked his way through the shadows of the city, he saw a crouching figure behind a dark tree trunk. He started to move away from the figure, when he heard his name called out in a gruff whisper. It was Chi Kal!

"What are you doing in the city, Chi Kal? I thought you would stay at the cave tonight."

Chi Kal gave an exasperated shrug. "That is what I thought, as well, but your father-in-law and his big friend decided they needed to get closer to the city in case you needed them. I tried to convince them to wait until morning, but Lemnoch is too fearful for his daughter. They are a short way from here in hiding while I came looking for you."

Yax followed Chi Kal to an alcove near the ball court where the other two men waited.

Lemnoch cried out, "Yax, what of Tutoma? Have you found her? Is she well?"

"Shh, Lemnoch! You must not give us away. Yes, she is well, and I am searching for the servants' quarters where she has been taken," Yax explained.

"I can take you there, Yax Kan," Chi Kal said. "I have a widowed sister who works for the priests, and stays in the servants' quarters most of the time."

"Tutoma was put into the custody of one named Yach'ka. Do you know her?" Yax asked.

"I think my sister has mentioned Yach'ka when she came to visit my wife," Chi Kal replied. "They must be together. Shall I take you there now?"

"That will be good, but I'm afraid there are too many of us to go unnoticed. Where will Lemnoch and Zak wait for the two of us?" Yax said.

Lemnoch interrupted with frustration in his voice, "We

will not wait at all! We will follow you now. I must see that my daughter is well."

Yax explained how he had a tentative agreement to buy Tutoma, and that she was being well cared for according to the greedy old high priest's orders. Chi Kal agreed that greed would be Beleb Cho's highest motivation, and this seemed to calm Lemnoch. Zaconiuh was more concerned about being captured tonight before they were better prepared to defend themselves.

Chi Kal explained, "We are near the edge of the city here, so we can get to the servants' quarters without being seen, but it is not safe for anyone but me to approach the women servants. Some of them may be so afraid of Beleb Cho that they would inform on us. You two will have to wait outside not far from there. Perhaps I can bring Tutoma to see you and Lemnoch, Yax Kan."

Agreeing on this plan, the four crept stealthily toward the servants' quarters with Chi Kal in the lead. He led them through the jungle adjoining the plaza on a narrow well-beaten path. They came out in a clearing containing three thatch-roofed buildings with flickering oil lamps showing through cracks in the walls. Chi Kal left the other three men in the forest a little off the path while he went to the furthest of the three huts to seek the aid of his sister.

As they stood in the forest, Yax felt a hot breath on his hand. He looked down and saw that it was Wi'tzin. He knelt by the cat and felt his side where the wound was and discovered that it had been licked cleaned, had stopped bleeding and was not very deep. He made a hand motion that the cat understood and Wi'tzin melted into the trees. Yax felt more confident with his powerful friend nearby.

Some moonlight filtered through the leaves of the forest, but there was not enough light to see facial features with the light of the moon behind someone. When Chi Kal returned, they recognized his expected shape and saw another smaller person walking beside him. Yax thought it must be Chi Kal's sister.

When they reached the place where the men were concealed, Yax was overcome with emotion, as was Lemnoch. It was Tutoma!

"Tutoma!" Yax gathered his young wife into his arms, and Lemnoch rushed to join the young couple. They whispered their love for each other, as tears were shed.

"Father, why are you here?" Tutoma asked in surprise.

"I had a feeling that you needed my help, my daughter, and Yax tells me I may be of some use. Big Zaconiuh came with me too," Lemnoch replied as he hugged his daughter. The shy Zaconiuh stayed back, but smiled and nodded at Tutoma to show his agreement.

Chi Kal led them all to a nearby work area where the servant women sat to do their weaving in the daytime. They were partly hidden and sheltered so they could speak more easily.

"Tutoma, you did well in not showing that you knew me when we were with Beleb Cho!" Yax said, "I'm sure your caution saved us both. I want you to stay with the servants where you will be safe until we can overcome the temple guards and remove any threat from you, and from these decent people who have been enslaved by the priests of Lubaantun. I will pretend not to be ready to leave tomorrow to give us enough time. You will probably be brought before the high priest again because I will be bargaining in a false effort to purchase you, so please trust in me."

"I will not be afraid as long as you are there," Tutoma said.

Yax laid out a plan for Chi Kal to gather his group of brave men together the next day with Lemnoch and Zaconiuh to bolster their numbers. Yax would need to have everything in perfect readiness for his plan to work. After he explained the details of his plan, including one more meeting near mid-day tomorrow with Chi Kal, the five huddled in prayer. Yax felt the Spirit confirm that the plan would succeed, and he was assured by the others that they would be ready, and that they, too, felt reassured that his plan would work.

With another embrace from Yax and her father, Tutoma returned to the quarters. Yax noticed that someone waited for her near the entrance and knew of their meeting. "Chi Kal," Yax asked. "Do you know who that was waiting for Tutoma? Was that your sister?"

"Yes, I know who it was, and it was not my sister. It was Yach'ka, the woman who was given the charge to care for her by the high priest. She is with us in our plans. Her husband is one of the men I have enlisted to help us overcome the guards," Chi Kal explained.

"That is wonderful! How blessed we are in this undertaking. The true God is assisting us at each step." Yax was elated at how their prayers had been answered so far. "Let us continue to follow the promptings of the Holy Spirit, that we may be successful in our plan. Hurry, now, go back to the cave to rest! We will meet again and shortly thereafter the priests and their guards will be delivered into our hands."

Yax rushed back to his sleeping quarters as they separated.

Although he did not encounter a guard along the way, he did see them guarding the temple in the distance. "If there are a total of fifteen guards in the city, and if two are at the temple, and two posted as sentries entering town the way he had come in, there were eleven more unaccounted for. There was probably one other entry point on the other side of the city, where two more were posted. They too would need to sleep," Yax deliberated. He would have to determine what the duties of the others were by tomorrow, but he assumed that the six at their post tonight, at least, would have to sleep during part of the day. He also had to account for all of the priests. Besides Beleb Cho and Uxpeq, he had only seen two others, but Chi Kal had told him there were ten. Perhaps one was an overseer at the salt farm in the coastal marsh, and he knew that one was the chief astrologer, spoken of by Chi Kal. They would not be as much of a physical threat as the temple guards, either.

After meeting Chi Kal and reviewing his plans for the next day, verifying that there was one priest at the salt marsh, Yax finally allowed himself some much-needed sleep. Sadly, his dreams were haunted by the glowing eye sockets of the crystal skull, and its jaws moved as it spoke to him, "Yax Kan, I know who you really are! I will destroy you and those you love. You will not be able to overcome me, or my priests!" In his heart he knew that this would only be a concern if he lost faith in his Father in Heaven. His restless night finally ended with a knock on the lintel of his room.

"Palak. It is me, Uxpeq. I have come to complete our bargaining. Have you eaten yet? The sun is in the sky, and I wondered if you were still sleeping or had been out in the city already." Old Uxpeq, although older than Beleb Cho, was not as heavy as his leader, but he was still winded from the exertion of walking to Yax Kan's hut.

Yax came to the door flap. "Uxpeq, I am glad you have come. I need to buy some other things for the journey, and would ask your help in finding the merchants for such items."

"Oh, there are no merchants here other than us priests. We take that worry off of the backs of our citizens. There are only four who do not deal with day-to-day tasks. One is Beleb Cho, our high priest, whom you have met. The other three are his two constant aides in the great temple, you probably noticed them, and the chief astrologer, who keeps himself closed up in a room in the temple all of the time. I and four others do all the bartering and other necessary duties in the city, although I am the superior over the others, one of whom I have sent to the salt marshes to oversee the transport of salt to the city. Tell me what else you may need and we will include it in our transaction."

Beleb had unwittingly given Yax the locations of most of the others that had to be captured.

"Hmm, that makes it difficult for me, Uxpeq. I understood from Beleb Cho that I was expected to conclude my barter for salt with the high priest, himself. You see, there is a slave girl that I wish to include in the deal, and Beleb Cho is the only one who would know about her," Yax said.

Uxpeq seemed disgruntled at the news that Beleb Cho would be taking a hand in the dealings. Although he had taken Palak, the trader, to the high priest himself, he had expected to be given approval to continue to barter with him after the high priest had discussed religion with the foreigner.

MARK OF THE JAGUAR

"Perhaps you can help me find a meal this morning, and we can discuss the other items I wish to trade for before I leave." Yax hoped to draw even more information out of the talkative merchant. He was clearly a priest in name only, considering his duties.

"Yes, yes. We have some excellent fruit and other delicious foods in the place of eating. Some of my brethren are there now," Uxpeq admitted in a begrudging tone.

As they walked across the plaza, Yax noticed one other man dressed like Uxpeq. He was ordering some servants about. Surely this was another of the priests accounted for, an overseer of those in servitude in the central city.

"Uxpeq, I hoped to take some *balche* with me for the journey, and whatever the female slave will need for cooking and sleeping. Can you get me those things by this evening?" Yax asked.

"Surely, we have everything you will need. Shall we make a separate trade then, Palak?" Uxpeq's eyes sparkled. Evidently not everything was held in common among the priests if Uxpeq wanted to procure a portion of Yax Kan's trade goods.

"I think that will be fine, Uxpeq. Also, after I have eaten I will need to make an inventory of my trade goods before I speak to Beleb Cho. Will you please find out how much I will owe you so I know exactly what I should take to the high priest's quarters for our negotiation?" Yax needed three things: to be free of Uxpeq, to acquire the *balche*, and to find the locations of the rest of the temple guards before his plan could be put into action.

They came to the eating enclosure and Yax saw four other priests. One appeared to be preparing food for the others, and had a cooking pot boiling in the far corner. He was evidently preparing a meal for later in the day, since they were eating only corncakes and fruit for their morning meal. Evidently, the priests did not feel comfortable eating food prepared by servants. *"Did they fear poisoning?"* Yax wondered.

Yax was introduced as the trader, Palak, but did nothing to encourage conversation. He wanted only to listen and glean knowledge while he ate.

In a few minutes a guard that Yax had never seen before came in and asked for a cooking tool which Yax did not recognize. The guard indicated that he and another had just been relieved of duty at the temple and were going to eat and go to bed. That was the sort of thing Yax wanted to hear.

Yax quickly finished his meal and followed the guard at a distance. He watched until the guard met his companion and they both entered a long building that Yax decided must be their barracks. That was all that Yax needed for now, so he went to the temple to speak to Beleb Cho. This was just like counting the black and white stones in a game Yax had played with Zak in Lamanai; he just needed to keep track of how many pieces there were and in what positions.

He walked to the temple-top residence of the high priest, praying silently that no blood would be shed in the execution of his plan. He also prayed that the Spirit would direct him as he helping the people to be freed from the tyranny of this false priesthood and its skull of doom. Yax had guessed how the priests made the crystal skull speak, and he intended that the skull should speak again.

"Come in, Palak! Where have you been? I have waited all morning for you to return so that we could finish our business." As usual, Beleb Cho lay propped up on his furs, eating sweetmeats and delicacies.

"Sir, I was eating a morning meal and discussing some minor purchases I needed to make with Uxpeq. I came as soon as I was done there, not wanting to bother you too early in the morning." Yax needed to accomplish much before the evening came.

"We need to determine how much you are willing to pay for the slave girl, Palak. You are still interested, I presume?" Beleb Cho's eyes squinted until they were nearly closed from his wicked little smile. "Come closer, Palak, that we may speak more easily."

Yax moved closer and could now smell the rancid breath of the evil high priest. "Yes, your Excellency, I am still interested, and I hope that I have sufficient trade goods with which to barter for the salt and the girl. I have brought cacao beans, cowry shells, and vanilla beans to trade, Sir."

"Well," said Beleb Cho, "We are always happy to have the beans to make the royal beverage, and the shells are useful in trading with others. However we have shells of our own found in the salt marshes. Do you have anything more, Palak?"

"Would you be interested in a jaguar skin, Beleb?" He hoped he could now speak with more familiarity and less formality in order to gain the priest's trust. Beleb Cho seemed to be totally relaxed and self-confident. His guards were outside of the door flaps and his two assistant priests sat in a corner discussing some other business.

"Of course, Palak, we are always happy to have the fur of the great cat, but have you nothing more of value? Some jade or other jewelry perhaps?" The greed in the high priest's face made him look like an overfed glutton desperate for something more to eat.

"I only have one other thing, and I was saving it specifically to barter for the woman, my friend. I have these gold nuggets that I got in trade with the Zapotecs long ago." Yax poured the two remaining gold nuggets from their pouch, and he remembered the day they had been given to him by Sasak, the metalsmith.

Now Beleb Cho looked delighted. "Yes, that would be good! There is no gold in the area of Lubaantun, and it would be most appreciated. These things you have shown me plus the jaguar skin will pay for the girl, all the salt you can carry, as well as the other things you need from Uxpeq. Just tell him you have paid me. Guard!"

The guard nearest to the door flap entered, "Go to the servants' quarters and tell Yach'ka to have the foreign girl ready to leave in the morning with Palak, the trader!" Beleb Cho ordered. The guard hurried away wondering what the urgency was, if she was not leaving until morning, but his pay depended on doing what he was told without asking questions.

Beleb Cho turned to Yax, "Of course, Palak, if you wish to leave earlier that can be arranged, but I know you have things to gather together, and you will need to get the rest of your trade goods to me before you will be able to leave with the girl."

"Yes, that will be very good, and it is a pleasure trading with you, good sir. I will return later in the day with full payment, and will leave the gold with you now as a token of my intent," Yax answered and mused that he would be doing more important things than trade this day.

Leaving the High Priest's quarters, Yax went directly to the corner of a stone platform where he had earlier met Uxpeq. The old priest sat there with the goods Yax wanted. Again, Uxpeq shooed people away that had been trading for their rations of salt.

"Palak, here you are, and I am ready to bargain with you for these items you wanted." Uxpeq said.

"I have good news for you," Yax answered, "We will not need to barter, since the high priest has asked me to tell you that he has included all of these things in our trade today." The disappointed frown that came to Uxpeq's face was almost humorous.

"Of course, I saved this packet of cacao beans for you anyway," Yax said as he handed a bulging pouch to Uxpeq.

"Oh, thank you, kind sir! You have the heart of a generous trader, Palak!"

Yax picked up the four skins of the intoxicating *balche* and the few other supplies and carried them with him to his quarters. There he carefully measured into each of the skin bags some herbs that he had brought just for that purpose. These drinking skins would be integral to his plan. He left everything else under the bamboo cot and took the four skins with him to meet with Chi Kal at the appointed place.

As Yax walked casually around the outskirts of the town plaza, he came to a place where he could not be seen from the temples or the entry, and he could not see any other person within the town as well. Here there was a low palm that covered a hidden path described to him by Chi Kal. He moved the palms enough to get onto the path and within a few steps he found his fellow conspirator.

"Chi Kal, take these three *balche* sacks. There are sleeping herbs in each, and they each must be carried by your sister, or one of the other servant-women who are willing to help us, to the men standing guard at the two entrances to the city, and to the barracks where the night guards sleep during the early part of the day. In fact, have them go there first as they must get the *balche* before they leave the barracks," Yax explained to the listening Chi Kal, nodding his head. "Have the women tell them that the *balche* is a gift from old Uxpeq, the trading priest." It was the least the old codger could do, Yax thought with a grin.

"This should make it easier for your men to surprise and bind the guards at both the entrances and in the barracks, so we will not have to fight or have any blood shed. Be sure they are well bound and that their mouths have been covered so they cannot call out before I can complete the task at hand. Gather up the priests of the city and do the same with them. I will take this last bag of *balche* to the high priest's guards, and perhaps there will be enough for his two assistants, as well. For my plan to work, I must have Beleb Cho awake. I do not fear that he will be much trouble by the time I need his help." Yax could foresee the outcome as though it had already come to pass.

"We will follow your instructions, Yax Kan, but what of you? Do you not need at least one other person to assist you in overcoming the high priest and the other people in the temple?" Chi Kal asked with sincere concern.

"I will have more help than you think, Chi Kal. Just

have your men do their part and we will all enjoy complete freedom from fear this night!" Yax promised his new friend.

Then Yax made a sound in his throat that is hard to describe. He had learned it from another friend. Within moments Wi'tzin was by his side, rubbing his enormous head in Yax Kan's hand, clearly wanting to be scratched.

"So this is to be your helper," Chi Kal said, obviously still amazed at Yax Kan's rapport with the big cat.

"Yes, Chi Kal. You go now and get your men ready. We will act when the sun is a hand's span from the horizon." Yax gave this instruction and Chi Kal turned and disappeared on the hidden path. Yax knelt and spoke to Wi'tzin, "Well, little brother, this will be the biggest adventure you have ever shared with me, and the most worthwhile. You will again have the opportunity to help save Tutoma, as well as a city full of people yearning for freedom. Come with me now. We go into the city."

28

Justice and Emancipation

Yax again skirted the main plaza of the city until he was within sight of the great temple that featured Beleb Cho's residence on the top. He motioned for Wi'tzin to go into the brush and await his call, and the golden animal followed his unspoken instruction, not as a servant, but as an ally.

As Yax walked up to the temple, he recognized Zan Loc, one of the temple guards. He raised a hand to the guard in greeting and Zan Loc nodded in unsmiling response.

"Zan Loc," Yax said. "I am glad to see you again, and I know that I have not been the easiest guest to ever meet with your high priest. Perhaps I can make it up to you with this *balche*, eh? I will be leaving upon the next rising of the sun, and would give you this parting gift to thank you for being patient with me." He handed the drinking skin to Zan Loc and motioned to the other guard as he came up to the door flap of Beleb Cho's home.

"Stay here, trader Palak, and I will announce you to the high priest," the second guard commanded. He winked at Zan Loc when he left Beleb Cho's temple residence, he grunted, then disappeared.

"You may go in now."

"Palak, my friend, it is good to see you again. Have you brought the rest of the payment, then?" Beleb Cho asked from his reclining position on his stack of furs.

"Well, yes, I have it on its way, my friend," Yax answered.

A glint of curiosity lit the eye of the bulky high priest. "What, have you enlisted a servant to bring the goods, then, Palak?"

"Not a servant, but a friend, Sir. It will be yet a while for him to come. May I sit and discuss my coming travels with you, Beleb?" Yax was stalling for time as the guards enjoyed their libation outside the temple door.

"Surely, what is it you wish to discuss, trader?" In his arrogance, the high priest showed no fear or concern.

"I have plans to meet an acquaintance from the north to help me carry my goods to Palenque, and I wanted to know what you thought would be the best route back." With that introduction to the discussion, Yax led Beleb Cho in a long discourse that had little real meaning, but the high priest apparently loved the sound of his own voice and was more than willing to have time to advise this willing listener.

Not too much later, Yax thought he heard some snoring sounds coming from outside the door flap. While Beleb Cho continued to speak, Yax stood and walked toward the door. Peeking out the flap, Yax could see both the guards, one leaning against a wooden post and one seated, but both deeply asleep. Yax again gave the summoning noise and the golden jaguar ran up the side steps to the temple.

Beleb Cho tried to stand, but was unable to move as quickly. He soon lay sprawled on the stone floor with his mouth hanging open, gazing up into the golden eyes of a lively jaguar. The other two priests began to head for the door, but Yax grabbed each by the wrist and firmly asked them to be seated. A glance from the cat made the two men more than ready to comply. Yax asked Wi'tzin to sit by the high priest and proceeded to tie up the two priests, then tore up one of their sashes to make gags for their mouths. No use arousing anyone in the city before Yax was ready.

Beleb Cho began to regain a portion of his usually bellicose voice, "What are you doing, Palak? My guards will have your head for this!" he threatened in a weak whisper.

"No, Beleb, your guards will not be coming in very soon. They have found the joy of sleep too tempting to resist," Yax said with a serious look at the enormous glutton lying on his back. "Besides here is the jaguar skin I promised to you, although it is still covering the jaguar, my friend. You will need to be bound too, I'm afraid, but at least that should let you know that I mean you no physical harm." And then Yax tied and gagged the bewildered high priest.

A servant girl suddenly walked through the flap from the adjoining room, but stood in shock gazing at the jaguar.

"Are you acquainted with Chi Kal and his sister, young woman?" Yax asked her.

She nodded slowly and started to back out.

"Stay right there or my friend will be disturbed," said Yax as he gestured toward Wi'tzin. "You indicate that you know Chi Kal, and I know you serve with Yach'ka. Please go to her, and don't stop along the way to speak to any other. Have her bring the guest Tutoma with her back to the temple. Will you do that, girl? It will help in the deliverance of your people." Yax pulled aside the door flap that she had come through to see if any other servants were around, but he saw no one. He motioned to the girl and she ran by him, smiling at last.

"Well, old Beleb, it looks like your reign of terror has ended here in Lubaantun. But I don't intend to talk to you all day again. I have better things to do. Let's see, I will take back my gold first, since I don't intend to pay you for my own wife." He reached over the priest's bulk to where he saw the sack lying with the nuggets within. "And I am afraid I won't need any of your salt, either. Instead I will be releasing the slaves in the salt marsh and they can go there only when they desire to get salt for themselves and to support the other free people of this city." With that he motioned to Wi'tzin to stay and watch all three of the men, so he could do some exploring. First, though, he walked out and bound the two sleeping guards. They grunted in their slumbers, but he knew that the brew he had prepared was strong enough to keep them sleeping for much longer.

Then, Yax went back through two of the rooms to the entry of the room forbidden to him in his first visit with Beleb Cho. Seeing that the third room was without light, Yax grabbed a lamp from the second room. The he searched for and found the bundle containing the crystal skull, but that was not all he sought. *"Where was the entrance to another room below them?"* he wondered as he held the lamp up over his head.

Moving an intricately woven wall hanging, he found what he was looking for—a low entryway with a stairway down to a lower level. He thought he knew what would be there, but waited for Tutoma to arrive before he explored further.

Yach'ka soon arrived holding Tutoma by the hand. Tutoma rushed to Yax and hugged him. After their brief embrace, Yax explained what had been done, and Tutoma told him that she had not seen any other guards in the plaza as they came through, and only a few bewildered priests being rounded up by a group of armed citizens. When he explained what else he had planned, Yach'ka, who had been listening carefully, not sure whether to be afraid or joyful in the freedom being offered, was fearful again.

"Oh, no, sir!" Yach'ka cried. "You must not unleash the evil of the skull of doom, or we will all die!"

Yax tried to calm her, and finally told her to look at something with him. He lifted the bundle from its niche in the wall and opened the furs, while Tutoma held the lamp up. "This is only made of clear stone, Yach'ka, nothing more. It cannot harm you. Only the evil men who have owned it could do that, and they can't do that anymore. Will you trust Tutoma, and me, even though you have only known us for a few days, so that we may go ahead with our plan? The temple guards are all subdued by now, and you have nothing more to fear."

Yach'ka still looked a bit doubtful but Tutoma soon soothed her. They then introduced Yach'ka to Wi'tzin and it appeared she was even more assured that she was on the right side of this conflict, though it seemed to a smiling Tutoma that the size of her eyes might never again be as small as they had been before seeing the cat.

Yax asked her to stay with the three bound priests while

he and Tutoma explored the temple room below them. Beleb Cho was making whimpering sounds, but not so loud that they might irritate a great jaguar sitting next to his rotund body. Wi'tzin used his rough tongue to groom himself while waiting for further instructions from Yax.

Both Yax and Tutoma took oil lamps with them as they entered the stairway to the lower level. The stairs ended at the beginning of a passageway that Ixtan assumed would lead them to the front of the temple. About halfway down the passageway a sliver of light shown from behind a door flap. They silently opened the flap and there found an emaciated old man polishing an obsidian mirror. He looked questioningly at them, but said nothing and continued to polish the mirror as though it was the only thing that mattered in the world. He showed no fear or surprise in their coming.

Yax spoke to him, "Old man, I perceive that you are the chief astrologist, is that correct?"

The old priest looked silently at them again, then pointed to some drawings on bark paper that were clearly charts of the sky and numeric calculations. He also pointed to some observation holes in the walls around him. They must have been drilled through the stairway of the temple. Yax decided the old man must use them at night to view the heavens on this side of the temple.

After a few seconds, Tutoma spoke to Yax, "I think he is deaf and mute, Yax. See how he watches your mouth when you speak. He is harmless. Let us leave him for the women of the city to care for when we are done here, my husband."

Yax smiled at her compassion and nodded in agreement. They went back out the door flap.

When they reached the end of the passageway and turned right, they found another small room with a pungent smell of burnt wood and incense. A basin on a stone pedestal where a fire could be lit, a long stick leaning against the pedestal, a large hole above the fire to vent the smoke from a fire, and two holes in the ceiling.

"Look, Tutoma. Do you see those three holes? This large one must be hidden right behind the altar at the top of the stairway on the temple to draw smoke over the altar, and these two smaller ones go right up through the stone altar itself. This one angles up from the fire to cast an unholy light through the eyes of the crystal skull, and the other is for that pole to move the jaw of the skull up and down. Now we only need to discover how a voice is made to seem like it comes from the skull."

Tutoma lifted a cloth hanging on the wall of the room that must be behind the steps of the temple. There was an opening in the stairway stones of about a hand's width and on a little wooden table sat a large, cut gourd. Tutoma picked up the gourd and wondered why anyone would cut the bottom away, as well as the top of the stem, since they were usually used to carry water, food and other liquids. She handed it to Yax, "What do you think this is used for, Yax?" she asked.

"I don't know," Yax said. He held it to his mouth as though he were taking a drink from the stem end. "It surely will not hold water now," he said as he held it up, and then a look of surprise came over both Tutoma and him.

"Yax, it made your voice grow louder!" Tutoma exclaimed. "It must be what they use to speak for the skull. They probably hold it right here at this opening in the stairs."

"That must be right," Yax said. "And this is what I want you to do tonight." Yax went on to explain what they should do to truly break the spell of the crystal skull over all these people.

After they had been joined by Chi Kal, Lemnoch, Zaconiuh, and some others of their allies, they made sure that all the bound guards were taken to the top of the temple and tied together so that they could be easily watched. Then all of the priests were tied up and made to sit together at the top of the temple with Beleb Cho ignominiously placed at their feet, all in view of the people, who stood in the plaza looking on in amazement. Clearly, some were still afraid that they would be harmed by the god Hunab Ku, or the crystal Skull of Doom, but their curiosity drove them to watch and see what must surely happen to the most prominent of these rebels because of their audacity.

As the sun set, Yax had Chi Kal tell the people to sit in the plaza, as they did on a holy day with the priests. Then Yax brought out the crystal skull and set it on the center of the altar, where a stone protrusion fit the bottom of the skull and held it in place. The people gasped when they saw that someone other than a priest was handling the *sastun*, and they saw that the skull lit up and the eyes glared at them just as it always had. Yax made a small sound and motioned for Wi'tzin to come down from the top of the temple where he had been waiting, unnoticed, to stand by his side, and again there was an involuntary intake of breath by the crowd.

Yax then called out in a loud voice, "O Crystal Skull, thou that has made this people fearful for many years! Tell us now what we must do to be free of you forever!"

Slowly the jaw again began to move, and they heard a voice, but it was not the remembered voice of Hunab Ku coming from the Skull of Doom. Instead it was a lovely, lilting voice singing a song of freedom. It was a beautiful woman's voice, with no threat at all, only the promise of a bright future if they used wisdom and chose good leaders. Yax raised the skull from the altar, moved its jaw up and down, and cried out again, "O she of the beautiful voice, come forth!" Nothing happened for a few moments, but then, out of the residence on the top of the temple, walked a beautiful, smiling Tutoma, still singing her song of happiness. With her came Yach'ka holding a long pole. The people could also see now where a dark cloth had been removed from a hole in the stairway and the light of a fire shone from the room within.

Darkness had been turned to light! The people in the square began to speak to each other about the priests' evil deceptions. Now they were liberated. Truly free! They wanted Yax to lead them, and they all cried out for him to be made their king.

Yax stood before them with Tutoma and Wi'tzin by his side. First he assured them that Wi'tzin was just an animal friend, not a god, and then he taught them about a benevolent God, who would never harm those who did not harm others—a God that was the father of their spirits, and who loved them as His children. He explained the legends of Kukulkan, the bearded, light-skinned God, who was Jesus Christ, the Father God's Son, who had come to earth to allow all of them to one day return to him and the Father. Then he taught them about prayer to give their lives hope and meaning. After explaining all that he could about the things that he had learned that could give them something to look forward to in the future, even after death, he motioned to his friend, Chi Kal.

"This man, who was threatened with death if he ever returned to this city, came back anyway to save all of you from these evil, selfish, false priests and their mercenary guards. This man is the one who should be made your leader, but not made a king. Not because he is tricky, not because he is strong, but because he is good, kind and loving. My bride and I must leave and return to our own families and clans, but Chi Kal will stay here with you and lead you in happy lives, if you will follow him." Yax nudged Chi Kal toward the people.

As he took one step forward, all the people in the plaza raised their arms in assent and shouted his name, "Chi Kal, Chi Kal, Chi Kal!"

"I must tell you something, my people! This night I have experienced a witness to my heart that what Yax has told you about the one true God is true! I don't know how to describe it, but I know it is the truth!" Chi Kal said.

Again the people cheered, and Yax spoke again, "My friends, what your leader has said to you, he can say because of the Holy Spirit that has touched his heart. You too can feel that Spirit now, as I do. Can you not?"

They cried out their assent as one. They were free, and they would use that freedom to live better lives with Chi Kal as their leader.

Tutoma sings under Crystal Skull Altar

29

Salt Marsh

Yax and Zaconiuh took six of the brave men, now armed with weapons taken from the captured temple guards, and started the long day's journey to the salt marsh. The people working at the mine needed to be liberated and reunited with their families, so they no longer needed to worry about their loved ones being punished if they rebelled at the salt mine.

Of the six valiant men, one had been appointed their leader by Chi Kal under Yax Kan's direction. He was named Chun Chukum, named for the acacia trees in the area. He wanted to go to the salt marsh partly because his brother was held there as a slave, and he had not seen him for six months.

"When we get to the salt camp, we must be very cautious because those two guards are the most dangerous of them all." Chun Chukum explained, "They were sent there to work because the priests could not keep them from the throats of the other guards, let alone the people. They are very evil men, Yax Kan, and the awful priest that is with them is a criminal from another city, who would kill a man without pain of conscience."

"We will be very careful, Chun. We hope not to shed blood now, after success without bloodshed in Lubaantun," Yax answered.

"How will we capture them, then?" Chun asked seriously.

"I think I know a way. Tell me more about their camp and the work site, then I will ask God if my idea will work," Yax said.

Zaconiuh appeared to be listening to their conversation with great interest. He had seen the blessings of Yax Kan's God on the people of Lubaantun and seemed to be losing the veneer of skepticism.

Chun Chukum explained that the salt marsh was made up of little islands among the trees of the swamp with waterways between these islands. The camp was situated on the largest of the islands in the area, and the work site was a series of drying ponds on the surrounding islets. Once the saltwater had evaporated in the rock-lined ponds, the workers scraped the salt off the flat stones and after drying a second time in the hot sun, it was scooped into skin bags made from the stomachs of large animals or fish. One of the animals they hunted for this purpose and for food was the slow-moving dugong. It was a huge animal that lived in the water, but breathed air like a land animal. It also had a large reserve of fat that was prized for lamp oil and other uses.

The current contingent of workers had been kept on the island longer than usual, and Chun did not know why. They had been expected to return with a load of salt long ago. The priest on the island either had not sent a runner with a message or the message had not gone further than Beleb Cho, and the families were not told why their men had not returned.

Yax and his men found a place to camp far enough off the path to escape detection, and they hoped to act on Yax Kan's plan at first light. They could smell the fishy, salty odor of the sea, and Yax wished there was a breeze to cool them and give them fresher air. He thought it must be very difficult for the workers to spend all day every day working in the heat and humidity. Yax went off a little way into the sparse coastal forest to pray. He knelt in the sandy soil and said a vocal prayer, as that had been the best way in the past. He asked for the safety of Tutoma and her father while they were separated, and for protection for the eight of them who had come to help others. Finally, he asked that he would know that his plan was acceptable to God, and allow him and his friends to free the slaves in the salt camp.

He phrased it many different ways in his prayer, but while he knelt in the sand and felt sand flies crawling on his skin and heard the lapping of the water on the nearby beach, nothing else happened. As doubts crept into his mind, he felt he could no longer even remember how his plan would have worked. It had become so dark by the time he returned to camp that it was difficult to find his way back. When he finally made it back, Yax told the others that his plan would not work. Then he asked if they had any ideas.

Zaconiuh spoke, "As we have walked on the trail together, I thought of what would happen when we arrived at the salt camp. I prayed for you and thought we would do whatever you told us to do, Yax, but I could not help but imagine that it would be easy to make a mistake that would cost a life on either side. We only have to deal with three men, Yax, no matter how evil and canny they may be. I think that we must find ways to separate them, and then overcome them individually. With Wi'tzin's help we should be able to do that." He went on to explain more of a general plan of attack to the other listening men.

At the mention of his name, the cat looked up at Zaconiuh. Usually only Yax said his name in such a straightforward and respectful way, without awe or fear. As he noticed Wi'tzin's reaction, Yax felt warmth deep within his heart and knew this was the plan they should follow.

"That's wonderful, my friend! I'm glad God has shown you the way."

Zaconiuh went on to explain his plan in detail. "It is important to keep to the plan," Zak stated, "and that we all understand that the guards are focused on keeping the workers from getting away from the camp, and no thought is given to keeping others out. They won't be expecting anyone to try to get onto their dirty little island without being noticed."

Finally, the men all went to sleep. In the morning, Wi'tzin was lying next to Zaconiuh when he awoke, and the big man was momentarily caught off guard, but he soon relaxed when he saw the calm look in the big cat's eyes.

After sharing a scant meal, according to Zak's plan they separated into three teams of three each, Yax and Chun taking Wi'tzin with them. After careful preparations on the trail's end, Yax Kan's group cautiously and quietly walked down the trail to the beach until they could just see the camp in the first light of dawn across a narrow waterway. No one appeared to be up yet, but they remained cautious. One group of three men, including Zaconiuh, positioned themselves on the north side of the trail, far enough away not to be noticed as they each squatted behind the shrubbery. The other three men did the same on the south side of the trail.

Silently, Yax, Chun and Wi'tzin slipped into the water and swam across the narrow channel toward a side of the island that had some low shrubbery for cover. From there Chun crept into the camp to find his brother among the huddled group of slaves. They were all lying in a bamboo stockade set further from the fire than the two guards and the priest, the three sleeping figures by the fire pit and closest to the end of the island toward the road.

Chun spied his brother, who was fortunately sleeping on the outside of one small group of men, and he gave a short, low call, like the morning call of a brush hen. His brother, Twelve Turtle, who clearly recognized the call they had used as boys when hunting the birds, looked towards the brush and saw Chun motioning him to crawl toward him. With a brother's trust, Twelve Turtle, crawled out from under the low palm roof and over to Chun at the bamboo wall of the pen.

"Brother, what is it? Why do you endanger yourself to come here like this?" Twelve Turtle whispered when he reached Chun's side.

"Twelve, the city is free! We have taken it away from the priests and their temple guards, and your family is safe from harm. Look, by that bush over there is the man, Yax Kan, and he has an unexpected friend that you must not fear, or cry out when you see him, which would arouse those three over by the fire pit." Chun nodded to Yax, and Yax putting his finger to his mouth as a reminder to silence, motioned for Wi'tzin to come to him from behind a clump of bushes.

Twelve Turtle inhaled sharply in surprise, but put his hand over his mouth. With both eyes bulging, he looked as though he were trying to suffocate himself. Chun grinned at his brother's response.

Then Chun explained to his younger brother the part he must play in capturing the guards and the priest, and in releasing the other men to return to their loved ones in Lubaantun. Once Twelve Turtle understood, he reminded Chun that the two guards, Yaxam and Ixkeem, would not hesitate to kill someone to stop an escape. He crawled over to the gate as Chun cut open the latch from the outside, all with great care to remain undetected. Chun then closed the gate to look as though it was still locked.

Twelve Turtle and Chun moved away from the guards, keeping the stockade in between them and the line of sight of anyone at the fire pit. This time only Twelve Turtle got into the water and swam to the head of the path; the water was so shallow that he was able to push himself along the sandy bottom with his feet.

As Twelve Turtle got to the trailhead he purposely broke some branches and fell, as though by accident. He made enough noise to wake the guards, who jumped to their feet.

"Ixkeem, a slave is escaping! Hurry, run after him! Quickly, now! I will check the stockade to see how he got out," Yaxam yelled out. The priest also arose, looking toward the escaping Twelve Turtle with a glare of evil intent.

The guard, Ixkeem, ran to the shore and pushed a small

dugout into the water, paddling furiously toward Twelve Turtle, who was pretending to struggle to get to his feet, and then tripping again. Ixkeem wore a cruel grin as he moved closer to the slave.

When the guard had crossed the channel, he jumped out of his dugout and raced after Twelve Turtle. Then, unexpectedly, he tripped on a vine drawn tight across the path just as he arrived. The six men all ran at him out of the trees on each side of the path and one of them, who knew Ixkeem well and wore the marks of his lash, held a spear up and said to him, "Stay down, Ixkeem! We have been told not to hurt you if you do not resist, or this spear would already be in your heart for the evil that you have done!"

There was certainly no grin on Ixkeem's face now, as the men quickly gagged him and tied his arms behind his back, pulling him up with a yank. They wanted to prevent him yelling out a warning before Yax, Wi'tzin and Chun could finish their task.

*

On the island, as Ixkeem had hurried after Twelve Turtle, his surly partner, Yaxam, ran to the pen where the other workers, awake now, were huddled and watching. The priest stayed by the firepit watching him.

When Yaxam got to the pen, he saw that the rope latch had been cut from the outside, and began to look around. Both Chun and Yax then appeared from the nearby shrubbery. Yaxam turned to run, but saw the powerful jaguar standing in front of him.

"It is best that you stand very still, Yaxam, and drop your war club, if you value your hide," Chun told him. The guard narrowed his eyes angrily, but dropped his weapon at a rumbling grunt from Wi'tzin. Chun tied Yaxam's arms behind him as Yax stood by wielding his throwing stick as though he would use it as a club. Then Chun picked up Yaxam's war club where he had dropped it.

Watching the men tie up Yaxam, the priest, Py'ishka, turned to call to Ixkeem, but before making a sound, he saw the other guard lying on the shore, surrounded by men. Py'ishka began to run toward the other dugout in the water, but Yax made a motion to Wi'tzin, who swiftly ran after the priest and pounced on his back. He was about to bite him on the head, as was his natural way of killing prey, when Yax called to him, "Wi'tzin, no!"

The golden cat stood on the priest's shivering back, lashing his tail back and forth in excitement, as Yax approached to tie up the man. Chun walked Yaxam over to where Yax was working.

"These three will need to learn a little humility before they arrive safely in Lubaantun again. Our men will not stand for even a word of dissent from them without lashing out at them for what they have done to our people in the past," Chun said. "It is said that Ixkeem is so cruel because since his youth he had to bear a name that has a woman's prefix, but that is no excuse."

"I imagine they will not be very brave now that they are outnumbered, and once they understand that there is no one from the city that can rescue them." Yax answered, and then turned to the priest and the wicked guards. "All your cohorts are bound and under armed guard, you men! Do you understand?"

They pushed their captives toward the water's edge and loaded them into a dugout, where they sat in stony silence while Chun went back to the stockade to explain all that had happened to the other workers.

One of the newly freed slaves suggested that they should carry the stockpile of salt back to the city for their own use and to trade. "At last we will have some benefit from the sweat of our own bodies!" he said, clearly elated. They all cheerfully agreed and loaded the remaining dugouts with salt bags and poled them across the narrow channel to where their friends waited with the other bound guard.

The men traveled home, pushing their dazed captives before them. Now all of the citizens of the city of Lubaantun were free and able to make what they may of their own lives. This was something Yax Kan knew was indeed unusual for the common man of the entire *Mayab*!

30

Departure to Comalcalco

*T*here were many council meetings held before all of the
people could be persuaded by Chi Kal and Yax that
the guards and priests should not be killed or permanently
enslaved in the city by those whom they had forced into
servitude. Yax explained that the true God of Heaven would
not want the people to become like their oppressors.

A few of the priests were contrite enough that they
were allowed to stay and live in the city, so long as they
made a solemn vow that they would work along with the
other citizens to maintain their own livelihood. The ancient
astrologer was one of these. It was agreed that the rest were
to be imprisoned, except for those who were found guilty
of murder by the testimony of two or more accusers. These
were put to death according to their law, including their fallen
leader, Beleb Cho.

Those of the remaining temple guards and priests who
were too surly to trust in any way, were to be taken bound
to the rulers of other closest cities with a tribute gift of salt
and other goods, and asked if they would make some use of

the criminals. The fates of these irascible ones were left in their own hands to the extent that they could convince the king or his subordinate *cabals* that they could be productive, as soldiers or other servants. While Yax and the other men knew that these prisoners might end up dead, they were given more of a chance at life than they would have offered the inhabitants of Lubaantun in similar circumstances.

After assisting in reorganizing the government of Lubaantun to the best of his ability from his knowledge of the free government of Tulum, the best example of governing he had experienced, Yax with Tutoma, Lemnoch and Zaconiuh prepared to go home to Lamanai. They were given a feast of gratitude by the people of the city, and were escorted by Chi Kal and a few of his fellow citizens to the place where their dugouts were waiting by the river.

"We will never forget you, my friends," Chi Kal solemnly said in tribute at the feast. "And we will always be grateful for what you have done. Can you even imagine how much you have helped our people, even future generations, because of your unselfish leadership in freeing our city? It is an unknown form of charity in our world, Yax Kan."

"Chi Kal, we are glad in our hearts that we could help, and we know that it is what our God would have us do. I hope you will remember your Father in Heaven and trust in the power of his Son's sacrifice. It is the reason for our love for your people. No other power could help us see the value of the lives of men and women in our world. You should keep the crystal skull as a reminder of the selfishness of some men, so that your children will know that it and other false idols are harmless to the righteous, and have no power over them."

Zaconiuh and Lemnoch also made their farewells to their new friends, Chun Chukum and Twelve Turtle. Tutoma gave her regards to Chi Kal's sister and the other women that she had grown fond of. Chi Kal spoke with great appreciation for the big cat, and Wi'tzin stared at him with a look of puzzlement, as though he could not understand what the fuss was about. With the last of their good-byes, the group of four pushed off in their dugout canoes and Wi'tzin loped into the forest to follow at his own pace. The weather was unusually cool, and the rainy season was not far away.

On the trip home, Zaconiuh revealed to Yax and the others that he now believed what Yax had taught them about Jesus Christ, once known as Kukulkan, and that he would never forget the feeling of peace that he had experienced when he received answers to his prayers. He would remember to pray each day, now that it had been shown to him as the way to live a happy life. His humility did not seem at odds with his great size, as his friends listened with moist eyes to his gentle testimony.

Upon reaching Lamanai, Yax and Tutoma were again anxious to finish their preparations to start their journey to see Yax Kan's family. They repacked the dugout to travel north on their way to far off Comalcalco. Wi'tzin had not been seen since they had arrived in Lamanai, and Yax was anxious to see his friend again, and that he would follow them.

Lemnoch had a surprise of his own for them. He came to

them with the smiling widow Pepem by his side, taller than Lemnoch by at least two hands. "Tutoma, my daughter, I need to speak to you. You will soon be leaving to go far from here. I hope I will see you again, but it may not happen. This good woman, who has been so kind to us since our coming to Lamanai, has agreed to come into my hut and care for me, as only a woman can. I hope you are happy with this news?" he said with a question in his eyes.

"Oh, yes, Father! It is wonderful news! I was worried that you might be too lonesome with only Big Zero by your side. He is a good friend, but he cannot care for you as Pepem will." Tutoma hugged the smiling Pepem, who was uncharacteristically silent. "We will have a wedding ceremony at once." Tutoma pulled Pepem into the hut to discuss her father's needs and habits. Some giggling sounds came out of the dwelling and Lemnoch blushed through his sun browned skin.

"I will miss my daughter, Yax, but I know you will care for her in all things. I could not ask for a better man for my only child. I knew the day would come when she would leave my house, but I did not foresee until we met you, that she would go so far away." Lemnoch was stoic in his speech, but Yax knew his heart was full.

"You know that I will always love her with all my heart, and protect her life with my own, Father Lem." Yax used the shortened form of his father-in-law's name to show his affection for the humble man. "You have shown me how a loving father cares for a child, and I will also promise to remember that lesson as we have our own children. Thank you, Lemnoch, for such a clear example."

They grasped forearms and smiled into each others eyes, almost as true father and son. Now Yax had a third father figure in his life, to remember and to emulate.

───── ⟨∞⟩ ─────

As Tutoma and Yax were ready to leave, Yax was concerned. *"Where was Wi'tzin? Had he been injured or killed?"* He had not appeared in Lamanai after their journey up the river. *"Did he no longer wish to share companionship?"* These questions plagued his mind and he was emotionally unprepared to depart without an answer to them. On the other hand, he knew that the big cat could certainly find or follow them if he were alive and well, and there was nothing Yax could do other than try to call him as he had done in the past. The decision was made that they must depart and accept whatever might transpire with the beloved jaguar.

In the early morning mist, after Tutoma's long and tearful good-byes, and Yax Kan's fervent farewell to both Lemnoch and Zaconiuh, they paddled upstream in their dugout, filled with the goods that they would need and could carry on their backs. The journey to Comalcalco would be a long one, but at last they would begin a home as husband and wife with children of their own and an extended family to love and enjoy, as well. This would truly be an ending to their youth; a new beginning was before them. Their love and trust was strong for each other. They could only guess at how much time would pass and what else would transpire before they could settle down into the new life the one true God would give them.

───── ⟨∞⟩ ─────

HISTORICAL & EXPLANATORY NOTES

ANCIENT TRADE ROUTES: In Chapter 18 when Yax Kan reaches Tulum, there is mention of sea-going canoes traveling from places such as Xicalango and the Caqueti area near the Orinoco River. The ancient port city of Xicalango lies north of Tulum and across the Yucatan Peninsula, and is known to have been a major trading center; whether they sent goods by sea or across the peninsula is not known. The area of Caqueti in northern South America lies west of the Orinoco River; again there was apparent trade with South Americans anciently, and connections have been made with trade goods, but the exact locations are unknown.

CHICHEN ITZA: The city of Chichen Itza (or "the well of the Itza") was named such because of the conquest of a people known as the Itza (circa 495 A.D.) The site is now referred to as Old Chichen; it seems that no other name is known for the prior period. I have chosen to use only the first part of the name for the approximate period of this novel, approximately 665 A.D. to 686 A.D. The skull racks (*tzompantli*) of Chichen Itza give evidence of its bloody history. In addition, both infant and adult skeletons have been found in the bottom of the *cenote* (*Chen-Ku* or sacred well), along with other offerings to the gods of these bloodthirsty inhabitants. Surely the Spirit of Christ had fled the leaders of such a place as they practiced the dark arts similar to those described in the last chapters of the Book of Mormon (see Mormon 4:11-15, and Moroni 9:7-14.) Regardless of their failings the architecture in Chichen Itza is amazing. During the summer equinox the shadows move down the stairway of the great temple as though the winged serpent was slithering down the steps! (See EXPLORING THE LANDS OF THE BOOK OF MORMON by Joseph L. Allen, Ph.D., 1989, pg. 169.)

CRYSTAL SKULL OF LUBAANTUN: The crystal skull is an actual object that exists today, and is purported to be an artifact found by Anna Le Guillon Mitchell-Hedges on her 17th birthday during a 1927 expedition to the Lubaantun ruins in what was then British Honduras (now Belize) with her adoptive father, F. A. Mitchell-Hedges. It has been questioned by some whether it was planted by her father for her to find on that day, or whether it is an authentic artifact. In 1970 numerous crystallographic tests were conducted in the Hewlett-Packard Company laboratories in Santa Clara California, determining that it was cut from a single quartz crystal, being at least an approximate eight inch cube. It was bequeathed to Bill Hohmann upon Anna's death in 2007, and is presently in his possession. It may not be an authentic artifact from Lubaantun, as a similar crystal skull held by the London Museum is now admittedly a fake; however, other smaller crystal skulls have been found in ruins in Mexico and a crystal cup in Monte Alban; so it is possibly an actual artifact. Some believe that with ancient Maya technology it may have taken 300 years to create such a work. I tend to think that the ancient Americans had some tricks that are still undiscovered by modern man, and quartz crystal and obsidian (as in eccentric flints) were worked much more quickly than supposed. (For more information see THE CRYSTAL SKULL by Richard Garvin, 1973.)

GLYPHS: The ubiquitous glyphs, found in the ruins of Mexico and Central America, are nothing short of astonishing. These written and carved glyphs have been studied for years, and there is now some understanding of them, but it seems that there is more still to be learned about them than there is of the Egyptian hieroglyphs. Cut in solid stone for the most part, they tell stories of their kings and queens with exact dates for their respective reigns. Along with murals that depict the killing of captives, and the battles between city-states, religious rites are memorialized in stone in such a way that puts the monuments of later cultures to shame as to artistic and historic worth. The discovery of glyphs that signify drops of blood dripping from a hand with a circle (hole?) in the center, and the 'utchi' glyph meaning "And it came to pass…" are particularly significant to believers in the Book of Mormon. (See READING THE PAST—MAYA GLYPHS by S. D. Houston, 1989; MAYA SCRIPT by Maria Longhena, 2000; and EXPLORING THE LANDS OF THE BOOK OF MORMON by Joseph L. Allen, Ph.D., 1989.) Those glyphs that look like heads, known as 'head variants,' may be what Jacob spoke of in Jacob 1:4, as he described great and sacred things by engraving "the heads of them" on the plates. Head variants are also common in

Egyptian hieroglyphs, so they would be expected to appear in any "reformed Egyptian", or successor script.

HUNTING IMPLEMENTS & WEAPONS OF WAR: The different weapons and hunting tools in this book are based on actual implements used anciently. The swords (also "cimeters" in the Book of Mormon) used by the Classic Maya were made of wood with imbedded sharpened obsidian or other stone, not of steel like the sword of Laban in the Book of Mormon, and were deadly weapons of war. The blow gun with poisoned dart is used even today by indigenous people in the Amazon basin, south of the locale of this story, and the throwing stick or spear thrower (called an '*atlatl*' by the Aztecs) was used in the ancient world for hunting. The *atlatl* throws darts, arrows or spears with great force, and these could have been what were used in Alma 49:22 when arrows were being "thrown" in battle. (See WARFARE IN THE BOOK OF MORMON, ed. Ricks and Hamblin, 1990.)

IZAPA: An ancient city in Izapa, Mexico, just above the northern border of Guatemala, that is strongly influenced by the Olmec. The "Lehi Stone," or Stele No. 5, most celebrated by Latter-day Saints, is displayed in an open field with numerous other large stelae, covered by simple thatch shelters to protect them from any further disintegration. The stele's design is not as clear as it was originally, so it is good that this carving that appears to represent Lehi's dream (I Nephi 8:10-38; 15:21-36) was well photographed years ago, as well as a casting made, when there was less acid rain in Mexico to destroy these amazing finds. The carving of the boat as mentioned in the text is also there, but at another site a short distance from the Stele No. 5 location. (See EXPLORING THE LANDS OF THE BOOK OF MORMON by Joseph L. Allen, Ph.D., 1989, pg. 118-128.) Dr. V. Garth Norman, another prominent scholar of the Maya and especially as to Izapa monuments (drawing of Stela 5 herein was drawn by him) states in private correspondence to the author that a "high priest on a pilgrimage quest to the ancestral home land temple at Izapa...discover(ed) the deeper meaning of the tree of life related to the first ancestors of the Maya as recorded in the Popol Vuh, a thousand years before Palenque was built in the 6th century AD, as recorded in the hieroglyphics there." (See also BOOK OF MORMON REFERENCE COMPANION, 2003, ref. Norman, "Stela 5", pg. 740-745.)

LAMANAI: Like other place names and words in the ancient Mayan languages, Lamanai seems to be clearly related to the name Laman and/or Lamoni in the Book of Mormon. Another simple example is the city of Uxmal, similar in consonants and sound to the name Ishmael, both a personal name and as is often the case, a place name in the Book of Mormon.

LUBAANTUN: An ancient city in Belize, formerly British Honduras. The name means "falling stones" whether because of seismic activity in the area, poor construction, including a lack of use of the corbelled arch, or the lack of mortar being used in construction, is not known for certain.

MAYA v. MAYAN: Most people are unaware that the term "Mayan" is only properly used relative to the language of the Maya. It would roll off the tongue better for a speaker of English to say a 'Mayan city' or a 'Mayan man' perhaps, but 'Maya city' and 'Maya man' are more correct. Also, the plural is Maya, and not 'Mayas.' The Mayan languages and Mayan hieroglyphs are varied enough to allow ample use of this term. There are over twenty Mayan languages being spoken in Mexico and Central America today, including: Mayan, Nahuatl, Huasteca, Tzeltal (or Tzental), Tzotzil, Chontal, Chanabal, Chol (or Cholti), Mam, Ixil, Aguacateca, Quiche, Cakchiquel, Tzutuhil, Uspanteca, Pokoman, Pokonchi, Yucatec, Tzoltin, Kechuan and Kekchi. (See A MAYA GRAMMAR by Alfred Tozzer, 1921, and THE CODE OF KINGS by the late Linda Schele, and Peter Mathews, 1998, among other books.) Mayan words used in the text may come from any of these dialects, since I learned them as I read many different books. It was enjoyable to note in my travels that many of the parks and ruins in the Yucatan Peninsula of Mexico had signs written in three languages: Spanish, English and Mayan (one of the dialects). It is as if they had created modern Rosetta Stones all over the country! (See THE ROSETTA STONE by E. A. Wallis Budge, 1929.)

MEDICINES OF THE RAIN FOREST: The plants described in the book by Naz-Hani, the shaman, as having medicinal qualities, are actual medicinal plants described in books obtained from the Panti Medicine Trail in a rain forest preserve in Belize. Eligio Panti was a shaman and medicine man who purportedly lived to be over one hundred years of age. The book,—SASTUN, MY APPRENTICESHIP WITH A MAYA HEALER, by Rosita Arvigo, 1994, was his biography and discussed many of these natural remedies which are now being studied by medical researchers all over the world. (Also, see my article "THE PANTI MAYA MEDICINE TRAIL" by Mark Cheney in EXPLORE THE MAYA WORLD [later known as BELIZE CURRENTS], Vol. No. 31, pp. 16.) The Book of Mormon tells us that God provided such plants for the use and benefit of man in Alma 46:40. As an example, we know that quinine, which for years was used to combat the fevers and symptoms of malaria, is a substance taken from the cinchona tree bark, and was anciently called "Quina" or "Quina-Quina", which roughly translated means "bark of bark" or "holy bark" in the Incan language of Quechua.

OLMEC: The Olmec (or Olmeca) were a people more ancient than the Maya, and many LDS scholars believe they may have been the people known in the Book of Mormon as the Jaredites, who came from the Old World in barges approximately 2200 years before Christ, at the time of the biblical Tower of Babel (Ether 1-7.) The word "olmeca" actually means 'the rubber people' as stated in the story, referencing the game played with hard rubber balls perhaps six inches in diameter which were hit through stone hoops in ball courts found in many of the archaeological sites of ancient America. They left behind a legacy of huge stone heads, around six feet tall, of what is presumed by some to be likenesses of their kings, wearing what look like old-fashioned football helmets. Perhaps they were only the Olmec equivalent of the ballgame hall of fame! Most of these stone heads can be viewed in a park in La Venta, near Villahermosa,

Tabasco, Mexico where they have been gathered. There is one in the museum in Chapultapec Park, Mexico City, and another in the concourse of the Mexico City airport, which may be replicas. (See <u>OLMECS</u>, Arqueologia Mexicana, No. 087, and <u>EXPLORING THE LANDS OF THE BOOK OF MORMON</u> by Joseph L. Allen, Ph.D., 1989, pg. 56-67.)

PALENQUE: The beautiful, ancient, 5th century city of Palenque, Mexico may have originally been called *Xbalanque* (See Glossary). This is where the 'utchi' ("it came to pass") glyph was first discovered on the Temple of Hieroglyphs and where the great Pakal, or Lord Shield, was entombed in a sarcophagus carved and described by Yax Kan in this fictional account. The mysterious secrets of the carvings discussed herein actually seem to exist. (See <u>THE MAYAN PROPHECIES</u> by Adrian G. Gilbert and Maurice M. Cotterell, 1995, for more unusual findings that may point to more imagined 'magic' in this great artifact!)

PARABLE OF THE GREEN IGUANA: The folk tale told to Yax Kan by Naz-Hani about the green iguana on their journey south through the Tehuantepec Strait was adapted from a story about a snake as related in the <u>TEACHINGS OF THE BUDDHA</u> by Fronsdal and Kornfield, 1995, which I found in the drawer of a San Francisco hotel years ago.

SACBÉ: The Mayan name for road, which is derived from two Mayan words: **"sac"**, meaning "white", and **"be"** meaning "road". This name came about because the Maya surfaced the roads with white earth called **"sascab"** made into cement, the same white earth that was mixed with lime to make mortar. The roads or highways are mentioned in the Book of Mormon in 3 Nephi 6:8, and the mortar or "cement" is mentioned, specifically as to house building, in Helaman 3:7. (See AN OVERVIEW OF THE MAYAN WORLD by Prof. Gualberto Zapata Alonzo, 1983, pgs. 116 and 134.)

SCRIPTURAL REFERENCES: The calamities that came upon the earth at the coming of the Savior as referred to by Malochi, the priest of Tulum, are described in 3 Nephi 8:6-23. The description of the three Nephites who were promised that they would be allowed to tarry upon the earth until the Second Coming as explained to Yax Kan in Tulum is in accordance with the scriptures in 3 Nephi 28:4-12. The choosing of twelve "disciples" by Jesus when he visited the Americas in the city Bountiful is told in 3 Nephi 11:1-17, and the three disciples who elected to remain on earth until Christ came again, as did the Apostle John in the New Testament, are mentioned in 3 Nephi 28:4-40. In Mormon 1:13 it is explained that "the Lord did take away his beloved disciples" because of the wickedness of the people.

TEOTIHUACAN: The ancient site of the city of Teotihuacan is found lying approximately 30 miles northerly of modern Mexico City. Although it is known as an Aztec site, the connections to the Maya civilization are numerous. People known as the Mexica, the Totonac, the Tolteca, the Zapoteca, the Huasteca, and many other tribal or culturally differentiated groups have all been referred to as Maya at various times. The origin of the Maya people may not be

Nephite or Lamanite, but certainly by the time subsequent to the Book of Mormon (421 AD) there must have been little dissimilarity in their histories. There was surely a cultural mix of all of these groups through trade, war and religious intercourse. There is a preponderance of evidence that the Olmec influenced the people of Teotihuacan, and that the Teotihuacanos affected the people of Palenque, Izapa and other such cities. The 'jaguar lip' appearing on most Olmec statuary, appears on many pieces of Maya pottery and carvings, as well. (See THE LIVES AND TRAVELS OF MORMON AND MORONI by Jerry L. Ainsworth, 2000.)

TULUM: The buildings of Tulum (originally called Zama) were painted turquoise and red when the Spanish first viewed it many centuries after the time of this story. Today the paint is worn and washed away, and it is beautiful white stone once more, with only remnants of the original colors. The contrast between the stone temples and the two-tone blue Caribbean Sea is most amazing (two-tone because of the change from water over white sand then over deeper water). The motif of the Descending God is found in other ancient Maya cities of the Yucatan, such as Chichen Itza and Coba, but not so significantly set apart as in Tulum (also Tuluum). The city was built during the Classic Period following the close of the Book of Mormon, actually after the time frame of this book, but I used Tulum so that the reader may be able to relate this beautiful location to the plot and to the present time. The stucco relief of the Descending God is sometimes called the 'Diving God' and some tour guides say that it is a representation of the bee deity of the Maya. However, many believe that the carvings clearly commemorate the visit of a bearded man with feathered serpent and resurrection symbols at his feet represent Kukulkan, later called Quetzacoatl by the Aztecs, the wise, white and bearded god.

YAX KAN and other Mayan names and words: The Mayan names and words used in this novel are for the most part based on names, words and sounds within the many dialects of the Mayan languages, and, of course, some of them are historical names that have been assigned by epigraphers and archaeologists, e.g. Pakal (or Pacal) and Kan Balam (or Chan Balaam) based on reading the glyphs. A few are based more on the endings and sounds of Book of Mormon names. Any similarity to words meaning something in a Mayan dialect which would be inappropriate, due to my lack of knowledge, is truly accidental! (Books used in my research were A MAYA GRAMMAR by Alfred M. Tozzer, 1921; NUEVO DICCIONARIO DE LAS LENGUAS K'EKCHI' Y ESPANOLA by Guillermo Sedat S., 1987 ed.; and MANUAL DE REDACCION K'ICHEE' by Candelaria Dominga Lopez Ixcoy, 1994.)

GLOSSARY OF TERMS

(mostly Mayan)

ahau (pl. *ahauob*): Maya king or ruler, also known as the "Keeper of the Mat"

balam (or *balaam*): jaguar

balche: an alchoholic beverage made from corn and honey

cahal (pl. *cahalob*): Members of the ruling class, minor lords

ceiba tree: otherwise known as the kapok tree, its branches, trunk and roots represent heaven, earth and hell to the Maya

cenoté (or *dzonot*): a natural well in a limestone sinkhole

Chaac (aka *Tlaloc*): the Maya rain god

Chac-Mool: a sacrificial altar in the shape of a reclining man or god

Chichen Itza: ruins of ancient city in Yucatan peninsula of Mexico; called Chichen herein, meaning "the well" or "cenoté".

ch'ocua: greeting in Mayan

chu-lal: the sacred life-force in the blood

copal: a tree that is tapped for its resin to be used as incense.

ex: loin cloth worn by men of the Maya

haab: long year of 365 *kin,* or days.

Hokeb Ha: a cave near Blue Creek in Southern Belize

Hunab-Ku: the Maya creator god, also known as Itzamna

Huyab Caan: the 'Heart of Heaven', or the god of the hurricane, also called *Hurican*

Itzamna: the Maya creator god, also known as Hunab-Ku

Ixchel: moon goddess of fertility, and the hearth

kan (or *chan*): snake or serpent

kin: a day or period of sunlight, Maya calendar

Kukulkan (or *Kukulcan*): the white and bearded god depicted as a winged serpent, known as Quetzalcoatl to the Aztecs.

Lamanai (meaning 'Submerged Crocodile'): ruins of ancient (ca 1500 BC) city in northern Belize, an ancient name found in the glyphs of the city as *Lam'an'ain.* Submerged Crocodile is *lama'anayin* in the Yucatec Mayan language.

Lubaantun: ruins of ancient city in Southern Belize

mai leaves: the leaves of the mai tree used for incense and as an agent like tobacco for smoking

maiz: Corn or maize (Taino word)

manta: blouse or tunic worn by Maya women

Mayab: world or people of the Maya

metate: a dressed flat stone used for grinding corn and other grains.

mecapal: a tumpline or forehead strap securing a load on the back of a worker (see Mosiah 21:3;24:14-15,21)

Na-Te-K'an: Precious first tree, the name of the *"wakah chan"* or tree of life in Palenque.

Nim Li Punit: an ancient city of Belize

Palenque: ruins of an ancient city in Mexico (See *Xbalanque.*)

pulque: a brew made from the fermented hearts of maguey plants

sacbe (pl. *sacbeob*): cement road, as found throughout ancient Mexico and Central America

sastun: a seer stone kept by a shaman to discern future events, and other matters

Teotihuacan: ancient city, the ruins of which lie approximately 30 miles north of Mexico City

Tonatiuh: The Sun god of the Maya

Tulum: ruins of ancient coastal city in Yucatan Peninsula of Mexico, formerly Zama, from the word `*zamal*' or `morning.

tumbaga: a gold alloy used in ancient America

tun (pronounced 'toon'): the common short year of 360 days (or kin)

tutiwah: sacred food for priests and kings made from corn meal and fresh blood

Tzolk'in the ceremonial sacred calendar showing propitious dates (260 days)

wakah chan: the Tree of Life, represented by the great ceiba (kapok) tree, that reaches up to heaven and down to *Xibalba*

Xibalba: the underworld or 'hell' of the Maya afterlife

Xbalanque: possibly the ancient name of the ruins called Palenque today and in this book, transliterated by the Spanish as *palanca* or *palanquera,* meaning fence, stockade or fortress. *Xbalanque* is the name of a minor god of the Maya, one of the hero twins of legend in the Popul Vuh, sacred book of the Maya.

yahau kak: generic name of a chief priest, or "Lord of Fire" in Chichen

Yun Kaas: the beautiful corn god

zamal: morning or dawn; Zama, the early name for Tulum came from this word

ziff: a metal used in ancient America according to the Book of Mormon (Mosiah 11:3 & 8)

ABOUT THE AUTHOR

MARK F. CHENEY received a BS in Psychology and was a post-graduate student at the University of Utah. He has written numerous articles about the ancient Maya online and in the IMS EXPLORER newsletter.

Mark has traveled extensively in Mesoamerica and explored the ancient ruins including Teotihuacan, Palenque, Tulum, and Izapa, Mexico; Copan, Honduras; Tikal, Guatemala; and Lamanai, Belize, studying the glyphs, art, architecture and artifacts of the Ancient Maya.

Mark was born in California and served an LDS mission in Florida, USA. He and his wife, Sally, currently reside in Oregon. They have six children and 15 grandchildren. Cheney has given presentations at firesides on Ancient America and the Book of Mormon, and college classes on the World of the Ancient Maya. He is currently an LDS Sunday School teacher.

Mark of the Jaguar is his first work of fiction. He can be emailed at MFCheney@hotmail.com